THE LOST PROPHECIES

2 0 AUG 2013

Also by Michael Malaghan:

Greek Ransom

THE LOST PROPHECIES

MICHAEL MALAGHAN

ANDERSEN PRESS • LONDON

First published in 2013
by Andersen Press Limited
20 Vauxhall Bridge Road
London SW1V 2SA
www.andersenpress.co.uk

2 4 6 8 10 9 7 5 3 1

British Library Cataloguing in Publication Data available.

ISBN 978 1 84939 574 8

Printed and bound in Great Britain by CPI Group (UK) Ltd,
Croydon, CR0 4YY

For Mam: who nurtured my love of books,
in front of a warm fire on cold winter nights.

Prologue

Third Full Moon, in the year of the Sacred Scarab Beetle, 1310 BC

A series of immense statues lined the chamber; muscular human legs and torsos supported the huge skulls of crocodiles, which stuck out at right angles from the bodies. In the flickering glow of the oil lamps, their flesh-sawing teeth appeared to be gnashing.

Between the two lines of statues stood an oblong slab of red granite, and on that lay a man's naked body, staring up at the arched ceiling with a glassy-eyed gaze.

A white-robed priest was setting out equipment to commence the embalming process. Four brightly painted jars clinked as he placed them onto the granite surface in a row: ready to receive the man's lungs, liver, stomach and intestines. A razor-sharp knife to remove each organ went with them. Then he added three clay bowls, each containing its own ingredient: palm wine for cleansing; ground spices to repack the cavities once the organs were removed; and a mixture called natron salt, which would dry out the remaining flesh so that the bandaging of the mummy could begin.

As the priest took up his glinting blade to begin work, the naked man's pale thin lips fought to speak.

'Stop! I live.' The words were little more than a breath, a tiny disturbance of air.

The priest hesitated, the knife a millimetre from the man's naked breast. He glanced into his subject's living eyes without surprise, and intoned in ancient Egyptian: 'You have failed your pharaoh, and now you are to pay for your offence... You were to discover the Lost Prophesies, were you not?'

Again there was no movement from the naked man's lips, but just enough sound to produce: 'But it was impossible. The Prophesies are lost for ever...'

'Then you should not have agreed to seek them at all,' replied the priest. Without pity, he returned to the task at hand.

As the knife began to pierce soft tissue and muscle, the naked man's scream was but a whisper.

1

Squirrel and Stickleback

Cairo, Egypt, 26 October 2013

C allie Latham was fighting her way through the narrow, busy streets of the Khan el-Khalili bazaar in Cairo, leaving her brother Nick, and their distant relative Omar, further and further behind. It was insanely hot to be running and her T-shirt was sticking to her back, her dark ponytail swinging damply from side to side, but she was completely mesmerised by the city's unfamiliar sights and sounds.

As Callie was thirteen, and Nick twelve, exploring on their own was definitely *not* on their parents' list of 'Approved Activities'. They were supposed to be supervised at all times, especially after all the trouble they'd got into in Greece last year. Trouble involving an earthquake, a lion-headed man, getting shot at and running away from the police... It wasn't surprising they'd been grounded really.

Callie's mum and dad were archaeologists, which took them all over the world, and right now they were working on a temple south of Cairo, while Callie and Nick spent the first few days of their holiday with Omar, who lived here in Cairo. But Omar only wanted to show them lots of mummies at the small,

3

off-the-beaten-track museum where he worked. Callie had decided that unless you were Nick, who revelled in anything disgusting, gruesome or weird, it was not a good way to spend half term! She was a lot more interested in the history she'd read about in her parents' books: when the pharaohs had actually been *alive*.

The thick tide of locals and tourists sucked her past a coppersmith's, where an array of decorative lamps, hole-punched with stars and crescent moons and other intricate designs, hung outside. She made her way through a gauntlet of food vendors as a mouth-watering concoction of aromas – sizzling lamb, spit-roasted chicken and fried vegetables – competed for her taste buds.

Baaaaaarp! Baaaaaarp! A horn sounded emphatically, and Callie leaped aside as a battered red motorbike zoomed towards her, its rider balancing a roll of carpet across one shoulder. Dodging the motorbike took her to the other side of the narrow street, where she almost upset a table of fragrant spices whose reds, yellows, greens and golds appeared as bright as an artist's paint box in the sunlight. She ducked past a man carrying loaves of bread in a large basket on his head, apologising lamely in English and Arabic: 'Sorry... Sorry... *Aasef*,' and carried on down the nearest alley.

Hawkers attempted to sell her their wares from suitcases, everything from hats to herbs, babbling that they could offer her the very best prices. Everyone seemed to be getting in her way.

She passed a glass and jewellery shop bursting with glittering gems: honey-bright amber, lavender amethyst, mint-green jade. The shop merged with the clothes shop beside it where embroidered fabrics, fine silks, Egyptian cotton and

4

luxury leather were displayed. Callie toyed with the idea of going inside to buy presents to take home, but then spotted something far more engaging: a sparkly silver sign written in English.

The Magic of Egypt: Proprietor Rashid Gobb.

Beneath the sign were two symbols painted on the door: a squirrel outline followed by a stickleback.

They made Callie catch her breath because 'Squirrel' and 'Stickleback' were the nicknames her parents sometimes used for her and Nick. She was Squirrel because she was into climbing (there was a climbing centre near where they lived); and Nick was Stickleback because he had been awarded at least a dozen certificates for swimming. Callie detested swimming. She'd nearly drowned once on holiday.

She continued studying the two symbols. Their dad sometimes drew their exact copy on Christmas cards and letters to her and Nick. He'd seen them in his work once, excavating Egyptian ruins, and got really excited because the symbols were rarely seen. They were apparently famous amongst archaeologists as no one had been able to interpret them, not least because squirrels and sticklebacks hadn't existed in ancient Egypt. Callie certainly hadn't been expecting to see them on some random shop sign. She found the mystery fascinating.

Now she *had* to go inside! She gestured her intentions to Omar and Nick, who were still halfway down the bazaar, trying to catch up, and dodging past a man trying to sell them a rug. 'I'm going in here,' Callie mouthed to them.

'What?' Omar was panting and sweating profusely in a crumpled, parchment-coloured, linen suit. A middle-aged bachelor, used to his home comforts, he was struggling to keep up with his young relatives.

'I want to look inside,' said Callie, pointing again at the shop.

Nick grinned broadly, his spiky blond hair sticking up as usual, and he waved back that he understood, before turning to Omar to explain.

It was gloomy inside the shop, and it took a moment for Callie's eyes to adjust fully to the dusty atmosphere. There was a mind-boggling array of ancient Egyptian-themed toys and games overflowing on the wooden shelves. Including magic spells, tents patterned to resemble mini-pyramids and even a chess set with all the pieces representing Egyptian gods (the pawns were particularly impressive – two opposing rows of men with crocodile heads). Judging by the Ten Plagues of Egypt board game, pharaoh costumes and a Curse Your Enemies magic set, it seemed that The Magic of Egypt was a cross between a magic-trick shop and a tacky souvenir emporium.

'Omar's waiting outside,' Nick said, as he wandered in behind her. 'This place isn't "educational" enough for his liking.' He glanced around with an open, curious expression on his tanned face. 'Not your sort of place, either, is it – a tacky joke shop?'

'Not normally,' agreed Callie, looking about for anything else with a squirrel or stickleback symbol on it. 'But there was—'

Nick had already moved on. 'Now that's what I call a souvenir! A Do It Yourself Mummification Kit!' There was a pile of brightly painted boxes in one corner of the shop. '*Prepare your friends for the afterlife,*' Nick read the blurb. 'Hey, let's get one for Mr Garbitt.' Nick and his math's teacher had a fractious relationship.

'Haven't you had enough of mummies for one holiday?' Callie said scathingly. She was now staring at a full-sized ancient Egyptian chariot, with a basketwork cockpit painted in flowing arcs of gold and turquoise. It was mounted on two huge six-spoke wheels, and 'parked' at the back of the shop. All that was missing were a pair of fine horses to pull it.

'You mean you can actually buy a chariot?!' gasped Nick, climbing on board before Callie could stop him.

'I don't think you should do that.'

'Why not? I'm only trying it out.'

Before Callie could answer, a giant man, more than two metres tall, and with alarming bug-like eyes, came bursting out from the back of the shop. What little sunlight there was in the dusty room seemed to be bouncing off his misshapen bald head. He hurtled over to the chariot, his black one-piece robe flying about him like the wings of a giant bat.

'Off! Off! It is not a toy.'

'Sorry...' muttered Nick, who was more annoyed at being humiliated than sorry. He scrambled down from the chariot, staring defiantly at the enormous man.

Callie expected to be ejected from the shop, but the scary owner stomped back behind his dimly lit counter without another word.

'I think that must be Gobb,' she whispered, when she was brave enough to speak. 'I don't think he encourages try-before-you-buy.'

'Gobb?'

'That's the name of the shop owner... It says so outside.'

Callie took one last quick look around the place. 'I think we should go. With any luck Omar's museum will be shut by now.' She turned towards the door, but stopped suddenly in front a sheet of yellowing papyrus crowded with hieroglyphic text hanging on the wall.

'What?' asked Nick, coming up behind her.

Callie pointed at the papyrus. It was divided into vertical columns, wide enough to fit the tiny ink symbols. There were lots of bird and animal outlines, some unidentifiable shapes, and even several human figures – all of which were completely unintelligible to her. She could be looking at somebody's love letter, their will, or just a shopping list, but whatever it said, there were the squirrel and stickleback symbols again – right at the top. 'Us.'

'Oh, yeah,' said Nick. 'Like Dad draws them. I thought they were supposed to be really rare, though. Dad's only found them once, hasn't he?'

'I thought they were rare too till I saw them on the sign outside,' said Callie.

'Really?' Nick glanced towards the open door.

'Yeah. I was trying to tell you when you walked off to buy presents for Mr Garbitt.'

'Sorry... What's the rest of it mean?' Nick began scrutinising the papyrus.

Callie shrugged her shoulders. 'How should I know?'

'Can't you look it up in your Hieroglyphics for Nerds book?' Nick suggested, and sniggered at his own joke.

'I left *Hieroglyphics for Beginners*,' replied Callie tartly, 'at Omar's. But Omar can read hieroglyphics, can't he?' She could see him through the door, trying out a walking stick which miraculously turned into a rubber snake when thrown at the ground, like the staff of Moses. 'Omar!' She beckoned him into the shop, and, embarrassed, he stuffed the snake-staff back into a basket before shambling inside.

8

'We wanted to know what it says on this papyrus,' Callie explained.

'Hieroglyphs?' Omar's interest piqued. He slid a pair of gold wire glasses down his broad nose and focused on the papyrus, following a vertical line of symbols with his finger without actually touching the document.

'I've been reading about hieroglyphics,' said Callie. 'The word means "sacred carved letter". And the symbols always face in the direction you're supposed to read them in.'

Nick rolled his eyes long-sufferingly. 'It's not an exam, sis.' Callie ignored him.

'Ah! I see why you are interested,' Omar said after only a few seconds. 'Squirrel and Stickleback symbols, of course. Your mother told me of this little joke you have... Callie is Stickleback, and Nick, Squirrel.'

'The other way round, actually,' said Callie mildly. 'But do you know what the symbols stood for originally? Dad always says they haven't been translated.'

Omar nodded. 'And he is correct. In the few instances where they are found, they are found together, and on scripts from the reign of Ssin.'

'The rain of sin?'

'Reign as in rule, and Pharaoh Ssin, spelled with a double "S". She was a pharaoh from the eighteenth dynasty, approximately 1300 BC. And she was well named, by all accounts, being a particularly sinful ruler.'

Nick glanced automatically at his sister, who shrugged. She'd never heard of Pharaoh Ssin, either.

'And, no, I cannot tell you what the symbols stood for originally. The author of the scripts bearing the squirrel and the stickleback symbols used a form of hieroglyphics understood only by himself.' Omar smiled. 'And perhaps by Squirrel and Stickleback, if they were actual people.'

Callie peered at the papyrus again and thought the symbol with the bug's face, followed by a lightning bolt might mean, *Beware of Gobb, the ugly shopkeeper*.

'Here is the author's signature,' Omar went on, singling out a symbol at the very bottom of the papyrus: a hieroglyph constructed of three, five-pointed stars forming a rising semicircle. 'It is the symbol for the Seer.'

'The what?' asked Nick.

'An individual who could "see" into the future. In this case a boy, just a little older than you and Callie. He is legendary.'

Callie giggled. 'Maybe he knew me and Nick would turn up here then, and sent us a text.'

'Or an Email,' added Nick. 'An Egyptian mail.'

Callie was about to ask if they could buy the papyrus, when the shop door rattled firmly shut. There was a sharp clacking sound as Gobb slid a metal bolt across. Then he dragged down a faded lemon-and-lime-coloured roller blind. The few streaks of light angling over the displays in the window were all that remained to illuminate the shop.

'What's going on?' asked Callie hoarsely, looking at Omar. Omar had quailed.

The giant bellowed over his shoulder: 'Ali...Hussein... Come out here! I require your assistance.' Two men, almost as big as Gobb himself, came clattering out from the back of the shop. 'Hold our two young guests,' ordered Gobb, and the two men grasped Callie and Nick by the arms, while Gobb himself pinned Omar to the wall.

2

The Seer

The air in the shop now smelled strongly of rancid sweat, and the remaining shards of sunlight picked out a line of crocodile tattoos on the arm of Callie's captor.

'Do something, Omar!' she cried frantically as the man began to drag her away from the bolted door. 'Give them money or something.'

'Yes, yes. Of course,' Omar pounced on the idea, producing his leather wallet and thrusting a bundle of Egyptian notes of all denominations at the giant shopkeeper. 'Please . . . Please. Take this.'

'No! She stays with us!' Gobb roared, slapping the money away. 'The boy too.'

'Why? What are they supposed to have done?' said Omar, sounding scared and mystified at the same time.

'They will translate the papyrus.' Gobb tore the sheet of papyrus, with the squirrel and stickleback symbols at the top, from the wall – and thrust it at Callie.

'Pardon?' Callie thought she must have misheard.

'You will read it, Squirrel.'

'I'm not Squirrel,' Callie mumbled in disbelief. Was this man crazy? 'It's just a nickname.'

'No. You said you are called Squirrel and Stickleback. The Seer himself predicted your arrival in this year and in this location – before he became more secretive in his predictions.' The giant leered at them unpleasantly. 'I have been waiting for you in this stinking hole for months, because no mere servant could be trusted.'

'But this is all a big mistake,' said Nick desperately. 'We're just shopping.'

'Read it!' bellowed Gobb, making all three of them jump.

Not daring to do anything else, Callie stared at the papyrus. She hadn't the faintest idea what it said. Then she spotted the bug face with the lightning bolt next to it again. 'I thought that bit might say: "Beware of the shopkeeper with bug eyes",' she admitted hoarsely, worried about offending her huge captor.

'Good. Continue.'

'But that was just a guess.'

'CONTINUE!'

The roar almost deafened her. She stared at the papyrus again, willing the symbols to form a coherent sentence. 'Erm...'

There was a loud crash as Ali or Hussein, Callie didn't know which was which, went flying through the tent designed to look like a pyramid. Nick had taken him off balance and was now scrambling into the window display filled with the ancient-Egyptian toys and games. He started hammering on the glass pane, yelling at passers-by. 'Help us! Help us! They won't let us out!'

Several people stopped to squint through the window. A deeply tanned tourist started rattling the door handle. Muffled though his voice was, he was shouting: 'Come on! Open the door!'

With eyes bulging even more alarmingly than before, Gobb let up the blind with a snap and unbolted the door. 'We shall meet again, Squirrel,' he warned Callie chillingly. 'It is destiny.'

Callie, Nick and Omar hurried out of the shop explaining to the tourists that Gobb had been forcing them to buy a mummification kit they didn't want; the truth was altogether too bizarre.

'Great one, Callie,' commented Nick, 'the whole of Cairo to choose from and you find a shop run by three psychopaths. As if someone from thousands of years ago is going to write to us. It's completely nuts.'

Callie's heart was still thumping hard inside her chest. 'Not if he could see into the future and knew we were going to be there to read it.'

'Don't be stupid!' Nick said dismissively. 'It's just a coincidence, that's all.'

Omar was hurrying them onwards through the bazaar, which was still clogged with shoppers and traders; as late afternoon passed into early evening, the oppressive heat from the sun was fading.

'Anyway,' Nick went on. 'What would an ancient Egyptian have to say to us? Have a nice holiday, don't forget to visit the pyramids, ride a camel and meet a few psychotic new people along the way?'

Callie shrugged. 'I don't know.' It did seem improbable. Yet she was certain she had been able to interpret the most important part of the papyrus, and she wondered if the rest hadn't meant: *Get out of the shop quick.*

They'd entered a new maze of narrow streets, giving them occasional glimpses of the Nile, dark salmon pink under the setting sun. But Omar kept going until they reached an area of restaurants and kiosks at least half a kilometre away from Gobb's shop. He guided them towards a man serving food from a compact white trailer, where wonderful aromas of grilled lamb and chicken kebabs began to make their mouths water.

'We should get something to eat,' said Omar, finally breathing a little more easily.

Nick ordered a lamb kebab, and Callie: *'Koshari.'* She'd had the same dish a couple of days before and really liked it: a blend of noodles and rice mixed in a spicy tomato sauce topped with crispy fried onions. Omar ordered *koshari* as well, and Callie wondered if he couldn't think for himself after their ordeal.

When the hot food had been ladled out into polystyrene trays, Omar paid and then led them, slightly more calmly, towards the modern-looking Nile embankment, eating as they went. A pleasantly cooling breeze was blowing across the world's longest river and the lights from the many shops and hotels were reflecting prettily onto the glossy wide ribbon of water.

Thankfully the ordinariness of walking and eating takeaway food restored a little of Callie's courage too. It was almost as if nothing strange had happened. They walked on, listening to the sound of a boat engine as it puttered past on the Nile, then sauntered towards one of the city's fabulous minarets: a white marble, pencil-shaped prayer tower encircled at intervals by delicate gold balconies all the way to the top.

'I think those three were Followers of Ssin,' Omar said at last, making sure that no one was near enough to overhear him.

'The pharaoh you told us about?' asked Callie.

'Yes. The Followers are a modern-day reinvention of the bodyguard sect loyal to Pharaoh Ssin...Did you notice the tattoos one of them had on his arm?'

Callie nodded uncomfortably. 'Crocodiles.' She didn't like crocodiles at all. They were repulsive creatures.

'That is right,' said Omar gravely. 'Not only was Ssin the most hated of all Egypt's pharaohs, she worshipped crocodiles and sacrificed her enemies to them.'

'Brilliant,' said Nick ghoulishly.

Callie gave him a reproving look. 'What happened to her?'

'Ssin was defeated by a new pharaoh, Pharaoh Nemesis—'

'Nemesis?' said Nick. 'I've heard that somewhere before.'

'From a Greek myth. It means retribution and revenge. The real Nemesis had his court magician conjure up a sandstorm which lasted for thirty days and nights, burying Ssin alive under the desert as punishment for her crimes against Egypt and its people.'

Callie shuddered, trying to imagine what it would be like to be buried alive.

'The Followers of Ssin believe that their pharaoh still lives, and will one day return to power,' said Omar, lowering his voice as they were passing a fruit seller.

'That's stupid, though,' said Nick. 'Isn't it?'

'The scripts I told you about, written by the Seer, the boy prophet,' Omar used his thumb to wipe tomato sauce from the corner of his mouth, 'are rumoured to be a set of instructions for the *real* Squirrel and Stickleback, whoever they are or were, to find his secret predictions called the Lost Prophesies.'

'And the Lost Prophesies are important because?' Nick crammed the remaining quarter of his kebab into his mouth in one go. 'This was all thousands of years ago, right? Everything this Seer kid predicted must have already happened by now.'

'Not necessarily. No one can say how far the Seer delved into the future or what he saw,' said Omar darkly. 'It is thought that he foresaw every major event that was going to happen in the future; which side would win every war; discoveries yet to be made; cures to every human illness and disease; every prime minister in every country around the world; people who would be born thousands of years after his time.'

Like us, thought Callie. The moist, damp evening air suddenly swirled icily around her. They continued walking along the embankment, threading their way through locals and sight-seers, but still only talking when they were safely out of earshot.

'There are also legends about other things the Seer may have prophesied,' Omar went on. 'The secrets of eternal life and of eternal youth.'

'Isn't that the same thing?' asked Nick frowning.

'No. With eternal life one continues ageing, with eternal youth one always remains the same... The Followers believe that Pharaoh Ssin had the secret of eternal life, but was seeking the secret of eternal youth. For that secret alone, the Lost Prophesies would be worth more than all the treasure of the pharaohs.'

'Think I'd rather have all the treasure,' said Nick, a greedy expression on his face, as if he was trying to work out exactly how much that might be. When Callie glanced at Omar, she noted a similar expression behind his brown eyes.

He masked it immediately, and concluded disappointedly: 'It is a pity you are not the real Squirrel and Stickleback.'

'Why did the Seer give up his secrets to two people in the future, though?' asked Callie. 'Why not to someone back then? A friend or a relative?'

'Or why not use his power to keep himself alive and come and tell them in person?' added Nick.

Omar shrugged. 'Because he predicted that it would happen another way? Fate is a tricky master.'

'Oh.'

Omar now guided them away from the Nile and towards the smart area of the city where he lived. 'Come on, I want to get home.'

Omar's grandly appointed house was set in a row of elegant buildings with walnut-hued stonework. Each imposing house rose to a spectacular four storeys, their balconied windows spilling yellow light onto the avenue of alternating mango and rubber trees. And it was all barely a step from the illuminated modern high-rise buildings of central Cairo.

They stepped into the spacious hallway, which was a chequerboard of red and black glazed tiles. Real palm trees, in enormous brass plant pots, stood in each corner. Omar led them into a large reception room, which was filled with an eclectic mix of colourful Egyptian rugs, mahogany furniture, two maroon leather sofas and an extensive library – taking up an entire wall from floor to ceiling. Omar made his way round the room switching on the non-matching lamp stands, and dragging the heavy velvet curtains across a large bowed window.

'There is a copy of one of the inscriptions the Seer wrote to Squirrel and Stickleback in one of my books, if you are interested?' he said hopefully.

Nick rolled his eyes at Callie, but she shrugged; it might be interesting to *try* and interpret the inscription. It'd be something to do since Omar's house was completely devoid of television, and he wouldn't let them use the internet.

Omar crossed to one of the packed book shelves and retrieved a reference book with a tatty cover. He thumbed through the pages until he found a colour plate showing a pink granite slab cut into the floor of an Egyptian temple. The slab was carved with an inscription.

'Here...' He slid the book across the leather-topped desk, towards Callie and Nick.

'*Dear Callie and Nick,*' interpreted Nick, half joking. The familiar Squirrel and Stickleback symbols were followed closely by the sign of the Seer: three stars in a rainbow pattern.

'This hieroglyph means "motion" or "go to",' Omar explained, eager to make a contribution. The hieroglyph he was pointing at looked exactly like pair of walking legs. 'The last two symbols have no meaning at all...' his voice trailed off. 'That we know of, anyway.'

Callie and Nick leaned over the book, their heads almost touching. The mystery symbols were a rectangle within a rectangle, followed by a long, thin U shape.

'So it means, *Dear Callie and Nick, go to "rectangle" and "U shape"*?' said Nick, with a defeated shrug. He didn't think it was worth any more effort and wandered off to an armchair to play a football game on his mobile phone.

Callie plonked herself on one of the squashy leather sofas and closed her eyes. Had she seen those two symbols together before? If so, where?

Omar continued pulling reference books off the shelves one by one. In fact, he spent the remainder of the evening hunting for more Squirrel and Stickleback hieroglyphs, and found absolutely none. They were as rare as Callie's dad had said.

'Sorry, Omar,' said Callie eventually. 'I've no idea what it means.'

'Well, I suppose that proves that you are not Squirrel and

Stickleback,' Omar admitted with a deep sigh. He glanced at the pine case clock, which indicated that it was past ten o'clock. 'Time you were in bed.' He ushered them back into the tiled hallway, and this time pointed them towards the magnificent marble steps leading to the upper floors of the grand house. He wished them goodnight, and told them to, 'sleep well.'

A large air-conditioning fan was turning on Callie's bedroom ceiling as she sat down in front of the dressing-table mirror to rub moisturiser into her sunburned face. Her skin was peeling unattractively around her nose.

Her bedroom was an even more exotic mix of tastes and styles than the reception room downstairs. The mirror she was using was framed by a mosaic of multicoloured glass, which matched the globe-shaped lamp shade on a brass wall-mounting behind her; luxurious emerald-green curtains with golden-yellow tassels hung across the curving window. Callie loved the jam-packed book shelves that were taller than her, and the small set of drawers whose top was littered with various trinkets and bowls of fragrant-smelling *pot pouri*.

After a minute, she screwed the top back on the tub of moisturiser and studied the book shelf. During his search of the shelves downstairs, Omar had told her there was a book all about the Seer in her bedroom, if she wanted to learn more. She was certainly curious, and she'd already read the couple of books on climbing she'd brought on holiday with her.

She found *Egypt's Greatest Astrologer* wedged between some Egyptian poems and a catalogue from Omar's museum, and after prying it loose with her fingernails, she found it was written by a professor called Jed Severs.

The large, cosy bed squeaked as she climbed in, and she plumped a thick, soft pillow behind her back to start reading: *Chapter One – The Potter and the Pharaoh.*

The giant Egyptian with misshapen bald head and bug eyes, who'd been dogging their footsteps the whole way home, saw the light finally go off in the girl's bedroom. Then, committing the details of the house and its green panelled door to memory, he turned away and hurried into the enveloping darkness.

3

Sacred Crocodile

Season of the desert storms, 3,422 years previously

The Nile was a vein of *lapis lazuli* blue, surging between lush green banks of papyrus reed and yellow-bloomed acacia. A jumble of mud-brick kilns – large ovens resembling giant sand castles – cluttered the riverbank. Around the kilns were stacks of pottery, sorted into different shapes and sizes, awaiting 'firing': the process of baking the clay to make it strong enough for use.

An army of potters were busy under the hot sun. Wearing little more than modest white kilts around their waists; their bare skin was tanned to the same rich red colour as the clay they worked. A boy of fourteen, tall and strong, was mixing armfuls of soft Nile clay with tiny pieces of straw. His dark hair was shaved off save for one thick lock, which swung down by his ear as he laboured.

'Hurry, Fortune,' urged an older man, using the name given to the boy because he could tell people's fortunes and had startling visions about the future. Almost from his first toddling steps he had shown an ability to know things were going to happen before they did; throwing a tantrum to get everyone away from a kiln once, just before it exploded, and foreseeing a

21

plague of locusts and so saving his farmer uncle's crops from destruction. It was a rare gift he had.

'Sorry, Father,' replied Fortune, 'my mind was occupied elsewhere.' Fortune realised he must have frozen in his kneading of the clay and straw, while his dark, almond-shaped eyes had widened in fear.

Fortune's father had stopped working too. He had been patting clay between a rounded stone and a curved paddle to make a storage jar. 'One of your premonitions?' he asked with concern.

'It's Neb,' replied Fortune, naming a younger boy who normally followed him around as if *he* was the pharaoh, instead of Pharaoh Ssin, on her throne in the mighty palace high above the Potters' Fields. Unusually they had seen nothing of Neb all day.

'I just had a vision of him by the galley docks,' Fortune went on, referring to the busy stretch of the Nile where the war barges and merchant ships tied up. 'I think something terrible is going to happen to him.'

Fortune's father did not delay him any longer for details. 'Then run, my son. Run before it is too late!'

'Thank you, Father.' Fortune sprinted away from the kilns, with the strongest feeling that he would not be returning. He raced through the glass-blowers' stoves in the adjoining industrial area.

One of the glass-blowers raised a warning shout as he veered towards a table lined with tiny perfume bottles – they looked like standing up fish, zigzagged with stripes of orange, yellow and white to represent their scales. 'Careful, boy!'

'Sorry!' Fortune changed direction abruptly, glancing at the position of the sun in the sky. There was still time to save Neb.

He took to the reed beds at the very edge of the river, disturbing a pair of snowy-white ibises, which flew raucously into the cloudless blue sky. They beat their wings across the docks where men were working at a stone jetty – using the wooden cranes there to unload red granite hippopotamus statues from a stonemason's barge.

The pride of the pharaoh's navy: a war galley, *The Cobra*, with its curving prow and stern and wide deck, lay at anchor beside the jetty. Without the use of a single nail, the ship's cedar-wood planking had been stitched together with rope. A dozen sailors were on board loading provisions, and there was Neb, acting the fool in front of them all, tumbling on the dockside, pretending he was about to fall into the Nile.

'Can you swim, little frog?' roared a sailor with a barrel chest and a snub-nose, effortlessly tossing sacks of flour from the dockside to the deck of *The Cobra*. 'If you want to join the navy, you must be a good swimmer.'

Neb nodded his shaven head enthusiastically, eager to win the sailor's approval. 'I could swim right across Mother Nile if I wanted to.'

'Is that so?' The sailor guffawed. Then, with a startlingly sudden movement, he swung the boy off his feet. 'If you can swim there and back again, I will make you captain of your own ship.' He pitched Neb spiralling through the warm, dry air, and the boy hit the water with a thunderous splash, which caused the rest of the sailors to hoot with laughter.

'No!' cried Fortune, with so much fury that the entire crew turned to see him scrabbling down a shallow earthen bank in a cloud of red sand and dust. 'Neb, come back!'

In the glittering water, Neb surfaced without seeing his friend; as good as his word, he began swimming with frantic, rather clumsy strokes towards the opposite bank of the river – easily half a mile away.

'Neb, there's a crocodile!' Fortune yelled after him, reaching the galley. 'A crocodile!'

Neb heard nothing, intent on earning the captaincy he'd been promised as a joke, he continued splashing through the warm, crystal-clear water.

'There are no crocodiles on this stretch of the Nile,' the barrel-chested sailor barked at Fortune, as though if anyone should know, a member of the pharaoh's navy should.

'Today there is!' shouted Fortune, his feet clattering as he ran up the wooden gangplank and onto *The Cobra*'s deck without stopping.

'Hey, Goat Dung! You can't come up here,' roared the nearest of the sailors, affronted.

Fortune dodged past him, snatching up a thick wooden stave used for tightening sail ropes and stuffing it into the waistband of his kilt as he ran.

'Oi! That's ours.' The sailor rushed at him, but Fortune was quicker and already diving over the other side of the galley. He punctured the surface of the Nile like a spear. Three seconds later he surfaced again and started swimming after Neb, reducing the distance between them with every stroke of his muscular arms.

The other sailors were jeering him now, baffled by this pointless rescue. 'There are no crocodiles, you young fool!'

Then they realised they were wrong: 'Gods!'

A monster launched itself from the muddy depths. It's deadly fanged jaws formed an open V shape, at once above and below the waterline, as it powered for Neb. Easily four times the length of the boy, the ugly, rutted scales along its back were as invulnerable as iron armour.

'Swim, boy! Swim!' Most of the sailors were suddenly rooting for Neb. Only the man who had thrown him into the water in the first place had taken the crocodile's side, and was now chortling to himself and smacking his lips. 'Go on, crocodile. Snap to it.'

There was a high-pitched scream. Neb had glanced over his shoulder, not alerted by the voices, but by a wave of water surging up behind him, propelled by the widening reptilian jaws. The boy panicked, fighting the water around him, trying to grasp handfuls of air above his head, and sinking in the process. Miraculously, it was that which saved him. The crocodile's side-swiping jaws snapped shut on several gallons of sparkling water, missing Neb altogether. But as he surfaced, gagging and screeching, the crocodile came round again with one swish of its 250 kilogram tail.

Then, another miracle for Neb: a jade-green eye, slit vertically by a reptilian pupil, seemed to flicker and calculate as it spied an even greater morsel – Fortune was splashing conveniently straight towards its re-opening jaws.

'Yes! Take *me*,' shrieked Fortune, thrashing the water in front of him. 'Come on, you hideous brute!'

The crocodile accelerated through the water: a segmented brown torpedo primed for slaughter. With alarming suddenness, Fortune's entire arm disappeared down the crocodile's pink throat. Deadly teeth sliced into his shoulder, producing fountains of blood. His scream was loud and chilling.

'Chop 'is arm off, and see if he swims in circles,' encouraged the barrel-chested sailor. But the crocodile did not complete its bite at all. It was retching, vomiting Fortune's arm free, and choking on the ship's wooden stave that was now jammed tight between its upper and lower jaws. The creature rolled away, twisting over and over, trying to close its mouth as water gushed over its tongue and into its stomach. It was drowning, the large flap at the back of its throat – to stop it swallowing gallons of water – held open by the obstruction.

Fortune swam away with nothing worse than a line of cuts incised along his arm.

'Fortune, you saved me! You killed the monster!' sobbed Neb, his hero worship complete. They were treading water together, water that was pink with Fortune's blood.

A less appreciative voice growled: 'You just killed a sacred crocodile!'

Fortune turned in the water and saw *The Cobra* gliding up beside them as its crew rowed for all they were worth. 'Don't you know that killing one of the pharaoh's crocs carries the death sentence with it?' The barrel-chested sailor was smirking merrily as he readied a boat hook to fish them both out of the water. 'I hope that little frog you saved was worth it.'

The sailor started to laugh, and Neb began to cry.

4

Plague of Flies

C allie had gone to sleep after reading only a chapter of *Egypt's Greatest Astrologer*, which hadn't really given much detail about who The Seer was or how gifted he had been. Now a blinding light reached into her sleep and plucked her out on the other side. Someone was in her room. She sat up, the sound of her pulse beating violently against her eardrums. The light was on, and it took her eyes half a minute to adjust.

'What do *you* want?' she groaned, when she realised it was only Nick, who must have been sleeping in his clothes since he was fully dressed, sitting on the end of her bed.

'I thought I heard someone poking around downstairs, and I wondered if you'd heard it as well.'

'No, I didn't,' said Callie, kicking impatiently under her covers to remove him from her bed. 'It's probably just Omar.' She pulled the cord hanging from the ceiling above her to extinguish the light, and then wriggled further under the cotton cover.

'It's twenty past four,' said Nick from the darkness. 'What would Omar be doing at this time of the night?'

'I don't know, do I?' Callie was frustrated. She heard her brother groping towards the door, and then a crack as he walked into something. She sighed.

'Can you try not to make so much noise? Some of us are trying to sleep.' If it was twenty past four, she wanted another five hours at least.

Then she heard the sound of pottery or glass smashing loudly downstairs and sat bolt upright again. 'OK, I did hear that.' She was about to haul herself out of bed to go and investigate, when she heard a strange voice shouting. 'That wasn't Omar.'

Nick let out a startled cry and leaped back as Omar entered Callie's room and thrust him aside. Their uncle looked ruffled and sweating; his black silk dressing gown swishing around him revealing gold-embroidered slippers, his wire-framed glasses slightly askew. He threw himself at the large bookcase to the side of the bed.

Callie gaped at him.

'Are you looking for something to read *now*...? Someone's broken into your house.'

Omar ignored her, dragging at the edge of the bookcase instead. There was a mechanical-sounding click and the entire unit swung towards him on a hinge – revealing another room on the other side. 'Hurry! Hurry. We must hide.'

Both Callie and Nick stared at him with open mouths.

'Come on! It is the men from this afternoon. The Followers of Ssin! A noise awoke me, and when I looked out of my bedroom window I saw them forcing open the front door.'

Heavy footsteps sounded on the marble stairs as if to confirm his statement.

Without stopping to wonder why such a room even

existed, Callie grabbed her clothes and purple rucksack and dashed through the bookcase door after Nick. Omar yanked it back into its original position behind them.

The concealed room she now found herself in was lit strangely from above, the glow of orange street light pouring through a circular skylight in the sloping ceiling. In a single glance Callie took in a pair of lavish thrones inlaid with bloodstone and topaz; solid gold statues of pharaohs; jewel-encrusted face masks; shimmering caskets painted with vibrant, colourful symbols; and the *piece-de-resistance* – a golden eye with a tennis-ball-sized ruby for an iris. When she was able to tear her gaze away from all the treasure, it was to see Omar, wearing a rather guilty expression.

'Does the museum know you've got all this stuff?' she spluttered, the intruders ransacking Omar's house briefly forgotten.

'It is a small museum... There isn't room for *everything*,' bleated Omar, casting anxious glances towards the secret way in. Obviously petrified that, not only would the Followers find them, they would also locate his secret stash.

'No wonder all that's left in the proper museum is dead people,' said Callie reprovingly.

'So, when you were talking about all the treasure of the pharaohs, you meant your spare bedroom?' put in Nick. He reached for a solid gold sword with a hooked blade.

Omar hissed at him desperately: 'Don't touch anything! And don't tell your parents!' He spun round as raised voices suddenly sounded in Callie's bedroom. All three of them held their breath, and Omar leaned forward to place a spectacle-rimmed eye to the back of the bookcase and peer through a tiny spy hole. Then he placed his ear to the wooden panel.

'What are they saying?' Nick whispered.

Omar turned a stricken face from the spy hole. 'They have come for you obvioulsy. They are convinced you are Squirrel and Stickleback, and can lead them to the Seer's prophesies and reveal the secret of eternal youth.'

'But we're not Squirrel and Stickleback!' hissed Nick. 'We couldn't translate the inscription you showed us, could we?'

'It doesn't matter whether you are or not!' whispered Omar. 'The Followers of Ssin *think* you are.'

Barely daring to breathe, Callie put her eye to the spy hole. In the soft lamplight beyond, the three huge men from The Magic of Egypt shop were poking around her bedroom. Startlingly, each was wearing a robe: simple white cloth for the accomplices, and blood-crimson for their bug-eyed leader. 'You didn't say they'd come in fancy dress,' she whispered.

'Fancy dress?' breathed Nick.

'They're dressed as ancient Egyptian priests or something,' Callie told him.

'Priests?'

'Keep your voices down!' Omar begged them both.

Callie nodded silently and put her eye back to the spy hole. Gobb was stooping to lift the cover on her bed. He stroked the cotton sheet where she had just been lying: testing it for warmth. Callie shuddered, her flesh crawling. One of the others, Ali or Hussein, found her pink mobile phone from amongst the bits and pieces on the dressing table. He passed it to Gobb, who after a cursory glance tossed it back among the trinkets. Callie was annoyed with herself for not grabbing it when she ran into the hidden room. Now she couldn't get in touch with anyone for help.

A pair of hideously bulging eyes came level with Callie's.

She bit down on her tongue to stop herself crying out, guessing the giant was only scanning the numerous titles on the shelf, not realising his prey was centimetres away.

After a few seconds he rapped out an order to his companions and led them from the bedroom. A moment later the Followers could be heard clomping around in another room, probably Nick's.

'I think they've gone to search the rest of the house,' Callie told the others, as she turned from the spy hole, trembling. Staring into that face had been revolting.

'We'd better wait here until they give up and go.' Omar sat down dejectedly in a corner, pulling his shiny black dressing gown over his embroidered slippers. Nick looked slightly relieved and flopped into one of the fabulous golden thrones and grabbed an oddly shaped pillow to stuff behind his head. Callie recognised what it was immediately: the ancient Egyptians had been in the habit of mummifying their pets, and Nick was probably now using somebody's long dead cat as a headrest. She didn't tell him. And Omar now had much more to worry about than Nick touching his stuff.

'I'm going to change out of my pyjamas.' Callie retreated behind the other throne with her screwed-up bundle of clothes.

'I think they're "media studies" and "physics",' said Nick randomly, as Callie reappeared in a beige skirt with big zipped pockets, a purple hoodie top, and pink and silver trainers.

'You think *what* are "media studies" and "physics"?'

'The message we looked at in Omar's book. I thought of it after we went to bed. The rectangle inside a rectangle is supposed to be a TV – *media studies*, and that U shape is a test tube – *physics*. They're identical to the icons on our school timetable.'

Callie and Omar stared at Nick as if he'd suddenly grown two heads.

It was Omar who found his voice first. 'Are you saying you *can* read the Seer's script? That you *are* Squirrel and Stickleback?'

Nick gulped, 'Maybe.'

'I knew I'd seen those symbols somewhere before. They were just so out of context I didn't make the connection.' Callie pulled a face. 'But why would the Seer write to us about media studies and physics? *Dear Callie and Nick, don't forget to do your homework during half term?*' It was inconceivable. And it certainly wouldn't impress Gobb and the other Followers.

'What if it's a clue to something else?' said Nick, sounding awed by his own discovery. 'Those legs you showed us didn't mean "legs", they meant "go".'

Callie's brain was churning. She turned hopefully to Omar. 'What about "med" and "phys"?' she asked. 'The words are abbreviated on our timetable.'

'Med phys?' Omar's brown eyes widened behind his glasses. 'Ssin's capital city was called Medphis. Though it was spelled with an "i" instead of a "y".' He furrowed his brow thoughtfully. 'It used to be located on the lower Nile.'

'*Used to be…?*' said Callie. 'Isn't it now?'

'As I told you, the city was buried along with its cruel pharaoh.' Omar stroked the dark stubble on his chin. 'But if the Seer predicted that happening, and he still wished Squirrel and Stickleback – you – to go there…' He stared off into a corner, obviously trying to fathom more from the simple message.

Callie was doing some thinking of her own. Were they really Squirrel and Stickleback? Strangely, it almost seemed possible now – because surely only kids at their school would recognise those specific symbols for media studies and physics, and how many others from St Joseph's Secondary School were in Cairo, at the right time and in the right place, and had the nicknames Squirrel and Stickleback?

Omar slapped his sweaty forehead with the palm of his hand. 'Of course! The boy prophet must have foreseen me too... and known that I would show you that inscription.' His eyes glinted in the orange street light, invading from above. 'What other conclusion could there be than he is directing us to the place where his prophesies are?'

Callie didn't like the way this was shaping up. Omar seemed so convinced. And there was more than excitement in his toffee-brown eyes, there was greed, he clearly thought he had the chance to add even more riches to his dubious private collection.

'The branches of the Nile have made hundreds of adjustments over the last several thousand years,' Omar went on. 'Medphis could be miles from the current course of the river.'

'Couldn't you make an educated guess?' said Nick, looking just as greedy as their host.

'Possibly... Ancient Egyptian geography *is* one of my interests.'

'Then you have to take us there.'

Omar nodded decisively. 'I will borrow my neighbour's car and we can start tonight. As soon as the Followers go.'

'Don't you think you should ask Mum and Dad first?' said Callie anxiously. She didn't think either of her parents would approve of Omar taking them off to a buried city with three maniacs dressed as ancient Egyptian priests chasing after them.

'Yes, yes, of course,' said Omar. 'I will contact them on the way.'

33

Callie decided to ring her parents herself, as soon as she got the chance. She put her eye to the spy hole again. Her bedroom now appeared to be in darkness. Maybe that was a good sign – she could go in and get her phone.

Then she thought she was going to puke. It wasn't that the light was off at all; her bedroom was black and crawling with flies. The walls, the ceiling, her comfy bed and every stick of furniture she had touched, sat or slept on, had disappeared under a seething carpet of ugly black flies, and thousands – tens of thousands – more swirled around the lamp shade, fogging out most of the light.

She was about to draw back in revulsion when something moved in the disgusting dark cloud. Gobb was sitting in the armchair at the bottom of the bed. Flies had settled over every centimetre of his misshapen bald head, almost blackening him from view. His ugly, bulging eyes were small islands blinking out of the black filth. And he was just sitting there, waiting.

Callie recoiled from the awful image. 'Gobb's in there. And there are flies... Millions of flies... I don't understand...' she whispered, stumbling over her words.

'Flies?' Nick took her place at the spy hole and then seconds later was making a retching sound. Omar was the last to look.

'They know that we are hiding *somewhere*, and are trying to flush us out,' he said in a terrified whisper.

'Where did they get all those flies?' rasped Nick. There were already a dozen or more large flies pinging off the skylight above him, attempting to escape.

'In the style of the biblical plagues of Egypt,' Omar said thickly, dashing over to a dark brown radiator, which stretched across the wall behind the two thrones. He felt along the line of metal fins, before snatching his hand away as if he had been branded by a red-hot poker. 'But a more modern conjuring trick. They have turned up the heating – as high as it will go. This is an old house. The attics and the wall spaces are infested with flies at this time of the year. Heat will encourage them out: through the pipes, through the ventilation ducts, from under the skirting boards...'

Callie swatted a large fly that had just landed on her arm and wheeled in alarm. The sound of buzzing had intensified to an angry din on their side of the bookcase. And to her horror, a mass of flies were crawling through a metal grille halfway up the wall. She opened her mouth to scream, but gagged on a mouthful of fat, black flies. She coughed and spat in nauseated revulsion, scraping at her suddenly fly-infested hair. She could not imagine anything more disgusting.

Nick began swatting dementedly with an irreplaceable ancient papyrus from Omar's collection.

'We *have to* bear it,' Omar took Callie by the shoulders. 'If we show ourselves, there are no passing tourists to save us this time.'

'Then think of something, before I scream the place down,' Callie warned him with her hand in front of her mouth. She couldn't stand this for much longer.

'Where does that go?' Nick was blinking up at the circular skylight in the ceiling. There was a hinge on one side and a handle on the other. 'Is it a way out?'

'Yes! Yes!' Omar jumped onto the nearest golden throne, no longer careful of his treasure, and grasped the brass handle above him. The skylight squeaked slightly as he opened it outwards, making them all turn in terror, but the back of the bookcase remained firmly shut. Gobb must be almost deaf from the drone of a million aggravated flies.

'Follow me.' Omar didn't wait for them, but pulled himself up through the circular frame. He dangled for a second, giving Callie an unpleasant flash of hairy legs under his dressing gown, before he finally manoeuvred himself the rest of the way out and disappeared with a muffled grunt.

'Go on, Nick,' Callie ordered, grabbing her rucksack as clouds of flies continued to swarm wickedly around them both. 'Go on!'

Nick leaped onto the throne and used the slats of its carved back as a kind of ladder to climb up through the window. Callie was just half a second behind him – having squirrel skills had benefits. Nick helped her out onto a short, sloping roof, which angled down to a paved area, and they slid thankfully down to where Omar was waiting for them.

Callie continued to flap at her clothes and claw at her hair until every last fly was off her. Finally she looked around. In the orange light from the nearby street lamp everything was the colour of Lucozade.

The paved roof was enclosed by an ornamental iron railing, curly and intricate, partitioning it from the other buildings in the terrace. As a roof garden it left much to be desired – there were a couple of untended terracotta flowerpots with dried-up soil in them and a pair of grimy white plastic chairs at an equally grimy plastic table.

Callie turned expectantly towards Omar. 'Can we get down from here? There must be a fire escape.'

Omar looked uncomfortable.

Nick looked over the railings. 'There isn't one, just an old drainpipe.' He peered nervously at the tree-lined street, a startlingly four storeys below them.

'I removed the original fire escape for practical reasons,' admitted Omar.

'How is that practical?' Nick hissed angrily.

'You didn't want anyone climbing up and discovering your *private* museum, did you, Omar?' said Callie, leaning over the railings to examine the drainpipe herself. The metal brackets fixing it to the wall were a *bit* like the steps of a ladder, though some of the screws were missing, and the drainpipe itself was beginning to rust. It might be possible to climb down, but she didn't think it would be easy for Nick. He wasn't great with heights.

'I will show you how to do it,' offered Omar, making it sound as if he was doing them a favour. He pulled his shiny black dressing gown tighter and climbed over the railings. 'Like this.' He began to descend confidently.

'Talk about a rat down a drainpipe,' muttered Nick.

'Shhhh! He'll hear you,' said Callie, wondering how Omar had acquired his climbing skills. Tomb robbing, perhaps? They were certainly finding out a lot about their uncle's character.

Nick peered at the drainpipe once more with an anxious expression. 'I don't think I can do it, Cal,' he mumbled. 'I'll fall.'

'Try not to think about that,' Callie advised. 'Think about, erm... school or something.'

'Now I know you're trying to kill me.'

'You know what I mean. Just don't think about the height... Here.' She unhooked part of the webbing from her rucksack, which included a toughened plastic ring clip on each end. She clipped one of them onto a belt loop on the side of Nick's jeans.

37

'What's that supposed to do?' he asked.

'Climb over, then thread the webbing behind the drainpipe and clip the other end to the other side of your jeans. It'll fasten you to the drainpipe.' She didn't add: *in case you fall.* 'You'll have to unclip it and then re-clip it each time you reach another bracket, so make sure you've got a good grip of the drainpipe when you stop.'

Nick nodded and gulped. 'Thanks.'

'Now climb out.'

Clinging to the ironwork with a sort of death grip, Nick swung one leg at a time over the railings. He fed the webbing around the back of the drainpipe as Callie had instructed him.

'Go on, start to climb down,' Callie said gently.

Nick grasped the drainpipe and, rather than actually climbing, started to slide down a couple of centimetres at a time, but at least he was heading safely to the ground. Callie watched until her brother had made it past the first of the brackets before shouldering the rucksack and beginning to climb down after him. Flakes of dark green paint, backed by rust, peeled off in her fingers as she gripped the drainpipe, and the brackets waggled in the stonework where there were missing screws, but it was a fairly easy climb.

Nick slipped down the final three metres all in one go and looked up at his sister in relief. 'I did it.'

'Well done!' Callie jumped down beside him and retrieved the webbing from her rucksack. But there was no time to relax.

Omar, who had been pacing anxiously, whispered, 'Come! My neighbour's car is along the street. He will not mind us borrowing it.' Before Callie and Nick could question him, Omar was ghosting across the narrow, paved garden and out through the open gate.

The street was deserted and almost as bright as day under the orange street lamps. Callie and Nick caught up with Omar at the side of a mustard-yellow battered saloon, with one orange door. It smelled of engine oil and diesel.

'The lock is a little tricky,' Omar whispered, keeping his back to them so that they couldn't see what he was doing to the car.

'We really have to talk to Mum and Dad about who they leave us with in the future,' hissed Callie. There was no way Omar's neighbour allowed him to take his car whenever he needed transport.

'I don't think we can afford to be picky right now,' Nick whispered back.

'It's stealing.'

They heard a slight *clunk* as the central locking succumbed to Omar's efforts. 'Callie you get in the front. Nick in the back.'

Omar leaped in behind the steering wheel and started rifling through the glove compartment. 'Now, where did Zelli tell me he kept his spare ignition key?' When the glove compartment didn't yield a key, he tried the side pocket of the door, and then finally felt under the seat. 'Ah-ha!' Omar waved a set of jingling keys at them. 'I remember now.'

He tried starting the engine, but it just made an unpromising *rarr, rarr, rarr* noise without firing up. He tried again.

A loud *bang* sounded as a cracked white plastic chair hit the windscreen with alarming force.

Omar screamed. Two terracotta flowerpots followed the chair, exploding on the bonnet with deafening *clangs*.

'They're on your roof!' yelled Callie, straining her neck to peer through the windscreen. Gobb, a swirling crimson shape, was lobbing garden furniture at them. The second plastic chair clattered loudly across the car, making Omar scream again.

'They have found their way through my treasure chamber!'

'Maybe they were in too much of a hurry to see what was in there,' said Nick, but Omar rounded on him furiously.

'Not see what was in there? Are you insane?'

'Sorry... I was just trying to be nice...' Nick quailed before Omar's unexpected ferocity.

Something else exploded deafeningly on the roof of the car, and then the white plastic table fell over the bonnet. Omar clutched at his chest as if he was having a heart attack, and then frantically turned the ignition key again. Still nothing happened. 'Come on! God help us!'

'Hurry up,' screamed Callie. 'He's climbing down!' Gobb was scaling down the side of the building. He was fearless and reckless, allowing the drainpipe to slide through his enormous hands. The car engine made another grating *rarr, rarr, rarr* noise.

'It is no good!' yelled Omar. 'We must run for it! Come on!'

He flung open his door and bolted from the car before either of them could stop him.

'Wait for us!' yelled Callie hysterically, trying to find the handle on her door. 'Wait!'

Omar darted down the nearest alley without looking back to check if Callie and Nick were behind him.

A loud crash on the street outside Omar's house made Callie swing round. Half of the drainpipe they'd climbed down was hanging from the house wall at right angles. The rest had just smashed onto the pavement. Gobb was still two storeys up, clinging to a windowsill.

He jumped the rest of the way, his crimson robe swirling around him, and landed in the garden. Then, seemingly uninjured, he was hurtling out through the gate and striding towards the car, his eyes bulging demonically in the orange lamplight.

5

Chased by chariot

C allie's hand finally found the door handle. 'Let me try starting it,' Nick shouted, already clambering over the back of the driver's seat.

'No. We don't have time.'

Nick ignored her. He turned the ignition key, depressing the accelerator pedal at the same time like he'd seen his dad doing with their own car. It worked! Suddenly there was a loud roar from the engine, and he was yelling: 'Which direction?'

'It doesn't matter!' Callie screamed back. 'Just get us away from *him*.'

The car lurched forward, scarcely under Nick's control, as Gobb banged his fists hard against the boot. He left a dent in the metal, but Nick was feeding the steering wheel through his hands now to get them going in a straight line. He stabbed the accelerator pedal again with the tip of his right foot and they speared forward and out of Gobb's reach.

Grand, sleeping architecture began to flash past them, and Callie was suddenly terrified they were going to crash straight into something. Their dad had allowed Nick to drive his car a few times on quiet country lanes, and once Nick had driven it in the supermarket car park (which had been totally unauthorised – and incurred a considerable amount of shouting from both their parents), but this was mental.

'Seriously, I don't know which way to go,' repeated Nick, sounding panicked as he clung on grimly to the steering wheel. A glance in the rear-view mirror told him that Gobb was falling behind.

'Just keep going! And put your seatbelt on.' Callie must have sounded like their mum, because Nick obeyed instantly; they veered towards a row of parked cars as he tried to snap it into place. 'Sorry...'

'Here, let me do it.' Callie fixed both their seatbelts and then looked round again for Gobb. He was standing in the middle of the street, glowering after their departing car. Watching him get smaller and smaller, Callie began to breathe again – they'd got away.

She realised they were driving without lights. 'How do you switch on the headlights?'

'Oh, hang on, I'll just flick through the owner's manual,' said Nick sarcastically.

Callie ignored him and started twisting paddles on the steering column. 'They're here on our car,' she said. First the windscreen wipers flashed across the windscreen, and then the headlights flared out in front of them.

'Wow, that's better,' said Nick, suddenly able to see the street in front of them in the blaze of light. They drove on for another minute before he wondered out loud: 'How old do you think you have to be to drive in Egypt?'

'I'm guessing it's older than twelve,' replied Callie. 'And I'm pretty sure they'd expect you to take a driving test first... It's a good thing nobody's about...' She glanced at the red needle on the speedometer as it inched up towards forty kilometres per hour. 'Do you think you should be going this fast?'

'It's OK. It's not as if I've never driven through a city before.'

'When have you ever driven through a city?' Callie sounded flabbergasted.

'All the time...on my computer.'

'This is *not* the same.'

The car suddenly swerved to the wrong side of the street as Nick's concentration was broken by something in the rear-view mirror.

'What? What are you looking at?'

'Do you remember that chariot Gobb threw me off yesterday?'

Callie guessed why he was asking and twisted round on her seat to look down the road behind them. An ancient Egyptian chariot was chasing them. Gobb was towering over the blue and gold striped cockpit, Ali and Hussein hanging on grimly beside him. In the chariot traces were two fine black horses which Gobb was lashing into a frenzy of speed. The clatter of hooves and metal-rimmed chariot wheels was deafening on the concrete road. And there was no question that they were catching up.

'Faster. *Faster!*' Nick encouraged the car to an even greater speed. More town houses flashed by in a blur. There was a loud bang, and a tinkling of smashing glass as they lost a wing mirror by veering into a parked car. Nick dragged the steering wheel back under his control again, and perched on the edge of the driver's seat to depress the accelerator pedal as far as it would go. Callie stiffened in her seat, terrified.

'We're not outrunning them, are we?' said Nick.

Callie kneeled up on her seat and peered anxiously through the rear windscreen. 'No! They're catching us up!'

Gobb seemed to know what he was doing, driving the two black horses with amazing expertise; unfortunately for them he was a master of the horses, a fearsome charioteer.

'Hell!'

'What?' Callie slid round to see a corner hurtling towards them. They were never going to be able to stop in time. 'Slow down!' she screeched.

'Don't you think I'm trying to?' Nick snapped back. He was angling himself across the driver's seat to reach the brake pedal, while trying to steer them round the corner at the same time. The car went into a skid, rocketing sideways on squealing tyres. There was a loud *thump* as they mounted a curb, then somehow the car swerved into another road and continued on its way. Nick's hands were shaking on the steering wheel, his knuckles white.

'I don't know how you did that,' said Callie hoarsely. She spun round again to see if the chariot would follow them at such an impossible speed. It was. Gobb was forcing the horses round the corner by leaning the entire chariot onto one furiously spinning wheel. The chariot threatened to topple right over, but then the airborne wheel bashed back down and the horses surged on.

'I recognise this place,' said Callie. They were racing past a city park hemmed in by dilapidated, cream-coloured buildings. 'We walked down here yesterday...But I can't think of anywhere we can lose the chariot.'

They roared by a row of shops with securely shuttered doors in every colour imaginable. Pictures of the items they

45

sold were painted onto the walls: fruit and vegetables, clothes, haircuts and electronics. The signs written in Arabic reflected back in the blaze of the car headlights. The road was wide enough here for the chariot to thunder up alongside them, the prancing horses drawing level with the bonnet of the car.

'He's trying to cut us off,' Nick realised. 'Shall I drive into him?'

'No!' shouted Callie. 'You'll kill the horses.' She couldn't bear the thought of destroying such beautiful creatures, even if it was to save herself.

'Then what?'

'I don't know.' Callie willed the car to go faster. Then a harsh, screeching sound erupted beside her. The round, metal boss at the centre of the nearest chariot wheel was drilling into the side of the car. Gobb was steering into them, determined to stop them at any price. Nick tried to steer the car away, and they scraped along a wall, clipping a series of curving arches outside a bathhouse one by one. Lights began to illuminate in the upper-storey windows – the entire neighbourhood awoken by the clash between chariot and car.

Finally the vehicles separated, but not before something heavy had crashed onto the car roof.

'What was that?' Callie peered fearfully at the fabric-lined ceiling above her head, where a large, convex dent had suddenly appeared. She screamed as a sharp-faced man, wearing white priest's robes, slithered down the windscreen. It was Ali, or Hussein, and he was clinging to the roof, while glaring menacingly through the windscreen.

'Don't hit the brake!'

Even as Callie screamed it, she knew that it was too late; Nick was stamping on the brake pedal. It was instinctive, but

46

totally crazy. The car skidded, grazed the metal shutters of a garage door with a loud clang and stopped in a screech of tyres. The white-robed man was catapulted forward, grasping wildly at handfuls of air. He cracked sickeningly on the road and rolled under the chariot as it shot past. A face contorted with terror rebounded from the chariot wheel, and bright crimson blood splattered his white robes.

Callie jerked her gaze away from the body, and covered her mouth to stop the contents of her stomach ending up in her lap. Nick yelled tearfully: 'What have I done? *Callie, what have I done?*'

'Stop looking at him,' commanded Callie.

'Is he OK?' It was impossible that he was. He was lying perfectly still in a pool of his own blood.

'No,' said Callie firmly. 'But it wasn't your fault.' She gave her brother's arm a gentle squeeze, and forced herself not to look at the priest's body again.

The car had ended up slewed across a small junction, facing one of the city's mosques. Starlight was reflecting off the spectacular copper domes, silhouetting the numerous prayer towers against a darkly sapphire sky. The chariot had stopped further on and Gobb was now reining his horses into a cruel turn. Both black creatures appeared to rake the air with flailing hooves, before crashing back down again at right angles, and jerking the chariot clattering round behind them.

'Nick, we need to go.'

He was still in shock: studying the front of a nearby clothes shop as if he was contemplating buying an outfit. '*Nick.*' Callie touched her brother's arm again gently.

'What…?'

'The chariot's coming back.'

'Oh.' Without another word, Nick put the car into gear and steered them past the gated entrance to the mosque. The tyres rumbled over cobbles as they drove beside a section of the ancient city wall in alternating layers of brick and stone, capped by battlements. The chariot followed them, Gobb still driving like a maniac, his remaining companion clearly pleading with him to stop.

'Speed bump!' warned Callie, squinting through the windscreen. Incongruously, right across the end of the cobbled street, was a very modern traffic-calming device.

Nick took the ridge without slowing: the tyres made a humongous double bang as first the front, and then the rear wheels hit the obstruction. Callie found herself airborne for a second, striking her head painfully on the car ceiling and crying out. She fell back, half dazed – straining her watering eyes to see what Gobb would do.

He took the speed bump every bit as fast as they had. The horses leaped it easily, not even missing a stride, but the chariot was far less flexible. For a moment Gobb was there: gripping the reins tightly, while the other Follower of Ssin screamed in panic; then suddenly, they were both gone in an explosion of splintering wood. The narrow wheels appeared to burst apart, flinging the cockpit into an unrecoverable death roll. It went spiralling across the cobbles and crashed into the ancient city wall.

When the wreckage of the vehicle came to a final stop, Callie could see a white-robed figure crushed and lifeless beneath it; of Gobb, in his crimson robe, she could see nothing. The horses thundered on by themselves.

'Where's Gobb?' demanded Nick, his eyes transfixed by the rear-view mirror.

'I...I think he must have jumped,' Callie stammered, scanning the wreckage and both sides of the cobbled street and seeing no-one else. 'Just go,' she croaked. 'Get us out of here.'

'Do you think the Seer knew *that* was going to happen?' whispered Nick in an oddly constricted voice.

Callie looked at him, having to force out her next words too. 'If we really are Squirrel and Stickleback then I guess he must have done, mustn't he? But Gobb obviously didn't.'

'Where is Gobb, though? No one just vanishes.'

'No.' Callie swallowed a lump in her throat. 'And he'll keep coming after us until we've led him to whatever he thinks the Seer left behind.'

'Worth more than all the treasure of the pharaohs put together,' Nick repeated Omar's words in dread. 'And we might be the key.'

They negotiated a few more streets in a kind of numbness, leaving the wrecked chariot, and hopefully, Gobb, far behind them.

'We should find somewhere to stop,' said Callie. 'We have to decide what to do now, anyway...'

They found somewhere a few minutes later, in the impressive waterfront district, where all the big, luxurious hotels overlooked the Nile. It had been a bustling thoroughfare with a badly tuned orchestra of car horns when they'd passed that way the previous evening eating their *koshari* and kebab. Now, at the coolest part of the day, there were only small pockets of activity: onion and garlic sellers setting up stalls at the corner of an alley, a robed man leading a camel. Nick brought the car roughly to a stop by the curb outside one of the hotels and turned off the engine.

'I'm going to deal with the bonnet,' Callie informed him,

49

flapping a hand towards the front of the car: the mustard-yellow paintwork was still wearing soil and pieces of broken plant pot from Omar's roof garden – and it was a good excuse to have a moment by herself. She lurched out, the cooling morning breeze refreshing her face a little.

She went over to an aluminium barrier running along the embankment above the Nile, and took a deep breath of the polluted air. Both banks of the river were dotted with slumbering motor cruisers and yachts. It could almost be a normal morning – if they hadn't just been in a deadly chariot race.

What they'd experienced was more awful than anything Callie could have ever imagined. They should be waking up later to start another day of Omar's museum and takeaway food. Now she wanted her parents. Now she wanted to go home. Now she wanted the last twenty-four hours never to have happened, especially the last ten minutes . . . She forced the image of the mangled bodies from her mind, and hoped that Nick was doing the same.

Nick . . . She'd better get back to him.

After another lingering look at the wide, gentle Nile, she used her sleeve to scrape the debris off the car bonnet. Then, trying not to notice the massive dent in the car roof, or the chariot-wheel scratches along the side, she climbed back in.

'Why us, Cal?' Nick was staring straight ahead. 'What have we done to deserve all this?'

'I don't think you *deserve* fate. I think it just happens to you.'

'So those two Followers of Ssin, they were meant to die like that tonight whatever else happened?'

'I suppose.'

'And we're Squirrel and Stickleback?'

'We must be,' said Callie. 'You interpreted the Seer's inscription, didn't you? No one else has ever been able to do that before. And there's no other reason that Gobb and his cronies would have come after us.'

'So what *do* we do? Just wait for whatever's going to happen to us to happen?'

'It might not be anything,' replied Callie thoughtfully. 'Or it might be something terrible. Either way, I don't think we can escape our own destiny.' She stared at the lights along the embankment and thought through their options. They could go back to Omar's. He was still supposed to be looking after them, and he was probably feeling guilty about leaving them now – at least, she hoped he was. But going back meant staying in Cairo, which didn't seem to be a good idea while Gobb was still unaccounted for. Or they could try going to the police. But what could they tell them? That they'd stolen a car and were responsible for the deaths of two Egyptians?

Nick was rummaging through the glove compartment – paperwork, a small first-aid kit and a pair of cheap sunglasses already on his lap.

'What are you looking for?'

'I thought there might be a map.'

'A map? Why?'

'So we can get to Medphis.'

'Omar said it's not on the map.'

'Oh, yeah. I forgot.' Nick stuffed everything back in the glove compartment and slammed it shut.

'Anyway, we need to tell Mum and Dad what's happened; get them to come and rescue us.'

'Phone them then.'

'I can't. My phone's at Omar's.'

'So's mine. And I'm not going back there. Who knows how many Followers of Ssin might turn up.'

Callie sighed. 'We *could* try Omar's museum later...'

'It's still a risk. The way he ran off, he's probably gone straight into hiding anyway.'

Callie was still staring at the hotel. 'There's bound to be a payphone in there.'

'Yeah, but can you remember Mum and Dad's number at the dig? Or their mobiles? Cos I can't.'

'No,' said Callie, shaking her head. Nick stared blankly through the windscreen again.

The sky had lightened, the dark blue suffused with the dusty orange promise of dawn. It might even have been called 'beautiful' in other circumstances.

Somewhere, within the complex of hotels, an engine rumbled into life. Then a minute later a single-decker coach, pale purple emblazoned with the words *Land of the Pyramids Tours*, manoeuvred slowly under an arch which separated the two wings of the nearest hotel. Some of the passengers visible through the bus windows were still yawning – looking every bit as if they had been turned reluctantly from their beds at such an indecent hour. As the bus drove past, Callie glimpsed the destination board displayed behind the wide, clear windscreen: 'Nag Hammadi,' she said in surprise. 'It's *fate*.'

Nick frowned. 'Why is it?'

'Nag Hammadi. That's where Mum and Dad are digging up ancient ruins! We can follow the bus all the way there.'

'How far is this Nag Hammadi?' asked Nick, glancing at the fuel gauge. 'Can we make it on one tank of petrol?'

Callie nibbled at her lip. 'I don't know. But we should try, shouldn't we?' She suddenly wondered if Nick had had enough of driving. 'Do you want me to take over at the wheel?'

It was about the only thing that could have made Nick laugh. 'Thanks, but no thanks. You've never even driven our car, have you?'

'Well, no,' admitted Callie, 'but how difficult could it be?' She stopped short of saying: *You're doing it*.

'It's difficult,' Nick informed her.

'OK. I'll leave it to you, then.' Callie suddenly felt relieved to be travelling with her younger brother. He was a road runner as well as a stickleback.

He started the engine easily this time and fiddled with the bar under his seat to slide himself as near to the pedals as possible. The seat slotted into its new position with a crisp-sounding clunk. Then they were underway again, following the purple tour bus in a stolen car, and both silently wondering if this was exactly what they were meant to do.

Whoever was driving the bus had impeccable road manners, indicating their intentions clearly before every junction, and never exceeding the speed limit. Even as other early morning traffic began to join them on the highway the bus made it easy to navigate through the city, and Nick's follow-my-leader driving was definitely improving.

In less than forty minutes, they had left the smoggy suburbs of Cairo and begun to travel through surprisingly green agricultural land under bright, hopeful sunshine. Crops were growing in the far-reaching fields on both sides of the Nile, the way they had for thousands of years. In the warm, dry breeze blowing in through the car window Callie could smell ripening strawberries, which reminded her they hadn't eaten since last night. She reached round to the back seat to retrieve her purple

53

rucksack and started rooting inside for something to eat. 'Here,' she said, unwrapping a sesame seed bar and guiding it into Nick's mouth. 'It's not much, but better than nothing.'

'Thanks. Have you got anything to drink?'

'Egyptian cola,' confirmed Callie, opening a half-litre bottle and taking a couple of swigs herself. She handed the rest to Nick, and continued going through her bag, checking its contents. The book her dad had given her for the trip: *Hieroglyphics for Beginners* was in there somewhere. But it was another book she pulled out instead: *Egypt's Greatest Astrologer*. She had stuffed the thin volume into her rucksack just before escaping her bedroom.

Perhaps there was something written in its pages which might help them. She opened the cover.

Nick was on red alert behind the wheel. Not only was he in a stolen car, he didn't possess a driving licence. The last thing he wanted to do was to attract the attention of the local police. He crushed the empty cola bottle and concentrated on following the bus. He was glad to have something to do so he didn't have to think about what Callie had said: that their fate might be something terrible. He was still in shock; he had just helped kill two, possibly three men, he had to force himself not to cry.

The bus turned into slightly heavier traffic, still keeping to the eastern bank of the Nile. Nick fed the steering wheel through his hands to follow. A felucca, a yacht-like Egyptian boat (both modern and ancient) with its rakish triangular sail, glided past under the road embankment, beating its way towards Cairo. As he was watching the felucca, Nick almost lost his place behind the bus. A black taxi, with stacks of furniture strapped to a roof rack, honked its horn at him as he changed lanes dangerously in order to catch up.

When the car was safely tucked in behind the bus again, Nick's mind drifted back to Gobb. What had become of him? One minute he'd been there in the chariot – the next gone. Was it some kind of ancient Egyptian magic? Gobb's shop *was* called *The Magic of Egypt*...

6

The Pharaoh's Palace

The Pharaoh's Palace, Medphis, 1392 BC

I t was a scream of suffering and indignity, and for a second it echoed eerily around the white marble walls of the palace's Enlightenment Chamber.

Fortune looked down at his bleeding fingers. There were ugly cuts across each knuckle of his right hand, and a dribble of bright red blood flowed down his index finger onto the ivory stylus he was using to write with.

Wazim the Pockmarked (he of the pitted skin and the nose which had once been broken and then healed to form an unusual twist), the Pharaoh's Grand Priest, Scribe and Torturer, was teaching Fortune to write hieroglyphs – the language of the elite, a source of power not normally shared with the masses. Wazim's teaching method was based on cruelty and punishment, and any error Fortune made was rewarded by an excruciating rap on the knuckles with the beaded crook Wazim carried as a sign of office. And the more Wazim injured Fortune's hands, the harder it was for him to draw the hundreds of different characters accurately. The Grand Priest revelled in the never-ending cycle of cruelty, resenting with all his heart that he had been asked to tutor a filthy potter's brat. They might have scoured him with soda to remove his fleas (which he hadn't had in the first place), and robed him as befitted a member of the Pharaoh's court – but he was still a dollop of river mud to Wazim.

It was half a year since Fortune had drawn the Pharaoh's eye by snatching his friend Neb from the crocodile's jaws; and in all that time, he hadn't been permitted to see his parents once. Even worse, he was still under threat of execution for his offence. Yet, intrigued by his gift of foreseeing the crocodile attack before it happened, the Pharaoh had suspended his death (temporarily) and sent him for training with Wazim the Pockmarked.

'What is this?' Wazim snatched up a small scrap of papyrus Fortune had been attempting to hide under his exercise page. Two figures were painted on the surface: a squirrel and a stickleback.

'You wretch. What is this nonsense?'

'Nothing...Just a doodle, master.' It was a lie. Squirrel and Stickleback haunted his visions: a girl and a boy from so many thousands of years in the future.

'I give you the power of writing, and you give me horse dung.' The back of Wazim's hand connected with the boy's cheek. Fortune bit down on a sob of pain; Wazim would only derive more pleasure from seeing him cry.

'As for being able to see the future,' Wazim told him, a speck of his saliva landing on Fortune's upturned face like the venom of a spitting cobra, 'You have no remarkable gift... In truth you are nothing but a curse on me from the gods.'

Wazim kicked out with his booted foot, sending Fortune tumbling off his wooden stool and onto the cold marble floor. 'Did you foresee that, young magic one?'

Fortune twisted out of range before Wazim's foot could strike again – his eyes burning with defiance and hatred. 'I have foreseen your death, master,' he stated clearly. 'It will be soon, and you shall die with pustules erupting all over your evil body. You will scream, and your existence will end in agony.' It was true, Fortune had dreamed it twice.

'Quite a speech.' Wazim leaped forward, a glittering blade suddenly in his hand – the sharp, copper edge finding Fortune's throat and drawing a line of blood. 'I predict your ending will be sooner than mine.'

'Wazim the Pockmarked!' It was a girl's voice – youthful, but full of authority. The teenaged Pharaoh Ssin, her dark braids swinging about her shoulders, had entered the chamber. In contrast to Wazim, her caramel-coloured skin was flawless.

Wazim threw himself into a kneeling position instantly, pressing his shaven head and hooked nose to the cold floor. 'Highness.'

Already on the floor, Fortune lowered his head in fear.

'Walk with me, Fortune,' the Pharaoh ordered after a moment of powerful silence.

She led the way into the sunlit courtyard with light, elegant footsteps. Fortune scrambled to his feet and fell into step beside her, while two Royal Guards, uniformed in red and white tunics and kilts, followed at an unobtrusive distance.

'Wazim the Pockmarked is cruel to you?' asked Ssin, her voice now soft and musical, almost hypnotic. As always, Fortune was instantly under the spell of her beauty.

'I seem to make him angry quite often,' he admitted candidly. He was still breathing heavily from the run-in with his teacher.

Ssin paused to turn her magnificent dark eyes, framed by

blue make-up, on Fortune. 'Have you really foreseen his death, and in such a dreadful manner? Or were you merely trying to scare him?'

'Both, mighty Pharaoh,' said Fortune. 'I see him coiled in agony, his flesh diseased.'

'Gods!' exclaimed Ssin with disgust and morbid fascination in equal measure. With a faint smile playing across her pretty, scarlet-painted mouth, she led Fortune through a giant gateway festooned with vines and into an amazing botanical garden stretching into the distance. Species of trees and plants more usually found growing hundreds of miles south were thriving here, irrigated by a series of channels diverting water from the Nile. A giraffe was feeding placidly from a treetop, its broken eggshell brown and yellow pattern shadowed by the leaves. Fortune eyed the beast nervously while the teenaged Pharaoh smiled indulgently.

'Tell me,' she said, continuing to walk, her hips swaying seductively, 'do you have any visions about me?'

'Sometimes,' said Fortune guardedly. He mostly day-dreamed about her, imagining how it would be to one day declare his love. But he was a potter's son, she was a queen; could he dare to dream?

'And what do you see? Great victories, a long life, or cruelty and revenge?'

'Oh, great victories and a long life,' said Fortune, far too readily to have thought about it properly.

'Mmm.' Ssin toyed with the gold and ruby necklace encircling her graceful, slender throat. 'And how far can you see into the future?'

'So far that it hurts my head,' admitted Fortune. 'Things I cannot understand or explain...though I don't see everything that's going to happen. I don't think anyone could.' He followed her through the sunlight-dappled trees, where a zebra was nibbling at the lush grass underneath.

'Great Pharaoh,' Fortune asked, emboldened by her friendliness, 'when may I see my mother and father again?'

The Pharaoh's beautiful face registered concern. 'You wish to return to wallowing in Nile clay.' It was an exclamation of dismay, rather than a question – but Fortune answered it nevertheless:

'No, I wish to stay here with you,' he admitted fervently. 'But I worry about my mother and father.' His visions on that score were unusually indistinct, and therefore troubling.

The Pharaoh turned to study him, weighing him up with narrowed, mesmerising eyes. 'Do not be concerned about them, my prophet friend,' she told him. 'Your good fortune is their good fortune. Your father is now in charge of all of my potters. He relaxes in the shade while others do the hard work. Your mother meanwhile receives food from my own kitchens as a special treat. So you see there is no need to worry about them.'

Fortune felt pleased by that. His father always complained that he was becoming too old for the back-breaking work at the kilns, and his mother loved nothing better than cooking new and exotic foods. 'Thank you, Great Queen.'

'You are most welcome.' Ssin stepped gracefully through another arch, taking them towards the sound of tinkling water.

Fortune followed uncertainly onto a wooden bridge, which formed a rainbow curve above a large, oval pool. Crocodiles floated like half-submerged logs on the murky water a metre below them. Ssin leaned over a handrail to admire her armour-plated pets. 'And what else have you seen?' she asked, returning to her most recent preoccupation – her future.

'A vision of eternal life,' said Fortune, and was pleased by her shocked expression.

'You're not serious?'

'I am.' Fortune nodded. 'It was a vision far into the future ... A dozen unlikely plant extracts, when combined with six animal essences can banish death.'

'And can it be done now? Here? Did you see enough?' The sunlight sparkled in Ssin's dazzling eyes as she contemplated eternal life excitedly.

'Perhaps.' Fortune desperately wanted to please her. He could remember the plant and animal extracts – but could they be found in Egypt? 'I could try.'

'Do not try. Succeed.' Ssin smiled. 'As pharaoh, should I not be a living god; eternal? Would you deny me everlasting life, you who loves me?'

Fortune reddened at the unexpected accusation, shocked that his queen should comprehend his feelings so well.

'I see the way you look at me,' she teased. 'Not even members of my Royal Court dare to think of me as you do. You, a potter's son, dare to love me.'

Fortune was still blushing, unable to deny that what the queen said was true. Her tapered fingernails touched his arm with butterfly lightness, making him tingle all the way to his toes.

'I did not say that I was angry,' she told him. 'Nor did I say that you should not hope for my affection. Give me what I desire, Fortune, and I will grant you your desires. Use your powers of vision, understand this discovery and replicate it. I will supply herbalists, botanists, naturalists and surgeons – the best in all of Egypt. Think of it, all at the command of a fifteen-year-old potter's son.' She sounded animated, more alive than ever before. 'When you have accomplished what I ask, then we can be together,' she added tantalisingly.

Swallowing, Fortune nodded. 'It will be done, Majesty.' Beneath him in the pool a deadly crocodile flexed its muscular tail and splashed away. Maybe the crocodiles had some message to impart, but Fortune dismissed it for another time.

7

Bandit Camp

They'd been following the road out of Cairo for the last three hours, continuing to track the purple and silver bus headed for Nag Hammadi. The car was becoming like an oven, slowly roasting them as the temperature soared.

'What's this idiot trying to do?' grumbled Nick, glaring into the rear-view mirror. A high-spec black jeep, coated thickly with dust, was attempting to overtake them in the face of oncoming traffic. 'There's no room!' Nick was forced to slow down or lose the front wing of the saloon.

The black jeep slotted in front of them then reduced its own speed to bring the saloon to within centimetres of its impressive-looking rear bull bars.

'What did he overtake for if he's going to go that slow?' fumed Nick. The bus would get away if they weren't careful.

'I don't know.' Callie was staring fretfully over her shoulder. Another identical black jeep was powering towards them from behind, effectively sandwiching them in between. 'I think they're trying to box us in.'

'It's not the police, is it – looking for this car?' said Nick, swallowing. 'We did steal it, didn't we? Or maybe they've spotted that it's being driven by an English kid.'

'They don't look like police,' said Callie. The driver of the following jeep was dressed in a white desert robe with a matching turban-headdress. The front-seat passenger was similarly attired, and he began gesticulating that they should turn off the main road. 'They want you to take the next turning,' she said hoarsely to Nick.

'Shall I try putting my foot down?' There was a distinct tremble in Nick's voice.

'It won't do any good. We're trapped, aren't we?' replied Callie. The second jeep gave them a warning nudge, the resulting bang shockingly loud.

Nick swore out of fear.

'You better turn,' said Callie panicking. 'Or they'll run us off the road anyway.'

Nick nodded briefly, and when two minutes later the leading jeep turned off the highway and onto a dusty desert road, he followed it. Every time he attempted to fall back more than a couple of car lengths the second jeep rammed them from behind. *Clang.*

'All right! All right!' Terror-stricken, Nick hurriedly closed the gap.

Callie scanned the horizon. The new road appeared to be heading straight into the desert. On the horizon straw-coloured hills stretched out in both directions. 'They're taking us away from prying eyes. Hardly the actions of anyone official.'

'Who are they then?'

'Isn't it obvious? More Followers of Ssin.'

Nick gulped. 'They're stopping,' he said and started to apply his own brakes.

'Better pull in behind him,' said Callie quietly.

Nick nodded, and the three vehicles came to a stop on the side of the desert road in the lee of a crested sand dune. The jeep doors opened immediately, and the robed men began climbing out. One of them, in ebony robes instead of white, seemed to be in charge of all the others: shoving them about and barking out orders. Underneath his black turban, a leathery brown face was thickly bearded. He flung open Callie's door impatiently. 'Get out!'

Wordlessly, Callie grabbed her rucksack and climbed from the car. Nick stumbled after her. The ring of men surrounded them instantly, and Black Robe's sharp, dark eyes flashed appraisingly: first over Callie and then Nick. He snatched Callie's rucksack, making her jump, and began a thorough search of each compartment in turn, unearthing the two books, a plastic bottle of sun cream, their passports and some cruise tickets they'd been planning to use later in the week. When he was satisfied, he thrust the rucksack and everything in it back at Callie. 'Pockets,' he barked.

'What's he looking for?' whispered Nick, barely moving his lips.

'I don't know.' Callie hurriedly turned out her skirt pockets to reveal nothing more interesting than a couple of tissues and a tube of lip balm. Black Robe nodded brusquely and turned to Nick.

'Erm... triangles of toasted Egyptian bread, tomato sauce and mayonnaise sachets, mixed nuts, dried apricots, a lump of white cheese... And a plastic knife and fork.' Nick gave a frightened running commentary as he produced each item from the multiple pockets of his jeans. Callie rolled her eyes. Her brother had been carrying all that and she'd fed him her last sesame seed bar.

'What?' Nick whispered at her.

'Never mind.'

'Get into the car. Back seat,' Black Robe ordered, abruptly. Callie and Nick exchanged a worried glance and did as they were told. The door slammed behind them and Black Robe threw himself into the front passenger seat. One of his men jumped in behind the wheel. After waiting for the dusty jeep in front of them to start moving, they pulled out after it. As before, the other jeep took up the rear, and within minutes the small convoy had turned off the road and was powering towards a distant range of hills, which appeared to be quivering in the afternoon heat.

'I think they're going to dump us in the desert,' muttered Nick.

'We're already in the desert,' pointed out Callie. 'And why? What would be the point of that?'

'Well, what do *you* think is going to happen?'

'Shut up! Both of you,' Black Robe shouted, whipping his head round angrily. Callie and Nick looked at each other, and fell into scared silence.

Around midday, their captors gave them deep-fried fava bean and herb patties and cold mint tea in a flask, which Callie and Nick both accepted gratefully.

Hours passed. Nobody had spoken since Black Robe had ordered them to shut up all that time ago, and Nick's face was now pressed up against the window, sleeping exhaustedly after driving them all the way from Cairo. Through the car's window Callie could see an unbroken vista of sand in every direction, and she was frantically trying to guess where they were being taken. They'd been kidnapped, but she was sure they weren't going to be held for ransom. Their parents weren't rich for one thing, and this was all too coincidental for that. It was something to do with Gobb, and them being Squirrel and Stickleback – it had to be. These men had to be Followers of Ssin.

Callie glanced through her side window again. The sun was dipping towards the horizon, and yet they were still driving, making her wonder if they would travel through the night. They were moving at an alarming pace, the vehicles skimming the soft desert sand too rapidly to get bogged down in it, utilising the sun-baked dips between the dunes where the ground was firmer. It was *almost* exciting: racing across the Egyptian desert with clouds of dust pouring out from under the tyres, except for one thing – they were captives and had no idea where they were being taken.

In another hour the car started bumping over a slightly rougher surface. The convoy was sweeping up a gravel slope between two craggy ridges that had been invisible until the last minute. After an engine-straining climb, they emerged onto a wide plateau ringed by tangerine-hued cliffs. The place would be just about impossible to find if you didn't know it was there.

They drove into the middle of the site, where the remains of a temple – not much more than a few stone columns scored with hieroglyphs – threw long shadows across a paved area. A few children of various ages, dressed in western clothes, were kicking some dead animal skulls around in one corner of the ruins, and a handful of dusty vehicles were already parked on a narrow strip of cracked stone. They drew up alongside them.

Black Robe and his driver left them in the car and headed towards a group of sand-encrusted black tents. Callie could see women preparing food on spits above open fires. She looked around. Nothing about the camp appeared permanent – there wasn't a single building; the tents could be folded up at a moment's notice, the jeeps driven into the desert like a puff of wind.

Calli nudged Nick with her elbow, and her brother's face slid down the window with a squeak.

'Where are we?' he mumbled, rubbing his eyes with his knuckles.

'I don't know... some sort of camp.'

She glanced out of the window on Nick's side and went distinctly pale. A row of crocodile-headed statues was only a few metres away. The nearest one was glaring right at her; with the setting sun shining blood-red through its jagged carved teeth, it appeared to be feasting on something very bloody. 'I hate crocodiles,' she gasped.

8

Eternal Life

The boy, who had once been a humble potter, was watching men labouring with hand scythes, cutting the ripe, golden corn along the side of the Nile for as far as he could see.

His high vantage point was afforded by the balcony of one of the most spectacular chambers of the entire palace, laden with lavish golden furniture and the most exquisite scenes of Egyptian science and discovery painted onto the walls. The room had been handed over to Fortune for his personal use by the pharaoh herself, and the long, solid marble table cutting the room in half was already festooned with everything he required to mix the elixir of eternal life.

Fortune's status in the court had been much elevated during the last year. Ssin had kept her promise of putting him in charge of the greatest surgeons, herbalists and scientists in the whole of Egypt. His power and influence had increased one hundred fold. Now none but the pharaoh herself stood above him. Even his former tormentor, Wazim the Pockmarked, no longer troubled him. The grim spectacle of Wazim dying had been frightful to behold; the man's pitted features a garden of angry boils, many of which had been weeping ugly yellow pus. Wazim had, as Fortune had correctly predicted, quite literally rotted away, though the boy had taken no pleasure in it.

Fortune had been permitted to see his parents once. They had been brought to the palace especially for a visit. Each had looked well, and told him that they were being advanced in the outside world because of him, because of his talents, and that he was to work hard on his learning, and do anything the pharaoh asked of him. In sadness he had watched them go away again, but he had done everything they had told him to: concentrated hard, obeyed the pharaoh's commands, and toiled unstintingly. And now the day had almost arrived: he was about to create life eternal.

The collection of eighteen separate plant and animal extracts had taken a full thirteen moons to gather. Great hardships and difficulties had been endured by each of the expeditions sent out by Fortune. There had been losses of countless equipment – ships, chariots, day-to-day items like uniforms, weapons and tents, and tragically, the lives of several men. Egyptian geography and the knowledge of the greater world beyond the Nile had been advanced by a thousand leagues in every direction. Then finally, early this morning, the very last extract, sap from a tree which only grew in the high mountains in the kingdom of K'om, had been brought to Medphis in safety, and the chemistry of everlasting life could properly begin.

The herbalists and doctors had been dismissed. None of them had been permitted to know all the ingredients, each working on two or three at most, and working in isolation, never being told the proportions required of each, or the names of their fellow scientists.

'I have no desire to make gods of my servants and lackeys,' Pharaoh Ssin had told Fortune early on. She had become more beautiful than ever, at the zenith of her physical perfection. Fortune loved her with an intensity which almost caused him pain.

Annoyingly, he could not tell what his future with Ssin held. It was a smoke-filled room to him. Perhaps his love made him like any ordinary person when thinking of the object of his desires. Where Ssin was concerned, Fortune was a person beset by doubts, with nothing to rely on but hope.

He turned from the window and studied the marble table top. Powders, resins, oils, grains were captive in shallow clay bowls covering the entire surface.

What had he to start with? The ground-up bone of the warthog, which was the colour of fine desert sand, went into the mixing bowl first, followed by the spice 'pearl dew', which was exactly as it sounded: satiny pink-grey buds.

He placed a set of silver weighing scales in front of him, accurate to the weight of a grain of sand, and continued working, measuring out the exact proportions he had foreseen in his vision of eternal life.

'Chopped coconut hair, rough and course; saliva from a bull elephant (which had been taken by a brave soldier while the elephant in question slept); dung from fire ants; and the nectar of a hummingbird.'

'How much longer will it take?' Pharaoh Ssin interrupted him impatiently several hours later. Her beautiful white, silk gown was clinging to her shapely figure. 'I seem to have endured an eternal wait for my eternal life.' She draped herself over him where he was sitting at the marble table, allowing dark strands of her hair to brush across his bare shoulder.

'Sweet little crocodile.' When they were alone together Pharaoh Ssin permitted Fortune to use his pet name for her. And with the preparations for the elixir at such a critical stage, Ssin seldom detained her guards when she met with him. 'Our mutual patience will soon be rewarded.'

'Show me all you are doing,' she said breathlessly, nibbling at his ear. 'I am fascinated by this new science and would learn more of it.'

Fortune giggled as the tip of her tongue probed the well of his ear. 'My beautiful, scientific highness.' He pulled her playfully onto his bare knee where it showed beneath his blue and white kilt, and continued with his work while supplying her with a running commentary:

'The ground-up root of a Lebanese cedar, four grains of copper ore, the bud of a lotus flower, one single grain of hemlock, the ground quill of an ostrich feather.' It had taken him weeks of study to ascertain the Egyptian equivalents of the chemical compounds which would be used by chemists in the far far distant future.

Ssin suddenly frowned. 'How shall we know it has worked?'

'Well, in a hundred years from now we shall definitely be sure.'

Pharaoh Ssin's beautiful face lit up at the notion of such a span of time. 'No other pharaoh has ever lived so long,' she said excitedly. She indicated the overflowing bowls of plant and animal extracts. 'Come on, come on. Don't stop working, my darling.'

9

Crocodile Head

allie jumped. Someone was yanking open the car door. 'Out!'

It was a boy around her age. He was fit looking, with a tanned face and short, raven-coloured hair. His alert, topaz eyes evaluated her in a couple of flicks as she tumbled out of the car, and she was annoyed to feel herself blushing. There was the hint of a smile as the boy looked away, and regarded Nick with a different, less predatory sort of assessment. Callie thought that in profile he resembled the paintings of ancient Egyptians she'd seen displayed in Omar's museum. The men too had the same strange look.

'My name is Ramy,' the boy told them in excellent English. 'I am to see that you eat.'

Callie wasn't thinking about eating. She was glancing around in the rays of the setting sun. As no one had bothered to restrain them, she guessed they weren't expected to run away; that in itself was worrying – there was obviously nowhere to run to. 'Where are we?' she asked the boy. 'Why have we been brought here?'

'Just food. No information.'

Ramy brought them to a striped blanket spread out across the desert sand a little way from the main grouping of tents. Tempting-looking dishes of food were laid out in the middle: various meats, cooked vegetables and flavoured rice.

'It's very good lamb,' he informed them, sitting down cross-legged on the striped blanket and waiting for them to do likewise. When Callie had reluctantly followed suit and Nick was kneeling, Ramy began to select morsels of food with the fingers of his right hand, in what Callie knew was the traditional way of the desert. Chunks of lamb, sultanas, nuts and onions in a kind of tomato sauce started disappearing into his slightly smiling mouth. Surrendering to hunger and the aroma of cooked food, Callie and Nick began to eat too. It was late evening, many hours since the bandits had given them lunch. Callie maintained a dignified silence.

'Those are stuffed vine leaves,' Ramy told her, as she picked up a green parcel, fat with rice and vegetables.

She wondered why he was attempting to make conversation with her. She was hardly going to make friends with her captors, was she?

Ramy shovelled more lumps of lamb into his mouth.

'Why aren't that lot eating?' Nick asked, pointing towards the half a dozen children playing amongst the temple ruins, where the shadows had lengthened significantly.

'They had their meal earlier,' replied Ramy, turning his head towards the other kids. Nick pocketed several of the stuffed vine-leaf parcels before Ramy turned back. Callie wished she'd thought of doing the same; they'd need food if they were to escape.

Ramy regarded Callie with an intense fascination in his eyes. She willed herself not to blush again.

'Now that we're eating your food, you can tell us why we've been brought here,' she said, fearlessly holding eye contact with him. 'We have a right to know.'

Ramy shrugged, as if he didn't care one way or the other. 'Orders... My family work for someone I think you know – a giant man, with a strangely shaped head and the bulging eyes of a locust. He ordered us to find you.'

Gobb! Callie's worst fears were realised. 'You're Followers of Ssin?' she asked.

Ramy frowned. 'No, we're not. But we have our own link to the ancients.'

'It doesn't matter. You're not very nice if you work for Gobb anyway.'

'We don't *want* to work for him,' Ramy flared.

'Then why do you?' Callie said accusingly.

'Because... he has *things* at his command.'

'What things?' asked Nick.

'Dreadful creatures... half human... half...' Ramy seemed afraid even of saying it out loud. The last threads of sunlight now disappeared behind the hills, the remaining crimson sky reflecting the apprehension in his eyes.

'Half human, half what?' Callie pressed. Though she wasn't really sure she wanted to hear the answer.

'Half crocodile,' Ramy snapped. 'Would you argue with someone who had crocodile men at his command?'

Callie searched his face for deceit and saw none. 'No, I wouldn't.' But how could such things exist? Maybe Gobb had played a trick on Ramy and his family, making them think that he had crocodile men working for him. 'Are you sure?'

'I was with my father one time, and he met with Gobb and a crocodile-headed man. I was scared and ran away.'

Ramy looked ashamed of himself. It must have cost him some pride admitting his fear to her. Callie was sure he was telling the truth.

Callie shivered. A creature that was half man... half crocodile. She knew that the ancient Egyptians had *believed* in half-human, half-animal gods – cats, jackals, hawks. Could they be real? She glanced across the temple ruins to where the crocodile-headed statues stood sentry-like in a long row. Twilight had given them a supernatural air, and little eddies of fine sand were blowing up in places, appearing like ghosts.

Ramy pulled a leather cord from around his neck, on the end of which was a blue glass bead with a yellow and white centre. 'This is an amulet, to ward off the evil eye,' he explained, holding it out for Callie.

'But it's yours.'

'I do not need it. I have the protection of my family.'

Callie didn't know why, but she trusted Ramy; she took the thing and settled the cord around her neck, trying not to think of crocodile men.

'When is Gobb coming to fetch us?'

'Tomorrow, I think. He ordered my uncle to hold you here while he deals with matters in Cairo.'

'Matters.' The two dead bodies, Ali and Hussein, thought Callie with a shudder. Tomorrow didn't give them long to get away. She rolled the glass-bead amulet between her fingertips, still wondering why she had accepted it.

'Where were you going in the car?' Ramy asked.

'Nowhere. Just running,' lied Callie. She didn't want to give anything away.

'What happened to the man you were staying with?'

Callie started. Ramy was apparently well-informed.

It was obvious now that he had been charged with finding out as much as he could about them. 'No idea. He ran away and abandoned us.'

Ramy gave up and got to his feet. 'I will take you to the tent where you will sleep.'

He led them across the sand to the smallest open-fronted canvas shelter, where two thin mattresses had been placed beneath the woollen canopy. Someone had lit a fire outside to take away the cold bite of the desert night.

'The latrine is that way.' Ramy pointed behind the grouping of tents. 'Don't get lost. We are fifty kilometres from the nearest village, and there are wild animals in the desert.'

Callie didn't let him see her disappointment. *Fifty kilometres from the nearest village!* If that was true, escaping was going to be even harder than she'd thought.

They watched him heading off to his family's tent, where he stood for a moment with Black Robe, probably relating their conversation to him. Once again, no one seemed to think they were worth restraining.

They pretended to settle down until Black Robe and Ramy had finished speaking and gone off to their respective tents. Then they headed for the latrine, using the excuse to slip through the camp.

Twilight had given the whole encampment an eerie feel. The sand stirred like phantoms where the breeze off the desert met the plateau and the ring of cliffs. An old man wearing a beige robe was drawing water from a well; women, their hair covered with scarves, were calling their children back to the black tents. Nobody seemed to pay any attention to the two foreign kids, loitering at the edge of the camp and staring across the sea of darkening sand. Callie was trying to decide if

Ramy had been telling the truth. 'Do you think we're really fifty kilometres from the nearest village?' she whispered to Nick.

'It's possible. We travelled a long way to get here, didn't we? But I don't reckon the desert's "full" of wild animals. Not much would survive out here. It's too hot and dry for most animals. Just scorpions and snakes, probably.'

Callie wasn't comforted. Scorpions and snakes were more frightening than jackals or wild dogs. Nick checked his pockets for a third time. He'd managed to snaffle enough stuffed vine-leaf parcels for half a day, but they had no water between them. Callie looked back towards the camp. The old man had gone from the well, but even if they were able to draw water themselves, they didn't have anything to carry it in.

'Perhaps we'll be able to find water on the way,' said Nick, reading her thoughts.

'I hope so...'

When they were sure no one was watching them they started to run.

The rock under their feet ran out within metres, and their trainers began to plough into thick, strength-sapping sand. They fought against the unnatural suction but only went deeper, their ankles and calves disappearing into the desert. The remaining light seemed to have been sucked out of the sky at the same time.

'The sand's swallowing us up!' cried Nick, realising he was unable to escape the grip around his knees.

Callie reached out her hand to help him, but she was sinking as well.

A booming voice sounded out of the darkness. 'Now you see that I have the whole of the desert at my command.'

Callie screamed as Gobb's giant figure loomed towards

them, bug eyes protruding from an ugly face. Even in the darkness, his repulsive visage seemed unchanged. He had survived his chariot crash without a scratch. What was he?

Callie and Nick continued to struggle against the tide of sand now swirling around their waists.

'It is good to see Squirrel and Stickleback once more,' Gobb said huskily. 'But now you will rest.' He lashed out with a sweeping fist.

Callie flinched. But the fist did not make contact. Instead a powder the texture and colour of red smoke puffed into her face. She thought how odd that was, and how little it hurt – but then she began to choke.

Her vision blurred, and her head rolled forward into oblivion...

Callie came round groggily, with a disgusting taste in her mouth and stinging eyes. Whatever Gobb had thrown at her had made her lose consciousness, that much was obvious, but for how long it was impossible to guess; though, long enough to be moved to a soft, spacious bed with pillows of the softest material in the middle of a large room.

Groaning, she propped herself up onto one elbow and looked around at her new surroundings – she wondered if she was in the private quarters of Gobb's shop back in Cairo, or his house. There were no windows, just a flickering light from little oil lamps set around the room in brass sconces. They were illuminating mural-covered walls, straight out of ancient Egypt: life-sized figures of dancers cavorted to music played on harps and cymbals.

A gold curtain rail fixed to the ceiling dissected the

room, and a shimmering azure drape was tied back to reveal a sunken oval pool, four times the size of a bath, on the other side.

A chair beside the bed could almost be called a 'throne' it was so grand – with gilded arms and side panels carved with intricate coloured hieroglyphs. Callie saw that her purple rucksack had been placed on the cushioned seat. A quick rummage told her it contained nothing to aid her escape – unless she could think of some genius plan using a hairbrush, a bottle of sun cream and *Hieroglyphics for Beginner's.* Their passports and cruise tickets weren't going to be of any help, either.

She swung her legs off the bed. The sudden movement was a mistake, and she had to grope for the nearest wall to prevent herself smashing face first into the tiled floor. She fumbled along to the door, battling to clear her head with a series of deep breaths. Surprisingly, when she lifted the metal latch, the door was unlocked. She eased it open quietly. She had to find Nick.

A long passageway illuminated by yet more oil lamps swam in front of her. It took her a few seconds to realise that the walls were adorned with unpleasant figures of crocodile-headed men marching one after another in a kind of grizzly conga. She shuddered, and instinctively clutched Ramy's amulet, which was still dangling around her neck.

'You're awake!' The voice right behind her almost gave her a heart attack. But when she spun round she saw Nick, looking none the worse for wear, slurping a ripe, green pear.

'Where did you come from?' she asked him.

'My room's down that way,' Nick pointed towards a corner at the end of the passage. 'There's a kind of dining area as well,

80

with loads of food laid out on a table – fruit mainly,' he waved what remained of the pear, 'plus some sort of honey cakes.'

'What happened after Gobb threw that stuff in my face?'

'Did the same to me, and I can't remember anything after that till I woke up here.'

'Wherever *here* is,' said Callie faintly.

'Obvious, isn't it?' Nick said confidently. 'It's an ancient Egyptian palace.'

Callie arched an eyebrow. 'I suppose it fits the bill.' The plaster reliefs on the walls, the luxurious furniture in her room and the oil lamps instead of light bulbs: it certainly had an ancient feel.

'It could be the hideout of the Followers of Ssin,' added Nick.

'You haven't found a way out, have you?' Callie asked, eager to change the subject.

'No. Not yet, and I've been right round this entire wing. There are what look like exit doors in the dining room, but they won't budge. Probably barred from the other side.'

'Show me. Maybe the two of us together can open them.'

Nick nodded and led her back quickly in the other direction. 'Check out the cool decorations,' he said, picking at one of the raised plaster crocodile men as he walked past. A section of its jaw crumbled away and smashed on the floor.

'Not really to my taste.' Callie hurried on; the image was just as unsettling with only half its protruding jaw.

Nick's dining area contained little more than a long wooden table, which, as he'd said, was spread with all manner of perfectly ripe enticing fresh fruit on silver platters.

A pair of massive wooden doors stood at one end of the room. Callie went over to them and yanked on one of two ringed metal handles while Nick pulled on the other. The handles rattled, but that was all.

'Told you.' Nick gave the doors a kick. 'Solid.'

'Have you noticed there are no windows?' said Callie, glancing around. 'There were none in the bedroom I woke up in, either.'

'Yeah. I wonder if that's because there's nothing outside to see.'

'Meaning what?'

'Meaning we're underground... You know, buried under thousands of tons of sand.'

Callie suddenly understood what he was saying: 'You think we're in Medphis!'

'It's a possibility, isn't it? Didn't Omar say the Followers of Ssin worshipped crocodiles? The walls are covered with them.'

Callie thought about it. A city dedicated to the sacred crocodile. Those mouldings on the walls were certainly convincing. She tried not to dwell on being buried under 'thousands of tons of sand' and selected a pomegranate from a glazed terracotta bowl, using a knife with coloured stones set into the handle to slice it in half.

When she looked up again, Nick was peering studiously at a coloured wall painting of an ancient Egyptian farmer, sowing seeds in a ploughed field. Then for some unaccountable reason, he suddenly poked the farmer in the eye.

'What did you do that for?' Callie stared at him, afraid he'd gone completely mad.

'I thought there might be a spy hole or something.'

Callie stiffened in alarm. 'You think somebody's watching us?' The room instantly took on the creepiest feel imaginable.

She spun round, now irrationally convinced that the dark-brown eyes of a painted ploughboy had blinked at her.

Nick continued prowling the room, stabbing figure after figure in the eye until he'd made a complete circuit. 'No. We're safe.'

Even so, Callie continued throwing fretful glances at the painted figures between digging out juicy pink pomegranate seeds with the point of the jewelled knife.

'When do you think Gobb'll come and fetch us?' asked Nick.

Callie shivered. 'Any time would be too soon.'

'It'll be all right, though, won't it?' Nick went on. 'He needs us, doesn't he? To interpret more stuff from the Seer.'

'And when we've interpreted it for him? He's not just going to let us go, is he?'

'Oh.'

'If we drag our heels interpreting, maybe we'll have time to come up with a way of escaping—'

They both started at a deep, grating sound directly behind them. The huge wooden doors which had seemed so immovable moments ago were being slowly pushed apart.

A giant creature: one with a human torso, and the scaly, forward-jutting head of a crocodile, was opening the doors. Muscles popped, and lime-green reptilian eyes stared. Wart-encrusted jaws, bearing innumerable fangs opened wide. Callie raised her hands with a blood-curdling scream.

10

Crone

allie continued screaming. She was rooted to the spot as the crocodile-headed monster bore down on her with stamping, heavy movements. Gore and slime coated its interlocking teeth. She could smell its rank and fetid breath.

'Callie!' Nick was trying to pull her away. She attempted to retreat, but the creature grabbed her and Nick by an arm apiece and dragged them towards the now-open doors.

Crocodile Head surged out into a wider passageway beyond the bedroom wing, Callie stumbling beside him, too numb with terror to cry.

Nick was angling his body as far away from the reptilian head as he could. 'What does it want?' he stammered.

Two shaven-headed boys, wearing nothing but short white kilts, changed direction the instant they saw Crocodile Head stomping towards them. They watched frightened from a small alcove as Callie and Nick were swept through a pair of gigantic decorated columns holding up the stone ceiling. But Callie realised that as the boys were watching, not running; they must be used to seeing Crocodile Head, even though they were afraid of him. Callie beseeched the boys with her eyes, but they made no attempt to help. She only just managed to keep on her feet as the crocodile man hastened them on through a wider gallery. Craftsmen in brightly coloured robes were painting human figures onto a mural of stars and planets.

Who were all these people living like ancient Egyptians, Callie wondered? And how could somewhere so vast be unknown to the outside world? Was it really hidden under the Egyptian desert? Was she really in Medphis?

The craftsmen moved respectfully aside for Crocodile Head, and he strode on to where the passage suddenly dropped away into a deep pit. Crocodiles, monstrous real ones, like those Callie had seen in the zoo, were writhing in filthy, foul-smelling water at the bottom. She yelled: 'Look out! Stop!' The creature was going to take them straight over and into the crocodile-infested water.

Callie pulled back with all her strength, but hers was nothing compared to Crocodile Head's, and she was lugged out over the pit. She gasped; by some magic they were suspended in midair, while still somehow walking. She looked down at her feet and realised they were clanking over a metal grate, indistinguishable from the dirty water below. She tried to concentrate so as not to put her feet through the squares, which were only a little smaller than her size-five trainers.

One of the real crocodiles exploded from the water beneath her with a splash, its jagged teeth clanking loudly off the underside of the grate. Callie was shaking uncontrollably as she reached the other side, but Crocodile Head kept on, now escorting them between two colossal statues of pharaohs, carved in pink granite. They came out into a massive chamber, greater in size than an indoor arena.

Callie almost passed out. The chamber literally dazzled. They were walking across silver tiles which flickered spectacularly in the numerous oil lamps. There was a vibrancy and brilliance to the decorated walls which depicted a river – surely the Nile. Turquoise-blue waves were set inside a border of tall green papyrus stems – the colours of such high-quality they seemed to burst forth, sinuous and living. The effect was more beautiful than any picture Callie had ever seen, but now she had no time to appreciate it – the painted river was flowing through the chamber, 'floating' them towards a gigantic throne sat high on a set of golden steps.

Priests, courtiers, soldiers and servants thronged the chamber itself, parting to let them pass – whispering to one another – until Crocodile Head brought them finally to the throne.

Callie trembled.

Some shrivelled thing occupied the jewel-encrusted throne and shockingly, like a footstool at the creature's feet, grovelled Gobb. Callie and Nick exchanged a terrified glance; someone here was so much more powerful than Gobb that they treated him like furniture.

Callie peeked up at probably the oldest living thing she'd ever seen. A pure white gown enhanced by chains of blood-red rubies suggested the object on the throne had once been a woman. Now her bare arms were bones held together with a papery stretch of dry skin. A golden cobra crown encircled a head so sunken it appeared dead except for the milky stare from opal-tinted eyes, highlighted by a band of dark blue paint. Her hair appeared to be a wig: raven-coloured and swinging in braids down to her bony, bare shoulders. But most disgusting of all was the plait of beard hanging from the wizened chin: the traditional false symbol that showed a female pharaoh's power. This beard appeared to be real.

'She's got a beard,' mouthed Nick, ducking slightly under Crocodile Head's right-angled jaw to grimace at Callie. She cautioned him to silence with a desperate look. This was not the time to stand and point.

Crocodile Head launched them sprawling onto their faces before the bearded creature, and planted a foot on Nick's back as he attempted to rise.

'Stay down,' Callie whispered to her brother, keeping her face lowered and staring at her own terrified reflection in the pattern of silver tiles. Out of the corner of her eye she saw Crocodile Head undoing a strap at the back of his neck. Then in one swift movement, he removed his grotesque mask. Beneath it lurked a very human head – shaped like a greasy potato. Callie caught Nick rolling his eyes at her. He must be feeling as stupid as she was: Crocodile Head was just wearing the sickest Halloween mask ever.

He bowed to the creature on the throne, 'Great Pharaoh Ssin, I bring you the infants.' He raised Callie and Nick as far as their knees. Callie gaped at the withered creature once more. *Pharaoh Ssin?* She asked herself. *The one buried in her city of Medphis thousands of years ago? Was she dreaming?*

Pharaoh Ssin prodded Gobb with a gold-sandaled foot.

'I am Pharaoh Ssin's Grand Priest,' Gobb told them. 'Last in the line of grand priests to her Highness, who have obeyed her will over the millennia both underground and in the outer world.'

The giant unfolded himself from his kneeling position and placed his ear beside her puckered mouth as she spoke. After a moment he began to translate her scratchy, ancient words.

87

'Test them. We must ensure they are who we believe them to be.'

Test them? thought Callie. They must be about to be given something to translate. She noticed a ring of hieroglyphs around a nearby column base. Twice she saw the symbols for the squirrel and the stickleback. She thought it was just a repeat of their names, but then realised what it actually meant: 'Squirrel climb, Stickleback swim,' she shouted.

'Swim where?' began Nick, but as he was still saying it, there was a loud clanking sound and the mirrored floor tilted suddenly beneath them. From her kneeling position, Callie launched herself forward, clutching at the rising edge of the section of floor. Nick wasn't so agile. He plunged down the mirrored floor tiles and made a spectacular splash.

The gathered priests, courtiers and soldiers dashed forward to gain a better vantage point, crowding the edge of a newly opened pool.

Callie swung herself along the upturned edge of the risen floor, using alternate hands until she could flip herself down before Ssin's throne. Nick met her there, dragging himself sopping from the water. They lay there panting, face down on the floor together. Only when they heard a collective shriek from their audience at the other side of the pool did they turn back. The crocodile pit with the metal grate must extend right beneath the throne room, because three monstrous creatures were now carving menacingly through the water below them, snapping their jaws.

Gobb heaved on a mighty chain, and the panel closed slowly over the crocodiles.

They had passed the test, interpreting the 'swim' and 'climb' symbols on the nearby column. Gobb returned to his stooped position beside the human thing on the mighty throne and continued to translate her words:

'Pharaoh Ssin welcomes Squirrel and Stickleback to her city of Medphis. Her city lives again: peopled by those with faith and loyalty. A few of us are even descendants of those who served her in antiquity. Pharaoh Ssin has waited for three-thousand, four-hundred and twenty-two years, seven months and four days...for you to come.'

3,422 years! Callie felt dizzy. She sneaked another look at the wizened object crouched on the throne. Did all these Followers really believe she was 3,422? Callie looked down again at her own reflection in the mirrored tiles. She looked deathly pale.

'You have learned already of the Seer: the boy named Fortune, he who writes to you,' the Pharaoh continued through her mouthpiece, Gobb.

Callie nodded.

'He knew you would come to us in Cairo. He left a record of this prediction, before he turned against us...He knew also that you would lead us to the Lost Prophesies, and to other things.' Gobb was speaking rapidly to keep up with his mistress. 'You will translate the secret hieroglyphs he created for only you to understand. You will serve the pharaoh or you will suffer.'

Callie swallowed a lump in her throat.

'And what happens after we've served you?' Nick braved a question, earning himself a brutal kick from Crocodile Head.

'Then we shall see what is to become of you,' answered Gobb cryptically.

Callie was terrified. What would happen if they *couldn't* read the hieroglyphs?

Pharaoh Ssin spoke one more time through Gobb. 'Today you will rest. Tomorrow you will begin.' Her frail, skeletal hand fluttered as she waved them away. Crocodile Head replaced his gruesome mask and dragged them backwards, forcing their heads down in a bow all the way to the entrance. The masses of priests and courtiers watched them depart in awe.

'There's no doubt, then, is there? You're Squirrel and I'm Stickleback,' pronounced Nick queasily.

Callie sat down on her bed and hugged her knees to comfort herself. 'Yes, we must be. The Seer predicted we'd come here, and here we are.'

'Does it say anything about us in that book you've been reading: *Egypt's Great Magician*?'

'*Egypt's Greatest Astrologer*,' Callie corrected him. 'And, no, it doesn't. Not what I've read so far, anyway. The thing is, if the Seer really did predict great discoveries and inventions in the future he kept that knowledge to himself so there's no actual proof that he predicted anything. There are definitely no ancient Egyptian computers or mobile phones. The author thinks that the whole thing is just an elaborate hoax.'

'That thing we saw wasn't a hoax,' said Nick, collapsing exhaustedly into the chair which resembled a throne. 'But she can't be three-thousand, four-hundred years old, can she?'

'Don't you remember what Omar said? That the Seer may have known the secrets of eternal life and eternal youth. Maybe he shared it with his pharaoh all those years ago, and that's her.'

'She didn't look that youthful to me,' said Nick, curling his lip in disgust. 'And what was that beard all about?'

'Women pharaohs wore fake beards to prove that they were masculine enough to rule,' said Callie faintly. 'But in her case I don't think it was fake.'

'That bloke's crocodile head wasn't a fake, either,' said Nick. 'I could smell rotting flesh. And they've got enough live crocs around the place to keep him supplied in hats for years.'

'No wonder Ramy and his family were scared into helping Gobb,' said Callie, fingering the blue, yellow and white bead around her neck. 'That mask is pretty convincing.'

'Very convincing,' agreed Nick.

'What are we going to do tomorrow?' Callie went on. 'If we can't translate the messages they show us?'

Nick was straining to rock the heavy golden throne. 'We could make up stuff, like, "This week it's going to be sunny," and, "You'll find love in unexpected pyramids..."' He finished with a loud scream as the golden throne toppled backwards.

'Look what you've done!' exclaimed Callie, leaping off her bed and dragging her brother unceremoniously out of the way. The golden throne had punched a hole, right through the bottom of her bedroom wall.

'Don't worry about whether I'm all right, will you?' grumbled Nick.

Callie ignored him and bent down to peer through the hole in the plaster and brick. 'You've made a way out.'

She could see a truly magnificent bedroom on the other side of theirs. A golden-framed bed dominated one entire end of the room, a solid marble throne the other. Jewel-encrusted furniture stood around the rest of the chamber. Vibrant embroideries of ancient Egyptian life hung from each wall, and the glazed tile floor glittered like the deepest blue water. A sunken, oval pool, dwarfing the one in Callie's room, was reflecting

91

flickering lamplight from behind amethyst-coloured curtains, tied back with a golden cord.

Nobody seemed to have heard the crash: probably because a fountain beside the hole was cascading loudly into an ornamental pool.

Right across from where Callie was kneeling, stood a pair of panelled doors dressed with two sheets of milky mother-of-pearl shell. 'Come on,' she said. 'That's our way out.'

Callie and Nick scrambled through the hole and stood up. The room smelled faintly of rose oil and cedar wood. Callie turned towards the sunken pool and noticed something odd surfacing from the water. It was almost round, and mottled with scaly brown spots. As she watched, it began to raise itself in the water, revealing a scrawny neck and shoulders, and an equally bony back.

Callie forced a scream of horror back down her throat; Pharaoh Ssin, naked and without her black wig, was taking a bath. She had heard nothing under the water, but now would only have to turn to realise that Callie was watching her.

There was a gurgle of water. The Pharaoh was lowering herself back into the pool, fully submerging herself again with a brief plopping sound.

Callie nearly died as a hand closed around her bare arm, but it was Nick – looking equally terrified, and dragging her towards the mother-of-pearl doors. She nodded, and started to tiptoe across the glittering tiles.

Something sparkled across the room as they moved: a glimmer of golden light that made Callie twist in alarm. The polished surface of a gold-plated painting positioned at the foot of the bath, reflected back the image of a beautiful young pharaoh. Horrifyingly, beside the golden painting of the girl, she saw the face of Ssin emerging once more from the water:

withered, full of fury, and hissing venomous, unintelligible words.

'*Hatra cartha, Salak nar.*'

At first Callie thought the words were directed at her, but then a pair of magnificent cheetahs, with butter-yellow and charcoal markings, stalked out from behind the amethyst-coloured curtain. Ssin was commanding them to attack.

Callie gaped at the razor-sharp teeth, the needle-like claws – perfect instruments for separating her flesh from her bones. She knew that cheetahs were the fastest creatures on earth; and yet she was contemplating trying to outrun them to those mother-of-pearl doors. Impossible. Yet she had to try.

'Nice cats,' she stammered. It was a stupid thing to say, but it slipped from her lips automatically. She edged backwards, pushing Nick, the two cheetahs stalking them, their bellies stroking the tiled floor. They were spitting and hissing. 'Please don't hurt us.'

A latch clicked behind Callie, and she was whipped backwards. The nearest of the cheetahs pounced at the same moment, its claws slashing through the back of Callie's skirt. But she felt no pain, and then Nick was slamming the doors to the Pharaoh's bedchamber behind them.

They were in a vast, enclosed courtyard with gigantic pot plants growing on all four sides. The only way out was through a round archway with the hint of an indoor garden beyond. They began to run across the white marble flagstones, but had gained only a few metres before the doors to the bedchamber clattered open again.

Pharaoh Ssin emerged vengefully, now wrapped in a white robe that clung to her hideously bony form. She screeched to the cheetahs at her feet, and two streaks of yellow and black flashed across the courtyard.

Callie yelled, sure she heard the exact moment the cheetahs left the ground, launching themselves to bring her down. She ducked, and fell sprawling several metres short of the archway, covering her head with all the protection her hands could provide. 'Please, no,' she squealed. In moments she would be as shredded as her skirt. 'No, no, no, no, no...'

The 'kill' stopped before it had even started.

Callie thought that someone other than her was screaming – a completely different note merging with her own. Her fingers slipped momentarily from her eyes as she sought the unpleasant noise. The two cheetahs were skulking away, yowling in pain and baring their teeth at a noise that seemed to be driving them as mad as it was her. The cats sped back into the royal bedchamber, their long yellow tails between their legs – and Callie continued to look for the source of the excruciating sound.

Pharaoh Ssin lowered a flute-like instrument from her puckered lips, and the sound ceased instantly. It was replaced by shrieks of demonic laughter, the rope of beard dangling from her chin bobbing up and down disgustingly. When she was finished amusing herself, she bellowed: 'Moldo!'

Crocodile Head, minus his gruesome headwear again, came running in through the arch, and looked shocked to find Callie and Nick in the courtyard. He dashed an anxious look at Ssin. 'Great Pharaoh?'

Ssin gave him an order in her scratchy, ancient tongue, and Crocodile Head lifted Callie back onto her feet.

'She's playing with us,' whispered Nick reassuringly. 'If she wants us to translate her hieroglyphs she's got to keep us alive, hasn't she?'

Callie looked down again at her torn skirt. 'Alive, maybe,' she gulped. 'But not necessarily unharmed.'

11

Beware of Gobb

'**O**uch! Ouch! Ouch!' Callie was yelping as she moved about her bedroom the following morning. Crocodile Head had meted out a singularly nasty punishment by whipping the backs of their legs thirty times each with birch branches. Callie's legs still bore the little red stripes made by the branches. It had been totally humiliating and painful, but she'd prefer being smacked with birch branches to being torn apart by cheetahs any day.

After the punishment, Crocodile Head and another man (with such bucked teeth that Nick had christened him Horse Face) had heaved an enormous marble statue of a hippo into Callie's bedroom to block the hole Nick had made in the wall.

Callie found her freshly laundered skirt with the rips made by the cheetah's claws almost invisible, having been mended by one of Ssin's servants. She gingerly pulled it on, along with her top.

Then, still smarting from the wounds on her legs, she made her way to the dining area to see what had been left for them for breakfast. Nick was already there, looking haggard – but still finishing off breakfast of oat flapjacks flavoured with honey, and an assortment of fruits. They'd decided last night that the food and everything else supplied to the underground palace must be brought in from above, probably by more Followers of Ssin, or maybe Ramy's tribe of nomads.

'How do you feel?' Nick asked her.

'My legs are still hurting.'

'Mine too...'

Callie helped herself to a bowl of dried fruit, realising that her hand was shaking. It wasn't just the thought of being punished last night, it was the fear of translating hieroglyphs today. What if they couldn't do it? What would happen to them then?

They were still eating when the massive wooden doors started to rumble open. 'Is it me, or is he actually grinning at us this morning?' said Nick, as Crocodile Head lumbered in to the room.

Callie glanced queasily at Crocodile Head's fearsome jaw as he took his now-familiar grip of her arm.

'How does he see through that thing, anyway?' Callie whispered.

'With difficulty, I guess,' replied Nick. 'It must be like staring down a tunnel of teeth.'

Crocodile Head took them in a different direction to the previous day. Instead of guiding them over the metal grate of the crocodile-infested pit, he turned right and steered them through another section of the palace entirely.

Chambers lit by oil lamps led off on either side of a wide whitewashed corridor inscribed with hieroglyphics. Callie glimpsed soldiers, wearing striped Egyptian kilts and leather armour, sparring with genuine swords in a gymnasium; then a little further on, servants preparing food in a kitchen with charcoal ovens. Followers of Ssin, keeping the buried city alive for their three-thousand-year-old pharaoh.

Finally Crocodile Head brought them down a small passageway decorated with familiar marching crocodile men, and to a tiny chamber at the end. Lifelike Egyptian birds – white ibises, vultures and storks – were painted onto the sky-blue ceiling of the small chamber, making it seem as though the birds were actually flying overhead. Crocodile Head propelled them forward with a grunt, then turned and left.

Gobb rose like a giant insect from a wooden table over-flowing with notebooks and sheets of hieroglyphics. He was still wearing his priestly robes, the exact colour of blood.

'Squirrel and Stickleback. Your worth is great indeed to be permitted to live after interrupting *her* bath.' He backed them towards a wooden bench and pushed them down roughly so that their legs stung. Callie willed herself not to wince at the pain, as she saw Nick staring up into Gobb's ugly face defiantly.

'Look around you,' Gobb commanded in his booming voice, while gesticulating at the walls.

Callie and Nick did as they were told. The walls were like the pages of an ancient Egyptian manuscript – column upon column of tiny painted hieroglyphs.

Gobb jabbed the nearest column of hieroglyphs. 'Most of these texts are nothing more than predictions of good harvests, successful trade missions, or inclement weather. But these' – he indicated an indented section of wall, set half a centimetre deeper than the general surface of the plaster – 'are very different. From the Seer to Squirrel and Stickleback, hidden under the plaster of the outer texts.' He gestured towards the base of the wall where a few crumbs of plaster had formed a little heap. 'There are six segments of the same message. You will interpret it in its entirety.'

'And what if we *can't*?' asked Callie again, tentatively. She didn't recognise a single symbol in front of her.

'Then you will assist Pharaoh Ssin in another way,' replied Gobb, sounding unusually reasonable.

'How?'

'You will feed her crocodiles.'

'I'd rather do that anyway,' began Nick, before spotting the expression on Gobb's bug-eyed face. 'Oh... You mean...' He gulped.

Callie lifted herself onto the palms of her hands to ease her stinging legs. 'Mr Gobb, will you tell us who that woman really is?'

Gobb stared at her as if he thought she was stupid beyond measure. 'She is precisely who she says she is: Pharaoh Ssin.' In the lamplight, his ill-matched eyes glittered red.

'But she's only *pretending* to be a pharaoh, isn't she?'

'*Pretending?*' Gobb roared. 'No one is pretending. You have met the original Pharaoh Ssin born in July 1408 BC.'

'But how *can* she be?' insisted Callie. 'No one could live that long.' Though she guessed what Gobb was about to say.

'Ssin learned the secret of eternal life many thousands of years ago.'

'You mean she can't die?'

'That is what eternal life means.'

'Then what does she want?' asked Callie. 'If she's already eternal, what's better than that?' Again she knew the answer. Omar had said the two things were not the same, but very different.

'Eternal youth...'

Callie flashed Nick a frightened glance. If Ssin were young

once more, and with this army of psychopathic Followers at her command, she could rise again!

'Now, you will translate the scripts,' growled Gobb, dragging them off the bench, and forcing them to the first section of wall. 'Ssin grows impatient after her long wait.' When Callie and Nick had stared blankly at the interconnected outlines for over a minute, Gobb returned to his table of notebooks. 'I will allow you the morning to decode it.'

It was another two hours before Gobb's patience ran out. 'Well? What does it reveal? You have had long enough.'

'I don't know,' stammered Callie. 'It's so difficult.' She had scribbled several pages of notes, but there was nothing she'd written down which made any sense. 'Can't you give us longer...?' Her eyes filled with frightened tears.

'What about you?' Gobb spun round to glower at Nick.

Nick shook his head apologetically. 'Sorry...'

'If you are not, after all, Squirrel and Stickleback,' spat Gobb, his bulging eyes blazing into them, 'all three of us shall die in torment!' He stormed from the chamber and they could hear him beating his fists angrily against the walls all the way down the passage.

'I didn't know what to do,' said Callie, after the dust had settled from Gobb's irate departure. 'I can read quite a lot of it, but I didn't want to tell him.'

'Same here,' said Nick.

'It starts here.' Callie rushed over to the bottom of the wall near the chamber entrance. '*Dear Callie and Nick, my name is Fortune, and this is my communication to you...* He used our school timetable icon for communications.'

'I know,' said Nick, nodding. Callie pointed to the next line of hieroglyphs in the middle of the same wall.

'Look, this box shape. It's exactly the same as my stationery box, where I keep all my letters and cards. So it means, "I am writing to you."'

'And that's our timetable symbol for history,' supplied Nick. It was crossed swords and the date 1066. 'So he's saying: "I am writing to you from history – from the past."'

Callie had to squat down to read the next line in the corner of the chamber. 'This mountain is the logo for my climbing club followed by his name again, the three stars in a rainbow over the top of it. So I think that says: "I have climbed, or scaled, the heights of prophesy."'

Nick nodded again. 'Modest.'

'True, though. He knew everything about us ... And it goes on: "I have a really important prediction for you" because it's our names again.' Callie felt her blood suddenly running cold. 'That sounds pretty ominous, doesn't it?'

Nick nodded as she moved somewhat unsteadily to the next part, wondering what important prediction could be for them.

'This definitely means: "I ask you to trust me."' She underlined a small hand being held within a larger hand. 'My year had a competition to design a symbol that meant: "Trust me," as part of an art project – and that was the design that won. Jade Simmons would be so pleased to see it here.'

'And this is: "Go to my hidden map room",' said Nick, moving to the next section of text, which was a few centimetres from the bottom of the wall. 'The school's icon for geography, and that's the hidden door symbol from my favourite computer game.'

'Did you work out this symbol?' Callie had stalled again at the next inscription, a sideways V shape with a sort of saw pattern inside it, and a stick figure with one arm up.

'First bit's how I draw crocodiles,' nodded Nick, swallowing. 'Mixed with my swimming badge for the five-hundred-metre crawl. So it probably means: "Swim with the crocodiles." That could be the test Ssin gave us yesterday.'

Callie shook her head doubtfully. 'But that's already happened. Why would he tell us now? In here?' Her face drained of colour. 'Unless it's a warning that Gobb is going to carry out his threat of feeding us to the crocodiles under the palace.'

'I don't buy it,' said Nick wrinkling his nose. 'We probably just have to follow the crocodiles on the walls. There's some right outside this chamber. "Follow the crocodiles,"' he went on with the translation, '"North, then west, then south—"'

'How did you get that last bit?' said Callie, looking baffled.

'The points of the compass are the different sides of our house – north, south, east and west. It took me ages to work it out, but it's pretty simple when you think about it. Look!'

Callie stared at the mysterious square symbols again and gasped. 'Of course! Each square has a different number and pattern of windows in it: north, west and south!'

'Thank you for your translation.'

Callie spun round, her eyes widening in dismay. Gobb was standing behind them, a satisfied look on his face. He must have been listening to everything, having only pretended to storm off so he could spy on them. And they'd just translated the entire message for him!

'Moldo...' the giant priest called, and Crocodile Head materialised in the entrance to the room. 'You may remove our guests now.'

Remove them, thought Callie queasily. *What did 'remove them' mean?*

Crocodile Head grasped each of them by the arm and marched them out of the chamber. Evil-faced carved crocodile-men flashed past on the walls, men they know knew led to the Seer's secret map room.

12

The First Prophesies

The Pharaoh's Palace, Medphis, Season of the Annual Flood, 1391 BC

Fortune was working in one of the many small prediction chambers dotted about the palace, the one with the painted blue ceiling inset with the images of white ibises, vultures and storks. His visions had been of a fairly mundane nature of late: to do with harvests, the weather and successful trade missions so he was recording them here.

His occasional, more significant visions he now kept to himself, mainly because he had grown to understand what Ssin was really like. Ssin was the spider, the reptile, the snake. She tortured and killed those who disappointed her, threw their broken, and sometimes still living, bodies to her pet crocodiles. The mists of vision had cleared for Fortune some months back and he now foresaw Ssin's future: every evil day of it. It had been a grave error trusting her, loving her, and now he had made her eternal – a tragic misuse of his prophet's powers.

It could be undone. There was a way. It was fate, not a force he could completely control, but one he could predict. Squirrel and Stickleback were his only hope.

He had just finished repairing the wall plaster and painting it over with a symbol of a hawk so that his words, hidden underneath, would not be found for several thousand years. It was preordained that they should be read by Squirrel and Stickleback. It was also preordained that a Grand Priest, called Gobb, would eavesdrop and hear the words too. Fortune had foreseen it all and could do nothing to prevent it. Fate was fate.

The alabaster door behind him flew open moments after he had finished, and Pharaoh Ssin surged furiously into his presence. 'You tricked me!' she screeched at him. 'Deceived *me*, your pharaoh!' She was flanked by two royal bodyguards, their muscular torsos displayed above their red kilts; she was rarely alone with Fortune these days. All former promises that she would give Fortune her unconditional love once he made her eternal had been forgotten or overlooked. Once she'd attained her eternal life, Fortune had become nothing to her.

She poked her soft chin to within centimetres of his; even after the months of betrayal, her nearness still intoxicated him.

'How have I deceived you?' he asked carefully.

'Look at this!' She rammed a fine strand of something at him, a thread of silver.

'I do not understand. What is it?'

'A hair, you fool! One of *my* hairs! And last week I found a wrinkle.' She pointed a sharp fingernail at the corner of her eye, but Fortune could see nothing amiss beneath the bright blue make-up – and apart from the single silver follicle, her hair was a lustrous black sheen of perfection. 'Why do I continue to age?' she railed at him. 'You promised me eternal life!'

'And such you have been granted,' stated Fortune, silently wishing it was not so. 'I have gifted you eternal life, not eternal youth.'

'There, then! There is the trick.' She leaped upon the statement as though it were a confession. 'This is not what I wished, not what I desired. Who would beg to grow ever older? What is the worth of eternal life if I should watch myself rot in my own mirror?' She was squealing like a scalded cat. She swept his paints and brushes angrily from his hand. 'Trickster!'

'But this is not your final destiny,' Fortune told her calmly. 'The breath of eternal youth exists.'

'What?' Ssin turned, seeing the possibility. 'You've foreseen it? Eternal *youth*?'

'Better. I have foreseen *you* breathing it.'

'Where is it?' the pharaoh now demanded greedily.

'It is hard to discern, that is why I have not shared the secret with you thus far,' said Fortune cautiously. 'There were mountains in my vision. I still know not where, but I would know them if I saw them for real.'

Ssin's mesmerising dark eyes widened with a passionate flame. 'I must prepare an expedition. You shall lead it and I shall accompany you, and with us shall travel ten of my finest chariot squadrons.'

She paced the chamber, racing on with her eager preparations. 'We must lose no more time. I become older with each passing moon. I shall not see myself turn into a white-haired old woman!'

She saw the hesitation in Fortune's eyes, and remembered the promises she had made to him and broken before.

'Leave us,' she ordered her bodyguards and, when they had withdrawn, she took hold of Fortune's hand in hers. 'I have misplayed you, loyal, loving Fortune; I have been ungrateful – because my advisors persuaded me that a pharaoh could not marry a humble potter's son. But I am the pharaoh! I shall marry whomsoever I wish. Just grant me what I desire and you shall at last see how grateful and loving your queen can be.'

Fortune smiled, pretending to believe her. 'When may we begin, highness?'

'By sun up tomorrow.' Ssin clapped her tiny palms together in delight, girlish pleasure lighting her face.

'I would like to see my parents before we leave,' said Fortune. 'It has been almost a year since I saw them last, and it could be a great time more before we return.'

Ssin's expression darkened. 'I cannot grant you this gift, Fortune. In a generous moment last month I allowed your father and mother to accompany one of my trade missions, to seek out fine pottery from some of the more remote parts of my kingdom. The mission is not due to return for many weeks.'

'Could we not delay our journey,' Fortune asked, believing nothing of what she said.

'No!' shouted Ssin angrily. 'I have spoken.' Her eyes blazed at him. She was not to be denied or contradicted, and suddenly Fortune saw right into her mind, and his insides burned. As soon as she left this chamber she intended to send soldiers to slaughter his parents, who were in their home, not on a trade mission at all. His one link to the outside world was to be eradicated. 'You may spend a week with your parents when we return,' she lied to him.

'As you wish,' rasped Fortune, staring queasily at his feet so as not to betray his true feelings of hatred. 'I am your humble servant.'

'Good. I shall make my preparations,' Ssin told him, kissing him lightly on the cheek. 'I suggest you make yours.'

Fortune waited a minute to be sure that Ssin had gone, and then he raced out of the chamber and along the white-washed passage. Sunlight blazed through the windows of a columned hallway. Modestly dressed servants were going

106

about their business, carrying pitchers of water or food on trays, one girl was walking with a stack of folded linen balanced on her head. Richly dressed courtiers stood speaking to one another in corners and cast black looks at Fortune as he hurtled past, his footsteps clattering on the tiles.

He cared not, dashing out into the full, dazzling sunshine, through a series of obelisks to a flight of descending marble steps. With a supreme effort, he checked his run as he approached the golden gates to the Pharaoh's private zoo and gardens – sauntering up to the bare-chested guards, as if everything today was quite normal.

'Here again, young prophet?' said the stoutest of the two guards, an amiable enough man called Golas.

'The gardens help me "see" things,' Fortune reminded him. He always used the same excuse.

'Speaking of seeing things,' said the guard respectfully. 'I wanted to ask you something...'

Fortune could have screamed, his impatience to rush on palpable, yet he forced the urgency from his face. 'Yes, Golas.'

'I was wondering about the Pharaoh's handmaiden, the beautiful Jarinda... Will she ever look favourably on me?'

'Your future, and Jarinda's are marked out together, great Golas,' said Fortune, just saying what the big man wanted to hear. 'You will marry before the next annual flooding of the Nile.'

Golas beamed, while the other guard started making embarrassing kissing sounds. 'Oooh, Golas, I love you.'

'Let the boy through,' Golas said good-humouredly. 'Maybe he'll have a vision about how many fine sons Jarinda and I will produce.'

The other guard opened the gates for Fortune, who slipped through almost fainting with relief – the beads of sweat running down his forehead thankfully unnoticed by either of the men.

The botanical gardens were as green as ever: overhanging palm-tree fronds shading the patterned walkways. The exotic animals which Fortune had got to know so well – zebras and giraffes – grazed within the high stone walls. But today he barely noticed them as he sprinted across the compound.

He plunged straight through some pink-flowered bushes which blanketed the outside wall where he'd been secretly working for some weeks now, since he'd begun to see the future of his pharaoh more clearly.

He scrabbled around in the red earth at the base of the wall, searching for the copper dagger he'd hidden there.

The blade glinted in his hand as he slid it between two of the chipped white blocks in the wall, and then started digging out crumbs of already-loosened mortar. After a few minutes' work, daylight began to creep around the block.

Fortune rolled onto his back, and used the soles of his papyrus shoes to send the block thudding onto the ground outside the palace. There was no time for finesse.

'*Ahhhh!*' A portly man dressed in fine merchants' robes shouted in alarm to see someone wriggling out from under the palace wall. But worse, he began yelling: 'What are you doing there? Why aren't you using the gate like everyone else? Are you a thief?'

A knot of the pharaoh's soldiers stationed along the outer ramparts of the palace heard the commotion and came running – drawing their swords as they did so. 'What's going on here?'

But Fortune was already scarpering, darting down the nearest alley. He weaved through wine sellers and meat vendors, and carried on running until he reached the brightly coloured stalls of Medphis market and its throng of shoppers. Fighting his way through, he ducked down another alley which brought him out at the temple of Ra, the Sun God.

He mumbled a prayer for his parents as he passed the high walls of the temple and hurried on past the gleaming white villas of the city's wealthiest inhabitants.

On he went through the vast city, tumbling through to the more modest districts of the general population. He knew from his recent visions that Ssin had not elevated his parents as she had promised him, it was just another lie she'd told him. At last he could see the glittering Nile and the mud-brick craftsmen's dwellings lining its bank. The chimney of his father's potting kiln was worryingly smokeless against the sapphire sky.

A chariot driven by two soldiers was clattering down Potters Street, towards him and away from the tiny home Fortune hadn't seen for more than a year.

He was too late.

Desperately, Fortune burst into the one-room dwelling without stopping. 'Mother...Father...?'

They were close at hand. Sunlight shone brightly through slits in the roof, and onto the dry matting covering the earthen floor. There was a small prayer shrine and wooden chairs to one side of the single room – and an awful smell of blood emanating from behind a roughly woven curtain. Fortune dragged it aside and recoiled. Two figures were curled up together in death upon the wooden cot.

He began to sob.

13

Follow the Stars

ɣ

Crocodile Head had taken Callie and Nick back to their private prison instead of to the crocodile pit as they had feared. Callie still felt too numb to cry, but she knew the tears would come eventually. She was sitting on her heels on the corner of her bed, while Nick was slumped again in the golden throne chair. Together they were trying to work out why they were still alive, and if it meant that things were going to work out OK after all. *But how can it work out OK?* thought Callie. Ssin wouldn't just let them go, would she?

'Why did the Seer have to choose us?' she said in a brittle tone. 'Couldn't he have picked some other kids? He must have known how much danger he was going to put us in by writing to us.'

'He didn't *choose* us, though, did he?' said Nick reasonably. 'He saw what he saw and that was us.'

'Well, I still hate him,' said Callie, hoping that the Seer had predicted her annoyance. 'Horrible boy, who knew every detail about us: where we'd live, our nicknames, stuff we'd do at school. Your swimming, my climbing. It's creepy...' She found herself wondering if the Seer had known what they'd look like, and if he'd thought she was pretty.

Nick preoccupied himself with picking at a piece of loose rubber underneath his left trainer. 'We've got to find out what's in that secret map room...'

'Why have we?'

'Because the Seer wanted us to.'

'Well, you'll have to ask Gobb or Ssin to let us, then, because I'm too scared.'

They both started at the sound of a scream. 'What was that?' Callie stared uneasily at her open door as another shriek erupted from somewhere nearby.

'More to the point: *Who* was that?' said Nick, gulping.

They held their breath a moment as the guttering lamp-light animated the faces of the painted musicians on the wall grotesquely. The cry became a wail and then, mercifully, died out altogether.

Callie was just relaxing again, when Crocodile Head appeared in the doorway. 'You will come.'

Callie was aghast; would it be her screams ringing out next? He pulled Nick out of the golden throne and then dragged Callie off the bed by her arm.

'We can walk on our own, you know,' said Nick, doing his best to sound brave.

'Where are you taking us?' Callie rasped. 'And who was that screaming?'

Crocodile Head ignored her, tugging them both into the corridor, on through their private dining chamber, and out the open wooden doors. As he steered them along the next passageway, Callie's felt her trainers slithering in something wet. She glanced down and let out a horrified sob; her feet were sliding through crimson slime.

'Blood...' mouthed Nick unnecessarily.

The grisly smear led all the way to the metal grate forming both bridge and cage over the pit of live crocodiles. Judging from all the blood, someone had been feeding them. Suddenly Callie realised that the unearthly screams they'd heard and the crocodiles were connected.

Callie tried not to look down as jaws snapped right beneath her feet. Teeth clanged on the underside of the grate. She made it to the other side feeling faint.

Crocodile Head brought them past the granite-statue-guarded entrance to the throne room, and round the next corner. Callie was only vaguely aware of the marching crocodile men reliefs on the wall, leading all the way to a jagged hole at the end of the passage where bricks and rubble littered the tiled floor.

'The hidden room,' whispered Nick.

Callie's confusion suddenly cleared. *Of course! 'Go to my hidden map room. Follow the crocodiles.'* The Pharaoh's followers had wasted no time finding it and opening it.

Crocodile Head gave Callie a shove towards the hole, 'In.' And after a swift glance at Nick, she obeyed.

She came into a long narrow chamber, more like a bricked-up corridor than a room. Several oil lamps had been placed around it and were shedding a soft amber glow onto the walls, where maps had been painted directly onto the plaster. Nick stepped in behind her, but Crocodile Head remained outside.

'Now what?' whispered Callie. 'What do they want us to do?'

Nick shrugged. 'Look around, I suppose.' He peered silently at the maps for a minute. 'I don't recognise anywhere, do you?'

'What did you expect? A map of the London Underground?' replied Callie, fear making her impatient. She didn't recognise anywhere, either. But the longer she stared she began to wonder whether maybe the London Underground wasn't too far off the mark. 'What if these maps aren't even of Egypt? The Seer might have hidden his prophesies in another country.'

'Possibly.' Nick studied one of the largest maps. 'Isn't that the Nile, though?' He followed a line of peeling blue paint down the map with his finger – tracking it from the very top to the very bottom. It fanned out at his feet into lots of separate blue squiggles merging with an even larger blue area.

'It *is* the Nile,' Callie exclaimed. 'It's upside down: the way the ancient Egyptians viewed their kingdom. The northern half, where the Nile flows into the sea, was Lower Egypt, and the southern half, where it rises, was Upper Egypt.'

'Right.' Nick inclined his head to view the map upside down, while Callie wandered along the narrow chamber, trying to imagine all the other paintings the other way up too. As she reached the end opposite to where they'd come in, she noticed a small section of text, etched into the stonework; Squirrel and Stickleback symbols were right at the top.

'Look. "Dear Callie and Nick," again.' The rest of the message appeared to be a mixture of elaborate shapes and genuine hieroglyphics.

Nick peered over her shoulder. 'Gobb couldn't read it because it's to us...' His frown deepened. 'Where is Gobb, anyway? Shouldn't he be here?'

'The Grand Priest is here.'

They spun round at the ancient-sounding voice and recoiled. Ssin was standing right behind them. And, startlingly, she was speaking to them in English. Callie realised with a shock that the evil pharaoh had been pretending not to understand them all along: probably hoping they'd let something useful out in front of her.

There was faint whimpering from the passageway behind her, as if someone was in pain.

'Bring him forward,' Ssin ordered, moving her grotesque form out of the way.

Two guards, one with a dreadful scar-induced squint, and the other they knew as Horse Face, dragged Gobb into the narrow chamber between them. They were propping him up, and Gobb was groaning, his bald head oddly bloodless.

'The Grand Priest misinterpreted our commands,' Ssin said in a detached tone. 'We did not instruct our servant to open the secret map chamber without our knowledge.'

'I merely wanted to reveal the chamber for you, my pharaoh,' Gobb burbled distressingly.

'Liar! You wanted to open it for yourself. You have masqueraded as my loyal priest while secretly planning to steal the prophesies!' Reaching up she slapped him cruelly across his ugly face.

Gobb produced another spine-chilling scream, which bounced off the narrow sides of the chamber. Callie winced. Why did he keep shrieking like that? Ssin's slap could hardly have induced such terrible pain. Then Callie found herself gazing downwards and thought she was going to be sick.

Gobb was being held up by Horse Face and the squinting guard because he couldn't stand up on his own. His feet were a slick of flowing blood from where his toes had once been; the tiles behind him were a trail of blood and gore.

Suddenly everything made nightmarish sense: the screams they'd heard, the blood smearing the grille above the crocodile pit...Ssin's men had forced Gobb's feet through the metal grille, and the crocodiles had feasted upon his toes.

Callie somehow managed to speak: 'Help him,' she begged, transfixed by Gobb's horrific injuries. 'Please. He needs a doctor.'

She hated Gobb. He'd threatened *them* with the crocodiles. But he had suffered that fate himself, and she couldn't now stand by and watch him bleed to death.

'*You* help him!' screeched Ssin, sending the thin plait of beard swinging on her chin.

'What?' Callie dashed away hot tears. 'How? I don't know what to do.' Gobb's bulging eyes were beseeching her.

'Translate the message.'

'Pardon?'

'Translate it, and we will spare our Grand Priest,' Ssin moderated her fury just a little.

Callie shook. How could they possibly interpret the message quickly enough to save Gobb? Yet they were his only hope. She glanced at her brother, who returned a small nod, and they swung round to the small block of text starting with Squirrel and Stickleback.

'That, that looks like a letter "Q",' Callie said hurriedly. 'But that doesn't mean anything to me.'

'It could be a magnifying glass...' Nick offered hesitantly.

Gobb wailed again.

'What's the next part?' Callie rushed on, trying to drown out the awful howl. 'They look like genuine hieroglyphics.' She realised with horror that *Hieroglyphics for Beginners* was still in her bedroom.

'It means City of the Dead,' Gobb cried out, biting down on another shriek of agony. '*Hurryyyyyyy!*'

Nick pointed at the remaining symbol: a sort of long tube thing. 'It's a telescope,' he stammered. 'It's from the box my telescope came in – exactly the same.' He struggled to find a meaning. 'Telescope? Stars... The heavens!'

'It's a star map,' shouted Callie, recognising the same compass symbol for 'geography' they'd translated before and decided meant 'maps'. She spun round to Ssin, whose narrowed, milky eyes were boring into her. 'It says: "Look closely at the star map to find the City of the Dead." Now help him!'

After a pause, Ssin nodded to Horse Face. 'See to our Grand Priest. He may prove useful yet.'

With another whimpering yell of pain, Gobb was dragged out of the chamber. Ssin was already casting around the narrow space for a star map amid the painted charts of ancient Egypt.

'There!' she croaked at last. 'There is a map of the heavens.' She pointed to a patch of faded midnight-blue pigment on the wall, squeezed between two larger cracked yellow panels of the Egyptian desert. At first it appeared to be a simple border between the other maps, but individual stars were picked out in spots of real silver – a constellation, a pattern of stars in the sky.

'This star is different... the colour brighter,' she mumbled. 'It is the western star of the Orion constellation.' She paused and licked her blackened teeth. 'Yes... I remember Fortune's mind. He was fond of boyish devices and tricks, playing with hieroglyphs to create his own writing.' She was talking to herself now, oblivious of Callie and Nick, standing petrified behind her. 'I understand. We must calculate the distance and the direction by applying them to these stars. But to what scale?'

Nick pointed to the final two symbols in the message. 'The

scale's fifteen hundred metres to one centimetre. That's the symbol for my fifteen-hundred-metre breaststroke certificate. And the other thing's a centipede: one centimetre, I used to get the two words mixed up when I was little, remember?'

Callie was still staring at the message. 'And...' she blurted out, causing the creature to glare at her with milky-lensed eyes. 'It isn't a magnifying glass. It's a hand-mirror. I bought one just like it for Mum last week. The Seer's telling us to read the star map the opposite way round – a mirror image.'

'A mirror image?' Ssin's eyes flickered over Callie's face for signs of deceit.

'I'm not lying,' Callie wept now; the consequences of crossing Ssin were seared into her memory for ever – the smell of Gobb's blood still clinging to the stale air. 'I don't want you to go to the wrong place, because you'll take it out on us.'

'Oh, that I will,' confirmed Ssin, her rotten breath ruffling Callie's hair. She nodded briefly. 'A backwards map. And upside down like the others. Yes, it is the style of the Seer.' She seemed to ruminate on the memory of the boy she had known so long ago.

'He has made me wait for many ages for this moment, hiding his little messages all over my palace, before running away. I went after him, of course, tore my kingdom apart searching for him. But the populace turned against me, burying me in my own palace. That was my torment: unable to die, and unable to leave the confines of an everlasting tomb; trapped alone for ninety-seven wretched years until those still loyal to me – the descendents of former acolytes – excavated me from my prison.'

She stared hard at Callie. 'Now, since you take such a keen interest in the health of my former grand priest, you may attend his operation.' She clicked her bony fingers, and Crocodile Head reappeared with an almost wicked leer on his gruesome crocodile mask.

Screams of agony were not uncommon in the Palace of Ssin. Its halls echoed regularly to the sound of pain. Gobb was merely the most recent in a long line of victims stretching back over three thousand years. He was lying at the centre of his own lamplit temple, being kept conscious with slaps and splashes of water in the face throughout the whole ordeal. A surgeon had not been called; a surgeon might spare him some suffering. So it had fallen to Crocodile Head and Horse Face to operate on him instead. It was apt, for it was they who had helped the sacred crocodiles carry out the amputation in the first place.

Callie was almost passing out with the stench of blood in her nostrils. Nick stood beside her, pale and silent. Each time they tried to look away, Crocodile Head dragged them nearer to the operating slab.

'One of the gods should have told Gobb it's no good trying to kick a crocodile in the gob,' guffawed Horse Face, his teeth sticking out in an angled leer. 'Never mind, old man, save you cutting your toenails again.'

Gobb shrieked once more, even though he seemed to be desperately trying not to show his agony. Crocodile Head was both cleansing and sealing the ragged edges of flesh halfway up his foot where his toes had once been, using a flaming brand. The scream became a gagging sound as Gobb scented his own burning flesh. It was smoking and melting like wax before his protuberant eyes, and still his evil surgeons would not permit him to pass out into oblivion, Horse Face slapping him hard across the face again. 'Wakey, wakey.'

'Tried to cross *her*, didn't you?' growled Crocodile Head exultantly. 'No more Grand Priest for you.' An appealing thought struck him: 'Maybe I'll get to wear the scarlet robe instead of a putrid crocodile's head. Let us be realistic: what use are you without your feet?'

Gobb was glaring back at his tormentor. Crocodile Head was right. Gobb would never be able to walk again unaided, much less run or drive a chariot the way he had before. Callie could guess what had happened: Gobb had succumbed to greed to make the lost prophesies his own, to gain his own immortality and eternal youth. In his moment of fevered madness he had wished to take everything for himself. And Gobb had been caught.

He was beginning to babble through his excruciating pain: 'My family coveted the Lost Prophesies for generation after generation, dreamed of them all the way back to Wazim the Pockmarked, who served Ssin before the Seer wormed his way into her brief affections. Salah the Disemboweller, Mytok the Sly, Komek the Hunchback – they all worked for this day, serving *her* secretly in the outside world and in her palace buried under the desert. An unbroken line of priests, one-hundred and seventy-seven generations long, dedicating their lives to Ssin; learning the ancient language, both spoken and written from infancy; keeping her name and cause alive among the Followers; maintaining the network who supplied her palace with all its food and manpower; dealing with a succession of archaeologists who'd strayed close enough to the truth to present a danger.'

'Stop your babbling complaints, Gobb, else we'll introduce

your fingers to my brothers in the crocodile pit,' yelled Crocodile Head cruelly.

Callie heard something sizzling and knew that it was Gobb's left foot. Horse Face was painting the melted stub with boiling tar. The pain must be unbearable. Then, at last, there was a respite, as Crocodile Head began to bind up the ruins of Gobb's feet in fresh linen bandages.

'A giant who can't even stand up,' hooted Horse Face, almost wetting himself. 'How are you going to get your kicks now, Gobb?'

Crocodile Head and Horse Face roared with laughter.

Callie screwed her eyes shut and forced herself not to listen to any more.

14

City of the Dead

M

The stars in the midnight-blue sky matched the Seer's star map in a perfect mirror image, as the squadron of twenty Egyptian chariots raced across the desert in battle formation. They were whipping up a storm of sand and dust. Crocodile Head was leading in the most striking chariot of all – gilded with fine gold leaf, and carrying the shrivelled Pharaoh Ssin in a splendid portable throne fixed inside the cockpit. The sheer weight of the throne required four horses instead of the usual two, and the wheels were carving deep tramlines in the moonlit sand.

With scarcely any notice, they had fled the buried city of Medphis. Callie had had at least the foresight to stuff most of her possessions into her pockets: *Hieroglyphics for Beginners, Egypt's Greatest Astrologer,* sun cream, their passports and cruise tickets. Her skirt pockets were bulging like saddlebags, but she had zipped them up carefully.

Medphis had been hidden by an optical illusion produced by rocky outcrops and sculpted dunes that made the entrance as good as invisible. Not even a single ruined column stood to betray its location. From a few hundred metres away, even the dunes disappeared in ghostly darkness.

Callie was glad to be finally above ground again, breathing the chilled fresh air of night. Two days they'd spent trapped in Medphis. She wondered if her mum and dad were still working in Nag Hammadi, or had returned to Cairo to find them gone? Would Omar have informed her parents of what had happened, or was he still on the run, terrified of Followers of Ssin and lamenting the discovery of his secret treasure room?

The chariot lurched to one side, and Callie was thrown like a rag doll inside the wicker cockpit. They were at the forefront of the V formation. The chariot's massive spoked wooden wheels were hammering into the uneven desert, but, thankfully her charioteer, broad backed and thick necked, appeared to know what he was doing – guiding his pair of silver-grey horses deftly round boulders and rocks that seemed to burst out at them in the speckled moonlight.

Callie glanced across at the flanking chariot where Nick was hanging onto the wooden side rail with the trace of a smile on his face – torn between terror and exhilaration. Callie started mouthing words to him – the same way they did at home, when their mum and dad apparently 'couldn't hear themselves think' and wanted them to be quiet.

Callie: 'Are you OK?'

Nick: 'Yeah...'

'Hang on.'

Nick mimed: 'Why don't we jump for it?'

Callie started waving frantically at her brother. 'Don't you dare!'

She indicated a chariot a little further back, being driven fiercely by Horse Face. Gobb, with his bound-up feet, was sitting, like some giant, bug-faced statue, in a kind of ancient wheelchair strapped to the chariot's deck. What agonies he must be enduring as he was rattled around by the chariot, Callie could only imagine. Surely he was regretting his greed now.

'At least he's still alive,' Nick mouthed at her.

Callie nodded grimly, and then pointed at the galloping teams of horses all about them. 'Why are we going so fast?'

Nick looked ahead at Crocodile Head's chariot. He was whipping the four black horses to suicidal speed, setting the pace for the entire squadron. Nick gestured at the crescent moon, now at its zenith above them: it was the middle of the night. 'He wants to reach wherever we're going while it's still dark,' he mouthed.

Callie nodded again, getting the gist of what he was saying. Night was the only time twenty ancient chariots *could* cross the desert – without being spotted by stray herdsmen, random tourists, or passing aircraft. At night the chariots were merely a sound like a storm, howling across the desert.

There wouldn't be much chance of escaping while they were travelling in the chariots, she knew, and Crocodile Head was showing little indication of slackening the pace. Hopefully they'd get their chance before Ssin discovered the prophesy of eternal youth, and had no further use for Squirrel and Stickleback.

Callie glanced across at Ssin at that moment, and found the creature's moonlit face glowering back at her from her mobile throne. Callie shuddered. If she didn't know better, she would almost think Ssin was regarding her with jealousy.

Callie was still staring when everything around her suddenly vanished. The sliver of moon had been swallowed up by clouds, and it was only the beat of horses' hooves, the scrape of chariot wheels, that told her she was still amongst the

123

others. She was straining her eyes to see where Nick's chariot was, when something huge exploded beside her. She heard wood being torn apart, men screaming, and felt debris of some sort smack into the side of her own chariot. Then she held her breath as the moon restored itself in the night sky. Two of the other chariots had collided. One was smashed to pieces, the other still careering out of control on one wheel. As she watched, it slammed into a low ridge of rock, and both driver and passenger were flung rolling across the sand. The horses shrieked in panic, but somehow galloped away unharmed.

'Nick!' Callie cried out in terror. She couldn't see him. But when she looked again, she saw that her brother's chariot had only fallen back a little to avoid the carnage. Nick waved weakly to show her he was OK, though he appeared to be wiping sick from his lips with the back of his hand. Callie searched for Crocodile Head's chariot again. Incredibly, he wasn't even slowing, but keeping his chariot flying into the night.

Two chariots had been lost, their soldiers were crawling out from the wreckage, but Ssin was leaving them behind. Callie gave up a silent *Thank you* that she and Nick were OK. At least the night was on their side.

It was probably another hour before the desert scenery began to look any different, sand suddenly giving way to rock. They'd reached a plateau, and the noise from the eighteen remaining pairs of chariot wheels became thunderous.

Callie cried out and made a desperate grab for the cockpit rail as a wheel hit a bump and the deck she was standing on leaped up. The chariot smashed down again, throwing her sideways, but miraculously she was still on board. Her heart thumped rapidly as she realised what had happened. She'd been falling asleep when she should have been hanging on.

'How much further?' she shouted to the back of her thick-necked charioteer. Her voice was ripped from her lips and lost in the rushing wind. She leaned forward and tried again, louder this time: 'How much further?'

If the charioteer heard, he chose to ignore her, or didn't understand. He probably wouldn't know how much further, anyway; like the rest, he was just following Crocodile Head. Callie had to stay awake, however far they were going. 'I can stay awake...I've got to stay awake...'

She attempted adjusting her stance; balancing the way she'd been doing so far seemed to involve using every muscle in her body – no wonder she was tired.

'That's better...' she told herself

She tried reciting the Periodic Table she'd learned in chemistry. 'Hydrogen, helium, lithium...erm...Why was she so rubbish at science?

'Beryllium, boron, carbon...'

Her eyelids began to droop.

The stars arched overhead, gradually changing position with the flow of time. The temperature had continued to drop to its nadir, and then slowly began to rise again with the coming of day. In the expanse of the heavens the sun god Ra awakened.

'Callie! Callie!' Nick rushed to wake his sister as soon as he was let off the back of his own chariot. They had drawn up amidst undulating sand dunes which were silhouetted against the rising sun. The men were feeding and watering the horses where they stood, still harnessed to the chariots, using nosebags and water skins. A black canopy on poles rose nearby to shade the hideous figure of Ssin on her private throne.

No such consideration had been shown to the traitor Gobb, who was beginning to roast like the rest of them under the strengthening sun. Squint Eye must have been ordered to guard Callie and Nick because he was leaning on a nearby chariot, leering at them.

'I thought you'd fallen off your chariot while I wasn't looking,' Nick said breathlessly. 'I was really scared.'

'Sorry,' Callie said lamely, who was now curled in a heap on the chariot's decking. 'I don't even remember lying down.' She attempted to stand up, but something kept her pinned to the deck of the chariot. 'Huh?' She glanced down and saw that a thin strip of leather had been fed through a couple of her skirt's belt loops then tied to the cockpit's wicker side.

'Your charioteer must've done that to stop you falling right off,' guessed Nick, 'an ancient Egyptian seatbelt. Nice.'

Callie started untying herself. 'How much further did we travel?'

'I don't know, but it took hours... And we lost another chariot.'

'How?'

'Puncture... Well, ancient equivalent of one. Those wooden wheels really don't suit rocky ground.' He ran his hand over the flank of the nearest of Callie's two silver-grey horses, as if he were grooming it. The animal's fine muscles quivered under his gentle touch.

Callie counted the chariots: just as Nick had said, there were now only seventeen of the twenty that had started out from Medphis, scattered amid the dunes and natural rock. 'I suppose we're just holing up here for the day because it's too dangerous to go on.' There seemed to be nothing else of significance – certainly nothing which looked ancient Egyptian.

126

Nick shook his head. 'No. This is the place on the star map. I couldn't understand what they were saying, but they were using some sort of old measuring instruments with lead weights, and consulting papyrus maps. Crocodile Head's been pacing out the site – trying to find a keystone or something.'

'What do you mean, a keystone?'

'See those circular slabs all over the place, like land mines?'

Callie followed Nick's gaze. There was something the size of a dinner plate, and of a similar colour to the surrounding sand, nearby. 'What about them?'

'They keep finding them and brushing the sand off. I've worked out that they're looking for a slightly different one – you remember the one on the star map which was brighter than the others?'

'Of course,' gasped Callie, impressed.

It took another ten minutes in the blistering heat before Crocodile Head found what he was looking for, and went loping over to Ssin to make his report. Under the protection of her ebony sunshade, Ssin ordered Gobb to be wheeled to the keystone in his creaking wheelchair. When he was sitting in front of the stone, he spread out his arms wide, creating a square sail with his crimson robes. Callie could just make out his lips moving, incanting something over and over. 'He's praying,' she gulped. 'That's not good is it?'

'I think it's all an act,' said Nick. 'You know, ritual.'

Callie shielded her eyes from the sun and looked over at Gobb again. His incantations had grown louder, ululating through the stifling desert air: ancient words which seemed to insinuate some dark intent. An expectant hush had fallen over the camp; even the horses at the front of Callie's chariot were champing apprehensively at the bit.

'It isn't working,' mumbled Callie.

'Give him a chance.'

As they watched, Gobb threw himself desperately out of the wheelchair: landing on his knees. He was frantic – trying to win back the approval of his pharaoh. He began scrabbling about in the sand, scratching at the keystone in an attempt to move it. Callie thought he must be tearing out his fingernails in his fit of madness.

'It's got to be some sort of mechanism,' concluded Nick. 'Maybe—' He didn't finish his sentence. The ground beneath them had started to shake.

Callie glanced down. Grains of sand were quivering around her feet – stirred out of their stillness. Men leaped up, horses stamped their hooves and whinnied anxiously. A deep rumbling sound deafened them all, and when Callie looked at Gobb again a narrow oblong of desert had collapsed directly in front of him. He remained motionless on his knees as a second oblong, precisely the same size as the first, dropped too, disappearing a little deeper into the earth.

'Steps,' gasped Nick. The steps continued to slam into place one at a time with loud thuds, until they could no longer see them disappearing beneath the surface of the ground, only hear them carrying on: *thud, thud, thud, thud, thud.*

'We have to get away,' said Callie. 'Before they trap us underground again.'

'Get away how?' They were surrounded by men and chariots.

'How do you think?' Callie indicated the chariot she was standing on. The horses were still in the traces. And for the moment everyone seemed occupied with the flight of steps

Gobb had just opened up in the sand. Even Squint Eye was looking in the opposite direction. They had only this one chance. 'Climb up,' she whispered to Nick.

He didn't need any more encouragement, but kicked the wooden blocks stopping the chariot from rolling away and jumped aboard. Callie grasped the long leather reins and gave them a swift flick, exactly like she'd seen her charioteer doing. The metal bits clinked inside the two horses' mouths, bringing them to alertness. Sleek muscles quivered along their hind quarters then tensed. Callie flicked the reins once more and the bigger of the two horses raked the air briefly with its fore-hooves before springing forward, taking the smaller horse with it. The chariot creaked and plunged after them. Callie leaned sideways on the reins, pressing her hip into the side of the basket cockpit to bring the horses and chariot angling up the nearest slope. Sand sprayed out from under the metal-rimmed wheels, carving out a steep turn. Shouts of alarm were going up from Ssin's men as they saw one of the chariots charging off. Squint Eye hurtled after them, while others jumped aboard their own chariots to take chase.

Still spurring the horses on, Callie turned to stare at the black canopy, searching for their kidnapper. What would Pharaoh Ssin do? The withered creature's hate-filled eyes latched onto Callie. Slowly the old woman raised a metal instrument to her puckered lips.

An awful wave of shrieking sound streaked across the distance between them, an unbearable sound both Callie and Nick had heard before: one that threatened to make the listener go mad.

The horses stopped dead in their tracks – not only those pulling Callie's chariot, but every other horse too. It was mayhem; braking, crashing chariots everywhere. And Callie was flying through the air, clawing wildly.

She was going to smash into the desert face-first…

15

Mummification

Callie's eyes were already open as she slowly regained consciousness. She was lying on a white marble plinth, in a chamber lit by oil lamps. She was not alone; standing sentinel in open wooden caskets, Egyptian mummies lined the four crumbling walls, giving her the horrible impression that she was being observed (even though the mummies' eye sockets were as bandaged as completely as the rest of them).

She guessed that she had been carried into the tomb that Gobb had just opened, and been placed among its long-term residents. This was not a place *built* by Fortune, just one *used* by him. Somewhere underground was another message.

Callie wanted to sit up but found she couldn't. At first she thought she'd been restrained, but it was something else: her body wasn't responding at all, every muscle was ignoring her brain. Even her gaze remained oddly fixed upon the same spot on the mouldy ceiling. She remembered being thrown from the chariot and began to panic, a terror greater than any she'd known before. How badly had she been injured? The dreadful word 'paralysed' sent shock waves through her mind, culminating in a silent scream. Then slowly she recognised an unpleasant smell and thought she understood: the scent of the same drug Gobb had thrown into her face two days ago was with her again.

She attempted to call out but her vocal chords were as immobilised as the rest of her. *Nick...* she thought the word rather than said it.

'Squirrel cannot move. Squirrel cannot speak.'

Callie would have jumped, if she could. The hated voice of Ssin was speaking to her again in English. The 3,422-year-old creature leaned over her – her prune-like, bearded face coming shockingly into focus. 'Did you believe I would not punish you for trying to escape? The Seer's little pet.'

A tear ran down the side of Callie's face; she silently called for her mum and her dad to come and rescue her.

Ssin's mottled, hollow face came sickeningly closer, and Callie could not recoil.

'You think me disgusting,' guessed the woman correctly. 'You despise me merely because I am old.'

'That's not true,' Callie wanted to say. *'I hate you because you're cruel and evil.'*

'Once I was young and beautiful like you,' Ssin went on, detecting no response from Callie. 'But time, so much time, erodes beauty, and decays the body... But do not fret, Squirrel, *your* ageing is at an end. I have need of you no longer, so you will journey to the Field of Reeds.'

The Field of Reeds. It sounded almost pleasant, Callie pictured a relaxing meadow with reeds swaying gently in a balmy breeze. But she knew otherwise; she'd spent enough time in Omar's museum to know that the Field of Reeds was what the ancient Egyptians had called the afterlife, the time beyond death.

The mummies encircling her appeared that little bit closer. No wonder they stared: she was soon to join their ranks.

Ssin summoned someone forward, and Crocodile Head moved solemnly into Callie's sphere of vision. He began placing equipment alongside her on the marble plinth: clumsily, as if his hideous mask restricted his lateral view.

'Organ jars,' Ssin commentated, as he clinked down four brightly painted vessels in a neat row. 'For your lungs, your liver, your stomach and your intestines.'

Callie willed herself to dash the jars onto the floor with a flick of her arm, but still no muscle moved.

A razor-sharp blade scraped onto the marble plinth top. 'A knife to remove them with,' Ssin went on, licking her puckered lips. 'Palm wine, ground spices and natron salt, for cleansing, stuffing and preserving.' Crocodile Head brought over three brimming clay bowls to the plinth. He lifted a long metal probe with a vicious hook on one end.

'Ah, my favourite' – Ssin cackled, her pearly eyes wide with sick anticipation – 'the brain-removing hook.'

Callie's eyes managed to register a flash of horror.

'Did you think the brain could be removed in one piece?' Ssin asked mildly. 'Oh no no no... Even *your* little brain is too big. Moldo here must twist and stir and liquefy the tissue until it runs out though your nostrils like snot. But, sadly, by then, you will be dead.'

Callie screamed... and screamed... and yet no sound left her parted lips.

Ssin nodded to Crocodile Head, who began to remove his mask to see better what he was doing. Now he could be precise, now he could be accurate. He began to line up the brain-removing hook with Callie's nose, his fingertips pressing into

133

her soft, pale skin. His nails were coarse and sharp. Callie gasped silently. *She could feel his touch!* She was going to feel *everything*.

'Enjoy the afterlife,' Ssin crooned.

'Pharaoh... Pharaoh, please wait!'

The words momentarily froze Ssin to the spot, then her scrawny neck snaked round to see who had dared to interrupt her. Horse Face came into view, looming in the lamp glow.

'What is it?' screeched Ssin, specks of saliva spraying through the gaps in her blackened teeth.

'The Seer still writes to Squirrel and Stickleback,' Horse Face stammered. 'We need them to translate more.'

Ssin wailed in thwarted wrath, slapping Horse Face with as much strength as she could muster in her withered arm. And then, with a look of extreme disappointment, she gestured curtly to Crocodile Head. The brain-removing hook slowly began to withdraw from Callie's face.

Callie didn't know how much later it was, but a vague sort of tingling had returned to her fingers and toes, and she'd managed to struggle into a sitting position on the marble plinth. The mummification equipment had all been taken away.

'You look awful,' Nick told her. He was slumped on the floor, leaning his back against one of the mummies, as if he had been dumped there.

'They were going to mummify me,' rasped Callie.

'I know, I was trying to get to you, but Horse Face was holding me right outside.'

'You saw Crocodile Head about to remove my brain with that hook thing?'

'Yeah,' replied Nick queasily. 'I saw.'

In the silence that followed, Callie examined the skin on her hands and arms which looked almost as white as the marble plinth she was propping herself up on. There was a long red graze from her elbow to her wrist, where she'd tried to protect her face as the chariot crashed. Nick seemed to have survived relatively unscathed – a minor scab on his forehead the only sign of injury that Callie could see.

They remained silent for another minute, contemplating the true horror of what had almost happened, before Nick staggered to his feet and lurched towards the tomb entrance where orange light filtered in. Crocodile Head must have been waiting just outside, because he materialised and thrust a tray of food at Nick before leaving again. Nick took it gratefully and brought it to Callie's plinth, where he sat down. There was barley bread, humus and some salted cold meat, plus melon slices, figs and dates. Nick selected a slice of cold chicken as Callie picked at the sticky brown dates.

'Do you know who I hate most in all this?' said Nick.

'Ssin…Gobb…Crocodile Head…?' replied Callie. There were plenty of candidates.

'The Seer.'

'Oh.' Callie frowned. 'The Seer. Why him more than the others?'

Nick's voice hardened: 'Because he's still writing to us.'

'So…?'

'So he knew you wouldn't be mummified, didn't he? Or why else would he have carried on writing to us both? But he didn't say: "Don't worry if you wake up surrounded by mummies with Crocodile Head preparing to pop out your brain because it won't really happen," did he?'

'No.' Callie suddenly felt as resentful as Nick sounded. 'No, he didn't... And I could have died of fright.'

'No, you couldn't!' Nick fumed. 'And he must have known *that* as well.'

'So, as long we're still finding what he's written to us we're not going to die?'

'That's how I see it.'

'But what about when he *stops* writing to us?' demanded Callie, fingering the glass bead amulet still hanging around her neck. She almost laughed – it was meant to protect her from evil. 'Does that mean we've had it?'

Nick nodded. 'Technically.'

'Technically? How can it be "technically"? We're either dead or we're not.' Callie eyed the Egyptian mummies lining the chamber wonderingly. Death surrounded them. How much longer would they escape death themselves?

'Are you sure Crocodile Head didn't remove your brain?' Nick asked her.

Callie glared angrily at him, not sure why he'd picked this moment to insult her.

'What is she after – Ssin?' Nick coaxed.

'The Lost Prophesies.'

'Much more than that. She's after the secret of eternal youth.'

'Great, a young psychopath instead of an ancient one.'

'No, Callie, it doesn't have to be her. Think about it, eternal youth means you *can't* die...'

'And...?' Callie still couldn't see what he was getting at.

'We've got to beat her to it. It's our one chance to survive: eternal youth. We have to become eternal before she can kill us.'

Callie's face twisted in horror. 'Do you mean you want to be like her, like that thing...?'

'No. Like us. We'd stay the same, wouldn't we? For ever.'

'You will come now.'

Callie jumped. Crocodile Head was back in the doorway, gigantic and ugly, waiting to take them to the Seer's next message. Callie rose unsteadily to her feet, worrying that Crocodile Head had overheard them. But what difference did it make anyway? Eternal youth wasn't in their grasp, and even if it was, did they really want to remain thirteen and twelve forever? She lurched after Crocodile Head, her mind now paralysed by a fog of confusion.

A narrow flight of steps stood in front of them, cut straight through the natural, black rock. Oil had been poured into the ancient wall lamps that now illuminated the way.

'Down,' Crocodile Head pushed them forward to begin descending. The flames in the oil lamps guttered in the draught they made as they passed. Their footsteps echoed eerily each time they passed another tomb crammed with mummies, and Callie shuddered at the thought of so many dead Egyptians buried in this subterranean world.

After more than ten minutes they were still plunging into the depths of the underworld. 'How much further is he going to take us?' mumbled Nick.

'I don't know,' whispered Callie. 'But at least I'm beginning to feel my arms and legs properly again.'

Crocodile Head 'encouraged' her to keep going with another push in the back.

She came to a stop some thirty steps later. She could descend no further – except into a final tomb facing the rock steps. The entrance was framed by painted flames: peeling red and yellow pigments licked around a bronze lintel that ran horizontally above the opening. The Seer's signature – three stars in a rainbow pattern – together with the symbols for Squirrel and Stickleback were engraved deeply into the dully tarnished metal. These familiar symbols were what had saved them from mummification.

Crocodile Head shoved them forward a last time. 'In.'

Ssin was waiting for them inside, her skeletal form perched again on her golden throne which must have been carted all the way down here. Beside her, slumped and deathly pale in his wooden wheelchair, sat Gobb. Callie felt an unexpected pang of sympathy for him. The pain of getting him all the way down those steps must have just about finished him off.

'My playthings,' Ssin addressed them in her sickly, scratchy voice. 'I read your minds. You think that by serving me you only secure your own deaths. This I cannot deny. But *fail* to serve me, and torment shall be yours instead. Consider my former grand priest here, before you make up your minds.'

Callie stared at Gobb's bandaged feet: neat little bundles – appallingly smaller than they had been before. It was more than enough to make up Callie's mind. She tore her gaze away from Gobb to survey the vault instead.

The flame motif from the entrance was repeated inside, curling up the walls in hues of rose and tangerine. Two more oil lamps were bringing the representations to life with their own fluttering glow.

'I can't see a message,' said Nick in a small voice. Apart from the painted flames licking the walls, there was nothing else to see.

'Beneath you,' croaked Gobb weakly.

Callie lowered her gaze. A series of intricate patterns were scratched into the highly polished black floor. It reminded her of an open book, the pages of which somebody had scribbled on, though perhaps some of the grooves were cut deeper into the surface than others.

'They're just scribbles,' said Nick, turning his head from side to side to look at the scratches from different angles. '*Meaningless* scribbles.'

'It is fire writing,' Ssin informed him impatiently. 'One of the Seer's silly juvenile tricks.' She motioned to Crocodile Head, who lifted a large stoneware vessel and dashed the contents onto the polished floor.

Glistening yellow oil spread in a tide, filling the grooves and following their patterns. Callie and Nick automatically retreated to the rear of the vault while Ssin remained safely enthroned and out of the oil with the rest of her followers and Gobb.

Crocodile Head now lit a thin papyrus taper from one of the oil lamps, and sent it flying towards the floor. As it landed, the oil ignited with a mighty *woomph!* and apricot flames leaped towards the ceiling.

Callie screamed, climbing a small stone curb which framed the floor. She pressed herself against the wall, but still the heat began to melt the toes of her trainers.

Flames were crackling about Gobb's wheelchair, burning the wooden wheels. He tried to raise himself onto the remains of his feet, and then snatched the bandaged stubs back from the rising flames. Only Ssin and Crocodile Head remained unmoved.

'Enough!' Ssin was glowering at them. 'Be still.'

Callie glanced back down at the floor and saw that

remarkably the fire was already dying down – the flames disappearing altogether where the oil was thinnest. Soon, only the deepest groves in the polished floor were still alight, and she saw that they were in the shape of two fiery hieroglyphs, one on either side, like opposite pages of a book.

'A tortoise and a hamster,' rasped Nick. He flashed an anxious glance at his sister; he obviously didn't know what it meant. Nor did Callie.

The flames petered out completely now, leaving only wisps of acrid smoke smouldering from the underside of Gobb's wheelchair.

Callie looked hopefully at him, but he shook his misshapen head. 'They are not *genuine* hieroglyphs. That is why *you* are here.'

'Well?' bawled Ssin, her patience running out. 'What does it mean?'

Callie searched for the squiggles which had a moment ago sketched out a tortoise and a hamster. But they were gone.

'I . . . I don't know . . .'

'Tell me!' Ssin commanded, blue arteries standing out on her mottled forehead.

Callie stared lamely at the floor. One of the grooves that had at first sight looked extinguished was still burning, almost imperceptibly, with a blue flame. 'Look.' She dodged back as the flame flared up in her direction. It raced swiftly across the glossy black floor in two directions at once, reaching the entrance and the back wall simultaneously. Then, after a small, explosive *pop*, an enormous slab of red stone came crashing down and thudded into place. Callie spun round. She and Nick were suddenly alone, and as one slab had come thundering from the ceiling another had gone rocketing into the floor.

A narrow, paved passageway had opened up in the rear wall of the vault.

They looked at each other, delighted – at last the Seer had helped them escape!

'I think the Seer wanted us to go this way,' said Nick panting.

Callie peered into the newly opened passageway. After barely a few metres it disappeared into complete darkness. She spun round. The red stone slab dividing them from Ssin had just made a sort of dull thud.

'Crocodile Head probably hitting it with his sword,' guessed Nick.

'See if you can unscrew one of those oil lamps from the wall,' said Callie, 'to help us see.'

Nick grunted with the effort, but finally one of the bronze oil lamps snapped off in his hand.

'Got it.' He led the way into the passage.

Cold, still air that had been trapped underground for millennia drifted around them, and the movement from the oil-lamp's flame created strange patterns on the pitted stone. Without even discussing it, both of them started to run.

'Any ideas about the hamster and the tortoise?' panted Callie, after they'd been sprinting for nearly ten minutes.

'All I can think of is that fable, where the tortoise beats the hamster in a race.'

Callie forced herself not to laugh. 'Do you mean the *Hare* and the Tortoise?'

'Oh, yeah. The *Hare* and the Tortoise…'

After running on in silence for a few more minutes, Nick suddenly blurted out, 'Benny and Sammy.'

'Benny and Sammy who?' began Callie, before her face

flooded with realisation. *Benny and Sammy!* Benny the tortoise, and Sammy the hamster; the pets they'd had when they were really little. 'Why didn't I think of that?' she said, feeling annoyed with herself. 'Benny Sammy, Benny Sammy. It even sounds a bit Egyptian.' She paused and pulled out the copy of *Egypt's Greatest Astrologer* from her skirt pocket and turned to the page at the front, holding it towards the lamp. There was a pretty reasonable map of Egypt, with a number of ancient sites marked.

'There it is,' she squealed, 'Benny Sammy... Well, Beni-Sami.'

It was marked beside the Nile with the words: *Site of Ancient Egyptian Library, 1330 BC* written underneath. 'A library, of course! The floor underneath the fire writing looked like an open book!' She showed the page to Nick.

'And if that's where the Seer is telling us to go, then he must think we'll find our way out of here,' said Nick, sounding more hopeful.

Callie nodded and put the book away.

They moved on, and for a moment all Callie could hear was the sound of their running footsteps. 'I've been thinking,' she said seriously. 'If you're right about eternal youth being the only way to save ourselves, and it means we stay the way we are now. Is that what you want?'

She could almost hear Nick thinking: *No leaving school, no growing up and doing whatever he liked. None of the advantages of being an adult.*

'No, I don't. But I don't think it's our choice, either,' his voice came back uneasily. 'How can we resist our own fate?'

Callie shrugged. 'I'm just not sure I want to stay thirteen for the rest of my life.' It was a grim prospect: nothing changing, for ever.

'Would you rather be dead?'

'Of course not. It's just a terrible choice.'

Neither of them spoke again until Nick said: 'That's not good.'

'What's not good?' Callie caught up with her brother. 'Oh.'

They had reached a dead end, or at least the bottom of a narrow shaft. Nick was holding the oil lamp above his head, and Callie could see that the sides would be impossible to climb.

'I suppose we should have expected to go up again somewhere,' she said despondently. 'We went a really long way underground to reach the Fire Chamber.'

'But we can't get up there! We're not spider people.' Nick tried waving the oil lamp about, but they still couldn't see how far they would have to climb. 'Not even you can get up that, Callie, there's nothing to use as handholds or footholds.'

Callie was examining the wall of the shaft. There were tiny holes drilled in pairs into the rock around every thirty centimetres and leading up. 'There must've been a ladder once, but it rusted or rotted away.'

'So we're stuck here?' concluded Nick. '*This* was our fate after everything we've been through. It's all been a complete waste of time.' He kicked the wall angrily.

'Hang on,' said Callie. 'The shaft reminds me of a chimney. It might be narrow enough to try something.'

'Like what? Waiting for Santa Claus to come and rescue us?' replied Nick sullenly.

'Just watch.'

Callie positioned herself in the centre of the shaft and stretched an arm out on either side of her, pressing her palms flat into the smooth wall until she was completely wedged. Then holding herself in position with her palms, she lifted both feet and pressed the rubber soles of her trainers into the wall on either side of her. She was now jammed into position thirty centimetres above the ground. Taking her weight on her feet, she moved her hands up to a higher position on the wall and braced herself again. She repeated the whole manoeuvre several times until she was three metres off the ground and looking down through her legs at Nick.

He returned an expression of disbelief. 'You have got to be kidding.'

'You can do it, Nick. It's really easy. And you're stronger than I am, anyway, you're a boy.'

'How am I supposed to carry the oil lamp? On my head?'

'We'll have to do without it. Leave it on the ground.'

Nick sighed, placing the oil lamp carefully at the base of the shaft. Then he got into position and copied her technique. 'Hey, it's not that difficult, actually, is it?'

'Don't get cocky,' Callie told him. 'Just concentrate on what you're doing.'

They climbed steadily for five minutes, three minutes in complete darkness, before Callie heard a sharp scraping sound directly beneath her. 'Nick!'

'It's OK ... My foot slipped, but I didn't fall.'

'Keep going. There are only a couple of metres more.'

'How do you know that?'

'I've reached the top. I can't see much at all, but I can tell that the tunnel carries on, leading the same way as before.' She lay down flat on her stomach so that she could reach into the shaft to help her brother up. Her fingers twisted into the collar of his shirt and she pulled him towards her.

'Well, if Ssin and Gobb manage to break through from the Fire Chamber, I don't fancy either of their chances of climbing up here,' said Nick, as he scrambled up beside his sister.

Callie heard the unpleasant sound of him hawking up saliva and then spitting down the shaft.

'Is that really necessary…?'

'Sorry.'

Callie turned and groped her way forward. After less than ten metres, she plunged into icy water, shocking the breath out of her. It was deep, too deep to stand, and she was soon struggling to swim. She began to splutter and retch as the water surged into her lungs. She was drowning, and her struggles were only taking her deeper…

16

Gliding like a Hawk

The temple of Amun-Ra (the sun god), 1391 BC

The temple was perched on the summit of The Red Gorge, a spectacular natural chasm through the Egyptian mountains far south of Medphis, and could only be reached by a zigzagging road which took almost a day to negotiate.

In the guest dormitory, paints and pigments littered the wooden floor in chipped pottery bowls. To hide his true identity, Fortune had cut off his dark ponytail and allowed the rest of his hair to grow out making him look like any other lower born Egyptian youth. He was learning to paint under the tutelage of Jofar the Painter, and was currently engaged in painting scenes of a holy nature for the priests of Amun-Ra. But right at this moment, he was slumbering on a straw pallet.

A stripe, made of sunlight beating through the slats in the ceiling, played across his naked body as he turned in his sleep. He was permitted to take a rest at midday, while the priests carried out their ritual of offering food and wine to the sun god. His tutor spent these little break times sketching the cliffs of the Red Gorge, and birds and flowers – details he added to the temple murals.

A trace of a smile fluttered across Fortune's sleeping lips; another premonition of Squirrel and Stickleback, standing by a black, obsidian statue of Osiris, the god of death.

He watched them, fascinated. The girl was remarkably pretty: her hair dark and glossy and twisted into a ponytail, her eyes bluer than the ocean. The boy's eyes were a little less blue and full of mischief. He liked the way their personalities differed: Squirrel strong-willed, defiant, athletic, but also vulnerable; Stickleback intelligent, brave, always hungry, and on occasion comical. They were discussing what to do next...

Before Fortune could find out what they decided, Jofar the Painter was shaking him gently. 'Nefrotu, wake up. Nefrotu...' Fortune had naturally adopted a new name to go with his new identity. He had jumbled up the letters of his old name, and as 'Nefrotu' was also the name of a popular pharaoh from twenty years before, many boys were named after him. 'Nefrotu, it is almost time to return to work.'

Fortune smiled up at the painter, who surely possessed the most pointed nose and chin in all of Egypt – and positively the kindest nature.

'You looked as if you were dreaming, young apprentice,' began Jofar as Fortune pulled on a white kilt spattered with dots of coloured paint. 'Do you dream of the future?'

Fortune tried to hide his surprise. Never had he mentioned his premonitions to kindly Jofar. 'Do you mean, do I dream I will be rich one day?' he said, to give himself some time to think.

'I believe you know exactly what I mean,' said Jofar, clucking patiently. 'In these past few months I have heard you mumbling in your sleep many a time. You speak of things that are yet to happen. You see the future, do you not?'

'Sometimes I have premonitions,' said Fortune carefully.

Jofar had been like a father to him. Perhaps, after all, there was nothing to fear from the painter. He'd never had any premonitions about the man betraying him.

'And do they come true?' Jofar asked with interest, collecting the pots of paints they'd need for that afternoon's work onto a wooden tray.

'Well, the ones that are about to happen always seem to come true,' shrugged Fortune modestly. 'So, yes, I suppose the others will – one day.'

'If I had such a gift I'd be writing down all my predictions,' said Jofar earnestly.

'I intend to,' replied Fortune. 'As soon as I can find a safe place to leave them.'

'Ah, sensible, very sensible,' agreed Jofar. 'Have you ever had any premonitions about our pharaoh?' he asked.

Fortune frowned, somewhat surprised that Jofar should ask not about himself, but about their pharaoh, whom he'd never even heard him mention before.

'Well?' pressed Jofar. 'What do you see? Great victories, a long life, or cruelty and revenge?'

Fortune staggered back. He'd been asked that very question before – and by the Pharaoh herself. He squinted fearfully at the painter; something of the chiselled chin and pointed nose had dissolved. As he continued to stare, a new face, the real face, quivered into being: beautiful and deadly – the hated face of Ssin. When he'd last seen her she had been planning to slaughter his mother and father in cold blood.

Fortune backed away until he reached the wall and could go no further. He feared her like he would fear a poisonous snake.

'It would seem my impersonation enchantment is no

longer effective,' guessed Ssin. 'Perhaps the real Jofar wakes from the drug-induced sleep I placed him in... No matter. You were about to tell me my future.'

'I predict that very soon you will be wearing the contents of this pot of paint,' said Fortune.

'What? What pot of paint?' Ssin snapped impatiently, realising too late that Fortune's fingers had closed around a bowl of bright blue colour. She tried to duck but the contents of the bowl splashed into her face, temporarily blinding her. Paint began to run through her hair, over the jewellery about her neck, and streak all the way down her fine, white robe. She let out a venomous howl, screaming for her bodyguards.

Fortune didn't wait for them to come in, leaping onto the table instead. From there he hoisted himself through the ceiling slats. Then he wriggled out onto the roof of the dormitory, and dashed to the very edge. The impressive temple tower stood in front of him, a square, white edifice, adding even more height to the already dizzying summit of The Red Gorge. Only hawks, wheeling against the satin blue sky, could reach higher than the top of the tower.

The Pharaoh's soldiers shouted up at him from the ground: 'Oi, you! Come down here at once.'

And end up as my mother and father did? Fortune thought. He took a few steps back to give himself a run up to the flat edge of the dormitory roof, and then charged forward – jumping into midair.

One of the soldiers turned to his comrade. 'What's the little dung-eater doing?'

It became apparent when Fortune disappeared from their sight. He'd made it straight from the dormitory roof to an open window on the second floor of the temple tower.

Fortune rolled to his feet, grimacing at the pain from almost every limb in his body, and apologising profusely to the poor priest at prayers he'd just scared the life out of. 'Sorry, Father. Sorry...' Then he hurtled towards a flight of stairs that would take him to the upper levels of the tower. His feet hammered loudly on the wooden steps he took two at a time.

Sunlight blinded him as the final ladder brought him to the tower roof. He closed the wooden trap door behind him and dragged a heavy pot plant on top of it to weigh it down.

Now there was nowhere left to run!

Fortune glanced around. The roof was enclosed by a low parapet, one corner of which was shaded by an awning made from woven white goats' wool. He'd been commissioned to build it himself for the priests a few weeks ago. It was his own design: an arrowhead shape with two thin but strong wooden spars forming a cross shape underneath – unorthodox for an awning, but perfect for a hang-glider. Fortune had dreamed of all sorts of flying machines in the future, but a hang-glider was the only one he had been able to construct himself. He had not known for certain why he had built it until now.

Bang. Bang. Bang. The giant pot plant was bumping up and down as the soldiers tried to force their way out onto the roof. 'Open up, you little sheep tic!'

Fortune pulled on the quick-release knots he'd used to fasten his hang-glider to the wall. He would be held in a kind of hammock underneath the canopy, which he'd disguised as extra lining to the awning. Face down and with his arms stretched out in front of him he could even steer the contraption.

The blood vessels in his forehead were threatening to pop in terror as he climbed up onto the parapet. 'Oh gods!' The three-hundred metre drop into the Red Gorge swam beneath him: deadly crags and sharp rocks – a hundred ways to die. And his courage deserted him. He couldn't do this. He—

A sudden gust of wind gave him no choice, and he was sent reeling over the edge. '*Noooo!*' The canopy made an unbelievably loud flapping noise and began to swell, and then he was flying. He remembered to start steering just in time to stop the hang-glider crashing into the side of the temple tower. He soared further out over the gorge, his stomach in his mouth, and realised with shame that the screaming sound was coming from him. He attempted to control his descent by steering the glider into looping turns, imitating the Red Gorge hawks he'd watched for hours and hours.

An arrow whizzed past his ear, and then another went sailing through the canopy. He glanced anxiously at the woollen material, but found nothing worse than a neat hole. Even so, he tried to widen the distance between himself and the Pharaoh's archers, while also keeping away from the treacherous rose-coloured faces of the gorge surrounding him. He looked back and saw Pharaoh Ssin's blue, paint-splattered face glaring after him, and managed a smile.

The air was icy on his bare skin, and flying straight into it made his eyes water. He blinked them clear to see a thin ribbon of water meandering between boulders some way beneath him. Hardly the limitless depths of the Nile, but if he could land in water he might spare himself a painful crash.

Fortune adjusted his course as the river accelerated to meet him, and made the hang-glider skim its silvery surface like a water fowl coming in to land. The water tugged at his hanging feet first, slowing him down. Then he exploded through the water: it was cold and surprisingly solid. The hang-glider disintegrated.

Choking up mouthfuls of water, he swam to the riverbank and dragged himself onto the nearest rock. Diluted blood dripped from his nose which had hit the water hard, but, by all the gods, he was still alive. He crouched for a moment, gulping in great mouthfuls of breath and scanning the cliffs for the temple of the Amun-Ra. Nowhere could he see it. He must have flown a mile. He started to walk. He probably had a day's head start; that was how long it would take the Pharaoh to drive her chariots along the temple road. By the time she got here he would be long gone.

17

On the Nile at last

Callie remembered what had happened. In the darkness she had plunged straight into ice-cold water and panicked. But now she seemed to be lying flat on her back, and in the inky blackness someone was pressing the palms of their hands on her diaphragm to expel any last water from her lungs. Callie pushed them away and croaked: 'Thanks. I'm all right now.'

Nick's frightened voice came out of the darkness. 'I was scared you'd drowned.'

'How did you get me out?'

'It wasn't easy. I couldn't find you at first, because there was no light. And then when I did, I had to pull you through an underwater chamber. I thought we were both going to drown.'

'Thank goodness you're Stickleback,' mumbled Callie gratefully, dragging herself to her feet. She was dripping wet and half frozen and, judging by the impenetrable darkness, still trapped in the tunnel. 'Now what?'

'We carry on,' said Nick practically. 'Carefully.'

It didn't take them more than ten minutes before they saw something up ahead, sparkling despite the darkness. A slab of mineral-frosted black marble was filling the tunnel and preventing them from going any further. 'Another dead end!' But Callie tiptoed carefully forward and ran her fingers along the smooth edges of the panel. A sliver of light was showing around the sides.

'What's that?' asked Nick. Four genuine hieroglyphs, in some sort of luminous metal, were inset into the wall beside the glittering panel: a square, a flattened oval and a pair of walking sticks.

'That's something I *can* read,' said Callie confidently. 'There is an alphabet section in *Hieroglyphics for Beginners*, so you can convert English words into their ancient Egyptian equivalents. P…RE…S…S…' She translated the symbols one at a time.

Nick reached forward and pressed the small oblong containing the hieroglyphs.

There was a click, and the entire panel began to sink slowly before them. Traffic noises invaded the tunnel as the panel slotted into the ground with a crunching sound.

They stepped out, blinking in the dazzling sunlight, hit by a welcome barrage of warm air. They had emerged in a tiny park, with feathery-leafed date palm trees springing from a parched lawn – a sort of oasis, in amongst the tumult of daily life.

'I'd have never realised we were this close to a town,' said Callie in astonishment.

'I saw lights last night while we were travelling,' Nick realised. 'But I didn't think it was somewhere we could get to.'

Opposite the park were modern concrete apartment blocks; cars flashed past, horns honking; people were hurrying purposefully; birds were twittering – all seemingly oblivious of two tired children who had suddenly just appeared in their midst as if from nowhere. Callie looked back and saw that a giant enthroned statue, carved from polished black stone, loomed above them: a long-limbed, long-necked giant formed the entrance to the tunnel.

Callie recognised it. 'It's Osiris, the god of the underworld.'

'It's freedom!' said Nick.

Callie started nibbling her lip. 'What do we do now? Do we go on or do we try to get back to Mum and Dad?'

Nick shrugged. 'I don't think it's that easy. Won't they have left Nag Hammadi by now? There's no way they wouldn't have tried to contact us in the last four days. When that didn't work they'd have headed back to Cairo.'

'I was thinking the same thing,' said Callie sighing. 'I suppose we ought to find out where we are, and then try to get to Beni-Sami... I think it's probably our fate.'

Nick nodded. 'This place is called El Gabir.'

'How do you know that?'

'Because it says so, look.' He pointed to a 1920s building opposite the park. 'Over there: *El Gabir Museum*. And a taxi just went past with "El Gabir Cabs" printed on the door.'

'Why do I seem to know that name?' said Callie, looking bewildered. 'And I wonder how close it is to Beni-Sami.'

She pulled out the now-damp *Egypt's Greatest Astrologer* and looked at the map again. 'Here's El Gabir, and here's Beni-Sami,' she said, pointing at the map. She measured the distance between the two with her finger and thumb, and then checked it against the printed scale bar. 'It's about a hundred kilometres.'

'Oh, that'll be easy to get to then, won't it?' said Nick ironically. 'We should be able to walk there by dinner time.'

Callie looked equally disappointed. 'Maybe we could rent a boat? I've still got all my holiday money in my pocket –

although it might be a bit soggy. Wait— What's the date today?' she asked suddenly.

There was a pause while Nick did the calculation in his head. 'It's four days since we left Cairo, so today's got to be the thirtieth. Why do you want to know?'

'Because it might be our salvation.'

'Why might it?'

'Don't you remember? Mum and Dad booked us all on one of those Nile cruise things. They said it would be an adventure for us when they'd finished their stint as visiting archaeologists.'

'An adventure?! I think I've had enough of adventure.'

'The ship was called *The Spirit on the Nile* or something. It was leaving from Cairo on the twenty-eighth, stopping in El Gabir on the thirtieth, and arriving in Beni-Sami on the thirty-first. It was all on the itinerary.'

'You don't think Mum and Dad are on their way here do you?'

Callie shook her head sadly. 'Why would they be? There's no reason for them to guess we'd meet them here is there?'

'Oh.' Nick frowned. 'Isn't it all a bit too convenient though? Transport waiting to take us exactly where we want to go?'

'No, of course it's not. It's preordained, isn't it? This was always going to happen. Fortune must have foreseen it – our entire journey – and when he was seeing everything that would happen to us, he must have known that he played a part in it by leaving us messages on the way.'

Nick had gone distinctly pale. 'Then he's trying to help us?'

'I'm not sure about that... He must have known how this was going to end though – even if we don't!'

156

Nick was still sceptical. 'We're not just going to be able to get onto that boat without tickets, though, are we?'

'The Seer must have foreseen that too,' said Callie. She pulled out two very battered, soggy cruise tickets, and their passports and official travel visas, from her pocket. 'I've been carrying them around for days,' she said wonderingly, 'for safe-keeping. And no one's ever tried to take them off me – don't you think that's somehow *meant*?' The whole idea made her feel quite sick.

'Fate, you mean?'

'Yeah. Fate.'

Callie stuffed the priceless bundle of documents back in her pocket, trying not to think about it. 'Come on. I don't know how long we've got.'

'Something tells me it'll be long enough,' rasped Nick as they started running towards the wrought-iron park gates. 'I can see the river, it's this way.'

They ran along beside a car park, full of vehicles baking in the sun, and down a short avenue lined with acacia trees with the sparkle of the river still in sight. It was a twinkling line on the horizon where the town was cut in two. They hurried on past gloomy offices, a vivid grocery and a clothes shop, and took a wide road past some Egyptian banks and insurance offices standing proudly in stately skyscrapers of shining yellow stone. Then, after less than five minutes, they emerged onto a promenade, fresh with a cooling breeze from a wide ribbon of water. The blue-green surface of the Nile sparkled under the afternoon sun.

'Fate,' croaked Nick.

A massive cruise ship, purest white against the indigo sky was berthed alongside a jetty.

There was a queue of passengers waiting to climb the single gangplank rising to the mid deck of *The Spirit on the Nile*.

'Returning from a morning's shopping in El Gabir,' said Callie. 'It was on the itinerary... We should get a few things ourselves while we can,' she added, heading towards a small row of souvenir stalls lining the waterfront. 'Food, water, toiletries, toothbrushes. And I've lived in these clothes for the last four days.' She was still writing a mental list, as she reached a stall selling a mixture of western and Egyptian clothes; shorts and branded-label tops were spread across the counter along with *galabiyyas* – the loose-fitting, one-piece robes, which must be sold here mainly to tourists. She handed Nick half of the Egyptian money she'd carefully carried around for days. 'See if you can find some of the other supplies.' Nick wandered off towards the nearest food stall while Callie started sorting through the T-shirts. For a brief moment it almost felt like a real holiday.

'How much is this?' Callie asked, holding up a purple top almost identical to the one she was wearing.

'Two Egyptian pounds.'

'I'll take it, please, and this one.'

She was buying bottles of mineral water when Nick caught up with her again. He presented her with a paper bag containing a supply of pastries soaked in syrup called *baklawa*. 'Got us both some.'

'Swap.' Callie handed him a change of clothes she'd bought in his size and favourite colours of blue and brown. Then they made their way along the quay, snacking almost without a care on a takeaway breakfast, and soaking up the strengthening sun. The queue on *The Spirit on the Nile's* gangplank had thinned out.

'Pretty impressive ship,' said Nick while they were waiting to board. *The Spirit on the Nile's* square cabin windows were huge, running in four long rows – the lowest, only centimetres above the waterline, while the entire roof section was an extensive sun deck that had striped awnings and hundreds of sun loungers ready for the passengers. At the bow end of the ship, the bridge roof bristled with satellite dishes and antennae. 'It's like a luxury hotel on water,' Nick went on. 'Not that we haven't earned a bit of luxury.'

Callie followed him up the gangplank, automatically hanging onto the safety rails on either side for dear life, and feeling queasy at the thought of the water beneath her.

'You are passengers with us?' The ship's boarding officer, cutting a dash in a crisp black uniform, blocked their way at the top of the gangplank. Everyone else was flashing him their boarding passes as proof they were passengers returning from the day trip. He regarded Callie and Nick suspiciously.

'Yes we are. Callie and Nick Latham. Here are our tickets,' said Callie, trying not to sound flustered. She handed over the printed ticket booklets, their passports and travel visas.

The boarding officer examined the documentation carefully, as if even the tiniest spelling error would render them invalid. When he looked up again something was obviously wrong. 'These tickets should have been surrendered when you first boarded,' he said reprovingly.

'Oh… Nobody told us,' said Callie. 'But you can see that everything's in order.'

'What are your cabin numbers?' asked the boarding officer distrustfully.

Callie thanked her lucky stars that she had scrutinised the tickets as well. 'Cabins C7 and C8.'

'Show me your keys.'

'Our parents have got our keys,' Callie said quickly.

'And why aren't you with your parents?'

'They're already on board, probably wondering why you won't let us on.'

The boarding officer didn't seem to like that answer, and the queue was now building up again behind Callie and Nick. 'Please,' she tried again. 'They'll be so cross with us if we don't get on now.'

With a sigh, the man handed back their papers and passports, and moved aside to let them board.

Callie and Nick had tracked down the reception desk in the spacious lower lobby, and picked up their cabin keys, which resembled credit cards, and were now eagerly exploring their own cabins, which had a convenient connecting door between them.

Thick, bright blue carpets matched the stylish curtains, and together with the mahogany beds and wardrobes gave the cabins an almost stately feel. There was even a tiny en-suite shower room and toilet in each cabin. If it hadn't been for a rather spectacular view of the glittering Nile through the cinema-screen-sized starboard window, they could have been in an expensive hotel room anywhere on land.

'This must have cost Mum and Dad an arm and a leg,' declared Callie.

'Maybe they sold Omar a few of their "finds" to pay for it.'

Callie laughed. She picked up the bag containing her toothbrush and a change of clothes and headed for her en-suite shower room. 'I'm going to freshen up...' She paused before closing the door. 'And I think everyone on board would appreciate it if you did the same.'

Nick rolled his eyes. 'Yes, Mum.'

When Callie returned thirty minutes later in clean clothes, Nick was drying his blond hair with a white pillow case. 'The maid's forgotten to put fresh towels in my bathroom,' he complained.

'We'll mention it to the steward later,' said Callie, slinging her damp top onto the blue carpet. The whole ship started to vibrate ever so slightly beneath her feet.

She ran to the window and peered out. They must have cast off, because water was churning along the side. 'We're under way,' she said, overjoyed at the thought of leaving both El Gabir, and ancient Egyptians behind them.

'What are the chances Ssin's given up?' asked Nick, as if reading her thoughts.

Callie shook her head. 'None. She's not going to give up on eternal youth after waiting for it for three and a half thousand years.'

Ssin was definitely still out there, and she was coming to get them. Callie didn't need to have visions to predict that one.

The diesel engines continued throbbing as *The Spirit on the Nile* manoeuvred out into the middle of the river.

'Come on. Let's at least *pretend* we're real tourists.' Callie grabbed a bottle of sun cream she'd bought in El Gabir and headed for the door.

18

Deadly Waters

The Upper Nile 1390 BC

The soft blue water of the Nile was passing slowly under the hull of the ship. *The Cobra*, the mightiest vessel in the Egyptian pharaoh's fleet, was sailing south more than 3,400 hundred years before Squirrel and Stickleback would pass the same way.

Parched hills stretched from the water's edge into the red mountains and, closer to hand, flocks of pelicans shared the fertile reed beds with wallowing hippopotami.

Pharaoh Ssin, young and beautiful with her rich dark hair and bronze complexion, was pinning Fortune to the deck of the galley with an elegantly sandaled royal foot. 'You have led me and my army far since you escaped the Temple of Amun-Ra, my flying friend.' Her voice was full with undisguised resentment. 'But now at last I have you in my grasp and you may regret your actions.'

She lifted her foot a little. 'But did you not once love me? Will you not give me what I ask for, for old time's sake?'

'Eternal youth?' queried Fortune.

'You have foreseen it. You told me so.'

'It is in the air which rises through the eternal mountain,' replied Fortune steadily. 'But its location shall die with me.'

A faint trace of a smile appeared on Fortune's face. The pharaoh repaid the smile with a look of hatred. 'Die with you?' She fingered her smooth, oval chin, and pursed full, red lips. 'Do you believe me to be a fool, that I would sacrifice your gifts for mere revenge? Not I.'

She turned to someone standing behind her on the wide deck. 'Captain Abasi, take us inshore. I wish to introduce Fortune to my sacred hippopotami.'

Captain Abasi, a short man with a horrific war scar from nose to ear, shouted out an order to his oarsmen, and the galley changed direction with a heavy thud. Then they began to glide towards the group of basking hippos. The creatures seemed harmless, even comical with their bulbous heads, but Fortune knew that when protecting their young they were more dangerous than crocodiles. One snap of those mighty jaws could swallow a full-grown man whole.

'Lift him,' Pharaoh Ssin commanded. Two of her Royal Guard, wearing blue striped kilts and headdresses, pulled Fortune upright. He had grown in the last year and he now stood taller than his Pharaoh.

'How much of you shall we allow my hippopotami?' Ssin asked in a petulant tone. She stooped to place her hand level with Fortune's bare knees. 'This much, perhaps?' She raised the hand to his thighs. 'Or here, maybe?' Her fingers reached his modestly kilted waist. 'Or what about half of you? You couldn't run away again then, could you?'

Fortune watched the reeds swaying in the gentle morning breeze, the afternoon sun bringing out the rose red of the distant hills. It was a fine day to die, that was why he had chosen it – permitting himself to be captured (after a convincing chase) at

The Great Library, where he had spent the last three months making preparations. He'd also been helping the librarian catalogue the many scrolls there, but today was his day to die. He had foreseen it.

Pharaoh Ssin had to bring herself onto her tiny tiptoes to whisper into his ear. 'Do not think of death, my potter's brat... The Royal Physician is close. He will save your wonderful mind – as I believe you will have foreseen.' She turned to the nearest sailor. 'You. Put a rope around him so we may fish him out before my hippos become *too* greedy.'

Fortune recognised the barrel-chested sailor and especially his lurid grin; the very man who had thrown him before the pharaoh for killing a sacred crocodile several years earlier. 'I'm going to enjoy this bit,' cooed the sailor, binding Fortune, and then tying the other end of the rope to his own wrist.

Fortune stared wordlessly at him. There was so much cruelty in this land of Egypt; he had experienced it personally. The memory of his slaughtered parents seldom left him.

'Nothing to say?' Ssin spoke pettingly. 'No last recollection of where the eternal mountain rises...? Not even a hint... No?' She was a coquettish woman, demanding treats she did not deserve, and Fortune felt almost sorry for her – for the countless centuries she would have to wait.

Ssin captured a braid of her ebony hair and used the tip like a paint brush on his face – drawing round his features: his nose, his mouth. Somehow the lock of hair seemed as threatening as the point of a blade.

As the Pharaoh played, Captain Abasi ordered his oarsmen to slow down the galley and allow it to carve into the reed margin on the bank of the Nile. The stiff stems began to clack along the wooden hull. 'All stop,' he instructed his crew,

164

and the galley glided to a final halt amid the angrily grunting hippos.

'Arghhhhh!' It was the barrel-chested sailor who cried out first, as one of the larger hippos lunged from the water. Nearly four tons of it broke the surface in a dreadful rush. As it splashed back again, it yawned its wide jaws, so that they snapped clean through several of the sturdy wooden oars like stems of corn. The sailors on that side of the galley scrambled back, falling over one another in their panic.

This great hippo wasn't finished. It submerged completely, and they heard it bumping along under the hull, with every intention of capsizing them. The deck swayed violently under Fortune's bare feet.

'Lady Tawaret,' Pharaoh Ssin said calmly, naming the Egyptian hippopotamus goddess of fertility, 'Is eager for a tasty morsel.'

Fortune smiled encouragingly. 'Then I suggest you offer her your old, fat rump, great Pharaoh.'

For a second, Ssin looked as if she had been slapped viciously across her beautiful face. Then she squealed in rage, throwing herself at Fortune. She weighed little, but fury and surprise took him completely off-balance, and he toppled into the water with a loud splash. The barrel-chested sailor, tied to him by the wrist, was dragged along too.

'Eat him! Rip him. Show him what it means to insult a Pharaoh!' cried Ssin, incandescent with rage.

But it was the sailor who gurgled up an explosion of blood as the hippopotamus impaled him through chest and stomach with deadly tusks.

More hippos joined in the attack, ripping savagely at the sailor and cutting the rope. The water bubbled with his blood.

Fortune felt himself sinking, taking the lifeline with him. Through the water above him he heard a shriek of realisation from his enemy; Ssin understood at last that he was gone. The blood which foamed in the water could be his, or perhaps he'd drowned – either way, everything he knew about the future went with him. Fortune began to swim down, parting the sinuous weeds, searching the murky depths as the dark forms of the hippos became more indistinct above him.

He began to panic, his lungs crying out for oxygen. The one breath he had taken would sustain him for less than a minute. If he could not find what he was looking for, this really would be the day he died. Where was it? The thing he'd weighted down and dropped into the water the day before. Had it drifted away? Then something of an alien shape stood out against the weeds, something spherical, and made of clay. *Thank the gods,* he thought, expending his final scintilla of strength to reach the object.

There was a tube made from a hollow papyrus stem sticking out of the pottery sphere, its exposed end plugged with wet clay. Fortune punctured the clay with a finger and precious air bubbles escaped the tube to rise through the thick, green water. In a few thousand years SCUBA (Self Contained Underwater Breathing Apparatus) would be a lot more portable, but the prototype he'd made for himself now would do him fine. He stuffed the reed gratefully into his mouth and sucked on its life-sustaining air.

Fortune grinned; it felt surprisingly good to be dead.

19

New Prophecies

ᛈ

Callie awoke to find herself reclining in a sun lounger on the top deck of *The Spirit on the Nile* as it cruised further down the world's greatest river.

She glanced up to see another cruise ship going past them in the opposite direction. Passengers on both ships stood at the railings to wave and call out greetings to one another. Callie looked round for Nick. He was in the sun-lounger beside her, scribbling intently onto a sheet of paper.

'What are you doing?' she asked. She didn't much like the up-to-no-good look on his face.

'Making predictions,' he informed her, continuing to scribble.

After another minute or so he handed her the sheet of paper. Callie read it with a wary expression: '*Prediction One: Callie swaps her bedroom with Nick's – because she doesn't need all that space for her collection of cuddly rabbits and film posters... Prediction Two: Callie hires Nick to be her style guru.*' She eyed her brother sceptically. 'Really?'

'I think I've got a gift for predictions.'

'I think you've got a screw loose.'

'Carry on reading.'

'*Prediction Three: Callie grows up, misses school so much – she becomes a teacher.*'

'OK, maybe that's at least *possible*,' admitted Callie.

'See,' said Nick, starting to fold up a second sheet of paper. 'I've got a hidden talent.'

'What's on that page?'

'Nothing.'

Callie snatched it before he could finish ramming it into his pocket. '*Predictions for Nick... Prediction One: Nick wins Gold Medal in the Computer Games Olympics.*' Callie sniggered. Her brother certainly spent a lot of time practising. '*Prediction Two: Nick gets a part in a TV soap.*' She looked up. 'Is that supposed to be: "Nick learns how to *use* soap"?'

Her brother pulled a face at her.

'*Prediction Three: Nick invents Danger Tennis...* Danger Tennis?' Callie couldn't believe she was even asking.

'Exploding tennis balls.'

'I might have guessed.' She almost felt relieved that Nick was acting as if everything was going to be OK, that they *had* a future which didn't involve staying the same age for the rest of their lives. She shielded her eyes and stared across the wide Nile as the setting sun brushed it with bright tangerine swirls. On the distant bank wild grass overflowed a narrow, earthen path, and green fields stretched away towards the red rock hills. 'What are we going to do about the real prophesies?' she asked, chewing worriedly at the corner of her lip.

Nick shrugged. 'Use them to make ourselves rich, I suppose. If we know stuff before it's going to happen we could win lots of bets. Or we could invent things before somebody else does.'

Callie threw him a disappointed look. 'I didn't mean how

do we profit from all this. I meant, what if we find out something really awful, like a meteor's going to hit the earth, or there's a nuclear war coming, or an alien invasion? How would we feel if we knew something like that?'

'Terrified,' said Nick immediately. 'But we could warn people, couldn't we? It would be our responsibility.'

'Would it make any difference, though? We haven't been able to stop things happening which just involve us, have we? How could we stop a nuclear war?'

'What do you mean then?'

'Maybe we shouldn't read the prophesies in the first place.'

Nick shook his head decisively. 'We have to read them! Don't you remember when we translated the message in the palace that part of it said: "Callie and Nick, I have a really important prediction for you"?'

Callie didn't think she could ever forget it. 'Yes.'

'Well we can't just ignore that, can we?'

Callie shrugged. 'No. I suppose not.' She stared at the golden swirls of the Nile again, wondering what the important prediction was. When she looked back up, Nick was staring straight past her, a look of terror on his face. 'What?' she asked.

Nick lowered his voice: 'I've just spotted one of Ssin's men.'

'What?' Callie spun round.

Not far from where they were sitting, a ferrety, shaven-headed man was leaning against a section of blue railings, watching the red hills at a particular point on the horizon. If he *was* a Follower of Ssin, he had swapped his kilt and armour for something a little less conspicuous: shorts and T-shirt and a white sunhat. 'Are you sure?' Callie said under her breath. 'I don't recognise him.'

'You didn't spend a night travelling in a chariot with him.' Nick ran his hand nervously through his blond hair. 'How did he find us?'

'They must have been watching the riverfront at El Gabir. Once we got away, Ssin would have sent out scouts looking for us, wouldn't she? We just didn't think that her army could be dressed in normal clothes.' She thought about the fussy official who'd examined hers and Nick's tickets. 'I'd like to know how he got past that boarding officer.'

'Could have climbed on board,' said Nick. The Follower was gazing intently at the skyline. 'What's he staring at? He must know we're here, so why's he looking over there?'

A line of feathery green palm trees stood out against hills which were already falling into shadow as the late-afternoon sun dipped lower on the horizon.

'There!' Callie pointed. Something was raising a column of dust precisely where Nick's charioteer was staring. It could be made by a jeep, or maybe a train of camels, but Callie knew it was neither. 'Chariots,' she said simply, and beside her, Nick nodded his agreement. Ssin and her army were tracking them.

Something flashed from close to the column of dust three times, and so blindingly it could have been aimed right at Callie's face. 'They're signalling to him.'

She looked carefully at the charioteer's hand and saw that he was holding a tiny mirror with which he was signalling back.

'He's telling them he's found us,' she guessed. Suddenly their great plan of reaching the lost prophesies and learning the secret of eternal youth before Ssin was scuppered.

'I think we should get back to the cabins,' said Callie.

Nick's charioteer turned to follow them the moment they stood up. He was directly behind them as they descended the stairs to the lower decks, but there were other passengers around and he could only shadow them down the metal steps. His footsteps clanked threateningly after theirs until they reached the blue-carpeted hallway of Deck C.

Callie was frantically wondering how they could reach their cabins without the Follower seeing which ones were theirs, when another of Ssin's men stepped out in her path. This one she did recognise: Horse Face, now dressed in a very bright floral shirt and white shorts.

They were trapped between the two men.

'What's the hold up?'

Callie turned round. A short, balding man was glaring impatiently at her. 'Get moving, girl.'

'Sorry,' Callie apologised, and seizing Nick's hand squeezed past Horse Face. As soon as they were through the double fire doors at the bottom of the staircase they broke into a run, pelting all the way down the hallway marked Cabins C1–C12 to cabin C7. Nick rammed his credit-card-shaped plastic key into the socket to unlock the door, and the pair of them burst inside. Callie slammed the cabin door behind them and leaned her back against it. 'Did they see which cabin we came into?' she whispered queasily.

'I don't think so.'

They listened, terrified as the sound of heavy footsteps went running straight past the cabin door and receded into the distance. Callie hurried over to the huge window and peered out, scanning the hills on the horizon for the tell-tale column of dust. 'I can't see anyone signalling anymore,' she murmured.

'With any luck they'll lose the boat when it gets dark,' said Nick hopefully.

Callie shook her head. 'They'll still be able to see us. This thing will be lit up like a Christmas tree. And even if your charioteer and Horse Face don't find our cabins, they've only got to wait for us to get off, haven't they?'

'Then we won't get off,' said Nick hurriedly.

They both jumped as someone rapped loudly on the mahogany cabin door. Callie stared, visualising Horse Face and the charioteer standing menacingly in the corridor: they were checking the cabins one by one.

There was a light click – and the brass door handle began to turn.

'Quick! My room,' blurted Callie. She plunged across Nick's bed and ran for the door connecting the adjoining cabins, but she didn't make it in time.

'Sorry... I knock... But no answer...' The cabin maid at the door to Nick's cabin turned as pink as her uniform.

'You surprised us,' explained Callie, blushing almost as much as the maid.

'You asked for more towels, yes?' The cabin maid was carrying a neatly folded stack of fluffy white towels, in a pyramid of descending sizes.

Callie had completely forgotten making a detour to the ship's reception desk earlier to request towels. 'Yes,' Callie said feebly. 'Thanks.'

The cabin maid placed half the towels on the end of Nick's bed, and then escaped through the connecting door, to deposit the rest in Callie's cabin. She called a hurried 'Goodbye,' and let herself out.

Callie collapsed face down onto Nick's bed, releasing a groan of embarrassment... 'God! That was stupid.'

ρ ρ ρ

172

It was nearly an hour later and Callie hadn't moved from the bed – apart from turning terrified eyes towards the door every time someone walked past outside. She hadn't even raised herself to go into her own cabin, too scared to be alone.

Nick got up from the floor, where he'd been leaning against the side of the bed, and picked up a plump pillow. He proceeded to dress it from the pile of dirty laundry – using Callie's T-shirt and purple hoodie. Callie blinked at him uncomprehendingly.

'Nick, I know you're scared too, but now's not a good time to start losing your mind.'

He ignored her and started forcing another pillow into his favourite football top. 'If we can get Ssin's men to think we've jumped ship, they'll signal to her to stop following it, won't they?'

'Maybe,' said Callie warily.

Her brother held up the two pillows. 'If we chuck these overboard when Ssin's men are watching, they'll think it's us.'

Callie stared at her brother aghast. He was perfectly serious. 'Nick, that'll never work.'

'You've not even thought about it.'

'I don't need to. A five-year-old would see through it,' Callie said disparagingly.

'Oh, thanks for your support!' snapped Nick, with a mixture of anger and hurt.

'Look, it's a clever idea...' Callie went on, attempting to rescue his feelings. 'I just don't think they'll fall for it, that's all.'

'Can you think of a better plan?'

'Unfortunately I can't...'

'Look, it's getting dark out there.' Nick flapped his hand towards the wide cabin window. 'If they see something which

173

looks a *bit* like us jumping into the water, they'll think the rest. Isn't it worth a try?'

Callie peered through the wide expanse of glass. The Nile was the colour of black coffee now, with reflected twinkles of light rippling on its surface from the ship's numerous windows.

'Darkness plays tricks with your eyes, doesn't it?' Nick ploughed on. 'OK, my plan might be absolutely bonkers, but it might also be absolutely brilliant.'

Brilliant wasn't the word Callie would have used.

'We could try it while everyone else is at dinner,' Nick persisted. 'We don't want any real passengers thinking we've jumped, otherwise the ship might turn back for us. Plus I'm betting Horse Face and my charioteer won't have restaurant passes – so they should be the only people still around.'

Callie let out a long, weary sigh. Nick's plan was the only one they had. 'OK.'

The carpeted stairs at the end of corridor C were deserted ten minutes after the restaurant had opened.

'We should hide our doubles at the back of the boat first,' said Callie, walking briskly up the metal steps with the pillow wearing her old T-shirt and hoodie tucked under her arm. She'd filled the hood with a cushion to make it look more like there was a head inside, and Nick had done the same with his. 'Then we accidentally on purpose bump into Horse Face or the other one – and get them to chase us, which shouldn't be too difficult.' She was speaking confidently but her heart was racing at the thought of another encounter with the two Followers.

'We have to get far enough ahead to throw these guys overboard and still hide, but give the Followers time to see our doubles floating away.'

Nick looked uneasy. It was his plan and there was a lot riding on it, and everything came down to timing.

They reached a pair of pine doors with porthole windows opening out onto the stern of the ship.

A warm evening breeze flapped at Callie's pillow as she opened the doors. There were lights on the deck above them, but where they'd decided to hide, behind the metal steps to the upper deck, was in perfect darkness. Callie peeped over the rail. The Nile was being spewed out into a gurgling trail by the ship's turbines. If Nick was right, the darkness combined with the churning water would be enough to make a couple of dressed-up pillows look like two kids. 'I hope this works,' she said, putting the pillows next to the rail. She knew that Nick was thinking the same thing. 'Let's go and find them before we lose our nerve...'

It took them another ten minutes to locate the two Followers. They were prowling the mid-section corridor outside the restaurant, obviously hoping to pick up Callie and Nick after dinner. They were in luck.

Callie spotted them early enough to give out a pretty convincing scream: 'Nick, run!'

They careered back down the corridor and burst out through one of the ship's double fire doors, the metal handles bashing loudly into the bulkhead. They took the stairs leading to the upper decks. Over the sound of their trainers pounding on the steps, they could hear the two Followers shouting at each other. Callie guessed it was something like: 'That way! Don't lose them!'

Callie was scared enough to really jump off the ship, but she dashed sideways at the top of the stairs. Nick was just seconds behind her, and together they lobbed the two waiting pillows over the rail and collapsed into the darkness behind the steps.

The doors swung open again as Horse Face and the charioteer hurtled out. They seemed confused not to see Callie and Nick immediately and ran to the railings together, leaning out and scanning the dark waves as they rippled beyond the reach of the many boat lights.

Horse Face pointed and started babbling in Arabic, the sound of which had become familiar to Callie during their imprisonment in Ssin's palace. She didn't need to speak it to understand that Horse Face was saying they should jump after the pillows, and that the other Follower was adamant that they shouldn't. They continued arguing, the charioteer shaking his head and retreating towards the steps. Callie willed him not to look round; he was barely a metre away – if his eyes were accustomed to the dark, there was no way he would miss where they were hiding.

There was a sharp crack as Horse Face slapped his companion hard across the face, but Nick's charioteer responded angrily, throwing a fist. The pair of them grappled for several moments before Horse Face, his massive front teeth forming a terrible grimace, made a grab for Nick's charioteer and hauled him towards the railings. He bent the charioteer's arm behind his back and forced him to climb over the rail, then he scrambled out beside him. They teetered on the ledge beyond the rails for a second before Horse Face pulled them both into a jump. They screamed all the way down, until an enormous splash cut out the sound of their voices.

Callie crept forward towards the rail. She could hear, rather than see where Horse Face and Nick's charioteer were swimming. They were making straight for the nearest riverbank, where there was a dim stretch of papyrus reeds by the water's edge. After less than a minute, she spotted two dark shapes wading through the reeds – thrashing the papyrus stems to try and flush out their quarry. A pair of waterfowl went clucking out across the dark horizon, and then Horse Face shouted. In the moonlight Callie could see that he was holding up one of the waterlogged pillows.

The plan had only half worked: Horse Face and Nick's charioteer were off the ship, but they knew that Callie and Nick weren't. Ssin would continue to follow. At the next stop, Beni Sami, their enemy would be waiting.

20

The Library at Beni-Sami

C allie hadn't slept very well, even though the bed in her cabin was as comfortable as any on dry land. After ridding themselves of the two Followers last night, they'd tracked down the ship's internet café. They'd suddenly thought of emailing their parents to tell them they were safe and now on *The Spirit on the Nile,* and that they'd explain everything properly as soon as they got back.

'They never check their emails,' said Nick. 'Dad's inbox is overrun with junk, and Mum tells everyone to phone her instead.'

'They might just look,' said Callie hopefully. 'They'll be desperate to hear from us.'

After writing the email, she started looking up the Library of Beni-Sami. It made sense to find out as much as possible.

'"Though still impressive, all that remains of this ancient Egyptian library is the outer shell of grey-green granite. The library is reputed to contain the Lost Prophesies: a set of predictions, spanning 3,400 years ..."' Callie read out loud from a page she'd found under: *library/prophesies/beni-sami*. Nick's mouth had fallen open.

'You mean they know they're there?'

'*Reputed* just means they *think* they're there. Obviously no one's ever found anything.'

Callie had clicked on another link and then scrolled through several photographs of the ruins: the outer shell of grey-green was exactly as the article had described. The structure looked to be crumbling around the windows, and there was no discernible roof, though the size of the building looked fairly substantial. 'There's a lot of it. How long do you think it'll take to explore?'

'Too long to do it in an hour-long visit,' said Nick practically. 'Besides, we can't be searching for prophesies and stuff while there are people around. We'll have to hide until everyone else comes back here. It's the only way.'

'Except,' said Callie, frowning, 'when there are people around, Ssin and her army won't be able to attack us.'

'We haven't got any choice, though, have we?' said Nick.

He might just as well have said: 'It's Fate...' thought Callie.

After they'd found out as much as they could about the library, they'd gone back to their cabins, eaten a snack and drunk a whole two litres of Egyptian cola between them. Callie had pulled out her copy of *Egypt's Greatest Astrologer* before climbing into bed, and read the final four chapters. As with the rest of the book, it was generally guesswork, with some tiny snippets of written evidence thrown in, which had survived over the centuries. Pharaoh Ssin had definitely recaptured her runaway slave. But while travelling on her war galley, he had fallen overboard. The Seer had drowned, or been killed by hippos – and that was the end of it. The conclusion that Professor Jed Severs had come to in *Egypt's Greatest*

Astrologer was that the prophesies had never been written down, if they had even existed in the first place. Sitting up in bed, Callie had felt very lost and alone, hugging her knees, and wondering if she should tell Nick what she'd just read. Tears began to leak from her eyes. If only her parents were here. If only someone else could take charge, and take all the horror of the past few days away.

She had then lain awake worrying about Ssin and Gobb, and all the others who could be waiting for them at Beni-Sami. She even thought of asking *The Spirit on the Nile's* captain to call the police, or to sail straight past the next stop. But she wouldn't be believed, anyway. They'd have to risk Beni-Sami. What other choice did they have? Even if they could reach an airport, get onto a plane, and fly a thousand miles away, Callie guessed they would still miraculously, somehow, end up back at the library ruins. It was preordained, wasn't it? It was a road that always led back to the same place: their future. She just had to hope that their future was going to be longer than the next few hours.

She had finally fallen asleep around four in the morning thinking about eternal youth. Was it their only protection against Ssin? Condemning themselves to everlasting childhood, a freakish existence of never growing up. That alone had been enough to give her nightmares.

In cabin C7, Nick had also suffered a sleepless night. Huddled in a blanket beside the wide cabin window with the lights out, he had watched the undulating black silhouette of the distant hills for hours. He counted a dozen moving lights, just spots, really, grouped together and tracking the progress of the ship. Clearly Ssin now wanted her presence to be known...

* *

The Spirit on the Nile put into the concrete dock at Beni-Sami a little later that morning, and everybody began streaming through the ship to disembark. Callie and Nick joined the exodus on the gangplank, emerging into bright sunshine and a persistent, driving breeze.

They immediately scanned the horizon for signs of Ssin or her army. Callie saw a few vibrant tourist facilities: a café, a museum and the obligatory souvenir shop – plus a kind of boat refuelling station where a battered red oil tanker with 'Marine Gas' printed along the side was parked. But apart from the local Egyptians manning the tourist spots with open, friendly smiles, no one else was about.

Callie whispered to Nick: 'So far so good. But keep a lookout. Ssin won't be far away, I'm certain of it.'

Nick nodded sombrely. He didn't need telling that the ancient pharaoh hadn't given up; he'd watched the lights from her distant chariots trailing them all night long.

Cold, caressing ripples of air continued to flap at their clothes. Callie glanced up at the sky which was sulphur yellow and cloudless right across the horizon. She tried to remember what time of year sandstorms blew across Egypt, and felt sure it wasn't for months yet: around January or February.

They were shuffling off the end of the gangplank behind the rest of the passengers, and Callie let out an involuntary gasp. The library ruins were now visible through the odd arrangement of trees: a pearly grey-green cube, four-storeys high. The granite sparkled at every point where sunlight caught its crystalline surface, and sixteen perfectly square but glassless windows were cut into the face of the building in four rows of four.

'It's a lot more impressive than it looks on the internet,' whispered Nick, shielding his eyes from the sun.

'I know,' agreed Callie, thinking it could take them all day to search it properly.

The passengers were being split into groups, according to the order they left the ship. As Callie and Nick were almost bringing up the rear, they were placed into the final group led by a guide wearing smart white galabiyya robes, and with a wrinkly but smiley round face. He detained them so that the other two groups could make their way up through the trees first.

While they waited, he told them the history of the great building, which had once been the largest library in the ancient world. 'Half a million scrolls were stored here in this one place, and it was consequently a great centre for learning and exchange of knowledge. Founded by Pharaoh Memuset in around 1600 BC, it thrived for over three hundred years.'

Eventually he said it was time to go, and began leading them up a sloping pavement, etched into the natural rock. More leafy palm trees shaded the approach to the ruins, their huge green fronds swaying fitfully in the strengthening wind.

After almost five minutes of climbing, they made it to the top, where the library stood glistening like green, frosty snow.

'This way,' their guide prompted, and led them towards a window in the right-hand corner of the structure. 'The entrance is indistinguishable from the windows – to preserve the visual symmetry,' he explained, and they saw that grey-green steps led all the way to the window itself.

Callie and Nick followed the others up the well-worn steps and into an L-shaped room – a full corner of the lower library. Plaster reliefs of ancient Egyptians reading, writing or just carrying scrolls, adorned the interior walls.

'You are looking at depictions of the original visitors to the great library.' The guide gave them time to view the reliefs and take photographs, before leading them on through a more conventional doorway and into a larger space beyond, where they could see that the library was a cube within a cube. The floors all the way to the fourth storey had disappeared, leaving empty sockets where the wooden joists had rotted away. Now, directly above them was a square of sky, tinged with swirls of yellow and grey.

'The thousands of papyrus scrolls would have been stored on wooden shelves,' the guide went on, sweeping his arm around the entire inner library. 'More literature than a person could read in a lifetime.'

Callie glanced round; the other two groups from the ship were still ahead of them: following their own guides, listening avidly to very different commentaries. She studied every passenger minutely in case any Followers had slipped into their midst. She breathed a sigh of relief: there was still no sign of their enemies.

'The ancient Egyptians produced writings on a vast range of subjects from music to mathematics, architecture to medicine, and yet very few ordinary Egyptians could actually read them,' their guide explained.

The tour continued, almost tediously, from room to room: each identical to the one before it, a perfect square, with a single window to permit in the natural light.

'Note the *unusual* hieroglyphs on the floor, which were excavated only a few months ago, beneath a layer of ancient paint.' The guide said encouragingly as they entered the final room. 'Look closely. What do the symbols remind you of?'

Callie did her best to catch sight of what everybody else was seeing, but there were far too many adults standing in front of her.

'Well, that's obviously a squirrel, and the other one looks like some kind of fish,' supplied a woman with an American accent.

'It's a stickleback,' muttered Nick. The man in front turned to look at him, and Callie was able to peer through the gap. The familiar symbols of the squirrel and the stickleback were engraved faintly onto the floor.

'Of course – squirrels and sticklebacks weren't known in ancient Egyptian times,' their guide went on. 'So perhaps a more modern visitor carved them here as a joke.' It seemed their guide wasn't as knowledgeable on Egyptian mysteries as Omar was.

A fresh gust of wind wafted in through the glassless window, and Callie saw that the other two groups were beginning their trek back to the ship. Their guide noticed too and clapped his hands together. 'So, who is ready for lunch?' he asked with a pleasant smile.

'What if he does a head count and realises two of us are missing?' Nick whispered.

'I don't think he counted us on the way up,' replied Callie.

They followed the others as they returned to the L-shaped room, but hung back as they started passing through the doorway disguised as a window. An elderly lady's straw hat was blown straight from her head by a flurry of gritty wind. The guide chased it gallantly across the paved area, and everyone else took that as a signal that they should follow him. Callie and Nick doubled back into the library.

Crack! Something crunched under Nick's foot as he stepped back. 'What was that?' He leaned against the crumbling wall so he could lift his foot and see what he'd trodden on. Jammed into the intricate black tread pattern of his trainer were the remains of a large, segmented brown arachnid, yellow gunge leaking from a crushed set of pincers. 'Cool! A scorpion!' Nick tried kicking his foot a couple of times to get rid of it, but it seemed welded to the rubber of his trainer.

'Here, use this.' Callie handed him the plastic key card to her cabin door to use as a scraper. 'And whatever you do, don't touch that sting!' The arched tail with its venom-loaded stinger was dangling dangerously off the side of Nick's trainer.

'Sorry, Scorpy,' said Nick, and flicked the mangled arachnid onto the stone floor before lowering his foot.

'Look where you're walking in future,' said Callie, 'Because I don't fancy sucking venom out of you if one of those things stings you.'

Taking extra care where she put her own feet, Callie led the way back to the room with the squirrel and the stickleback markings on the floor so they could look around properly. The wind was now squalling past the window, making it feel darker and colder than it had done before. She wondered if a sand storm really was about to hit.

'All it says is: *Callie and Nick...* Not a lot to go on, is it?' said Nick.

'What did you expect, a "Lost Prophesies Here" sign and a large arrow?'

Nick shrugged. 'It wouldn't hurt to help us occasionally, would it?'

'There's nothing on the walls or the ceiling,' said Callie, after a quick inspection. Each was as plain and nondescript as the next. She tried running her hand softly over the surface. 'Maybe there's a concealed mechanism or switch or something.'

Nick watched her hopefully, but after a minute or so, Callie shook her head. 'I don't suppose it *would* be that easy.' She bent down to examine the symbol for Squirrel etched onto the floor. Apart from being a lot bigger, it was exactly the same as every other Squirrel hieroglyph she'd seen over the past few days – no extra lines or subtle variations that she could discern.

She sighed and strode out of the room to check the doorframe for hieroglyphs, but there weren't any – only a very simple repeated pattern resembling downwards-pointing chevrons engraved into the stonework.

'You don't think we've missed a message somewhere, do you?' she said, going back into the room.

'We can't have, can we?' said Nick rationally. 'The Seer would have *foreseen* us missing it and not bothered putting it there in the first place.'

'Oh, yeah. That makes sense.'

'How about if we say: "We're stuck... We need more help?" The Seer must have foreseen that as well.' Nick glanced optimistically around the room.

Callie arched an eyebrow. 'What were you hoping for – a secret door to open up and let you in?'

Nick ignored her sarcasm, and sat down exhaustedly on the floor, leaning his back against the wall. 'You know, if the Seer was so good at seeing into our future, he must have known we were coming here anyway – on the cruise with Mum and Dad. So why did he allow us to chase all over Egypt first, coming up against a demented old hag who chucks us in with her pet crocodiles, sends cheetahs after us and tries to mummify us?'

Callie stared at him. He was completely right – they'd been heading to the library anyway, and it would have been much easier coming all the way on the cruise ship.

'Our fate's the same whatever happens!' said Nick.

'Couldn't we at least have had a nice holiday first?'

Callie bit her lip. 'I suppose we wouldn't have thought much about the symbols if we hadn't met Pharaoh Ssin first. But I wonder why Ssin didn't bring us straight to Beni-Sami. She must have known these symbols were here.'

'You weren't listening properly,' said Nick. 'That guide said they'd only uncovered them recently. He said it was painted over. Ssin probably doesn't even know about them.'

'Oh... That still doesn't help us, though...' Callie stood up to go to the window to see if the wind had died down at all, but as she moved there was an unpleasant grating sound. 'What...?'

She glanced around in panic. The entire room, walls and all, had started to sink the moment she'd stepped onto the squirrel symbol. She dashed a look at Nick. Exactly where he had sat down was the stickleback symbol. 'It's an escalator!' she cried. 'We just had to stand – or sit – on our symbols.'

Nick pulled a face. 'But any idiot could have done that... at any time...'

'Not *any* idiot, Nick. Us. It must be our weight,' said Callie. 'Our *exact* weight, in exactly the right place. It's ingenious. Both of us must have lost half a stone chasing round Egypt. If we'd come here straight away we would have weighed too much!'

The room went on descending, leaving the intact outer shell of the library behind. As the room settled with a loud, shuddering thump, all the light from above was extinguished. 'That's not good,' said Nick.

'Hang on.' Light flared from a small silver torch. 'I came prepared... I bought it yesterday from the ship's souvenir shop with my last two Egyptian pounds.' Callie aimed the torch beam through the door opening which had descended with the rest of the room, and a circle of light played into an underground chamber stacked with thousands of scrolls. 'Oh my God!' she gasped.

There was an entire secret level of the library, crammed with ancient scrolls, heaped up on lecterns, on little wooden shelves and stuffed into pigeon holes – each document perfectly preserved in the dark, dry atmosphere.

'Prophesies galore,' whispered Callie. She automatically dashed through the doorway, unable to resist the lure of so many precious papyruses.

Nick was only a step behind her. 'It'll take us weeks to read them all.'

'Months... Years.'

The grating sound started up as soon as they stepped off the squirrel and stickleback symbols, and the elevator room began to rise.

'No!' Callie shrieked, spinning back round. She made a grab for the floor she'd just been standing on as it rose up to her waist, but couldn't pull herself back in. 'It's going to bury us alive!'

Nick tried hanging on the edge of the rising floor, but had to let go as it slotted back into what was now the ceiling. He swore loudly, then grabbed the torch out of Callie's grip and waved it around. A pool of brightness landed on a second doorway with a distinctive chevron pattern around the stone frame. This time, the arrows were pointing up instead of down. 'The way out?'

They threaded their way through the piles of scrolls and manuscripts, and hurried into the second empty room. Callie squinted at the floor for the squirrel and stickleback symbols with an air of panic. 'There, look!' she said thankfully, positioning herself on the squirrel symbol. 'Hurry up. You need to get on your symbol as well.'

Nick remained where he was. 'Don't you think we ought to have a look at a few prophesies first?' he asked wryly.

Ignoring Nick's smirk, she marched back into the main chamber and stopped at the first set of shelves. 'Aim the torch over here.'

The beam fell upon a stack of ancient papyrus books. The volume on the very top was open, as if someone had just been reading it. Callie couldn't believe her eyes. 'It's the lost art of pyramid building,' she exclaimed. 'Step by step pictures showing you how to do it.'

'What's so great about that?'

'Haven't you ever wondered how they built them?'

'Oh yeah, *that's* what's been keeping me awake at night.'

Callie pulled a face at him. 'Well, maybe *you* haven't wondered how they built the pyramids, but experts have been trying to figure it out for thousands of years. You know that there's 2.3 million blocks of stone in the Great Pyramid.'

'I do now.'

'And some of the blocks weigh over ten tons. The ancient Egyptians didn't have cranes, and even if they did it would still be almost impossible to position so many blocks in such perfect order. And just think how high the crane would have to be to reach the top. Plus the corners are so precise; it's hard to imagine anyone achieving such symmetry!' She paused to turn over a couple of pages. 'So how did they do all that? Unless they used magic.'

'*Magic?* You're not serious?' Nick was suddenly interested.

Callie pointed to a coloured illustration of Egyptians

levitating stone blocks many times their own size. The picture showed two sets of large black circles – one placed on the ground, the other on the underside of the massive blocks of stone. 'They look exactly like two sets of magnets repelling one another,' Callie went on. 'They've even drawn little wavy lines coming out of them.'

'Magnets! To lift ten tons!' said Nick enthusiastically. 'We could make a fortune selling this info – and not just to archaeologists, but to building companies as well.'

Callie flicked through more manuscripts from the same stack, their subjects obvious from the vivid illustrations contained inside. 'Temple building for beginners...constructing papyrus ships...These manuscripts must be worth their weight in gold; the entire reference section for ancient Egyptian technology.'

Nick moved over to a wooden lectern where several scrolls were already lying open. 'An encyclopaedia of ancient Egyptian gods, some sort of music book and an astronomical chart. They're not worth anything...'

Callie rolled her eyes at Nick's apparent greed and kept on looking.

An atlas, a cookery book, an animal encyclopaedia. They were still unearthing every kind of text and scroll almost an hour later.

Callie groped for a high-backed wooden chair and flopped heavily into it. Something was wrong. Nick stared at her nonplussed.

'What's up?'

'These scrolls might be worth their weight in gold, but they're not the Lost Prophesies, are they?'

'What do you mean?'

Callie threw him a tortured expression. 'Look around, Nick. Everything here is about *ancient* Egypt: technology, science, religion. But where's all the stuff about the future? Space travel, mobile phones, next week's winning lottery numbers? There's certainly nothing about eternal youth. None of this is going to save our lives.'

21

Sandstorm

'**B**ut the prophesies have to be here somewhere.' Nick carried on searching. 'Come on, Callie, one of them refers to us.'

'How do we know the Seer wasn't just playing a game with us, *and* his pharaoh?' Callie said despondently, feeling crushed and hopelessly tired. 'Maybe he hated us. Maybe he hated her as well. Maybe he was a stupid boy playing a stupid game!'

'Then why's all this stuff *hidden*?' Nick demanded obstinately. He swept the room wildly with the beam of the torch.

'It must be just a part of the original library – secret texts and manuscripts, probably too precious to be pawed by ordinary Egyptians,' said Callie. 'But definitely not predictions.'

'What did the Seer come here for, then? What did he bring *us* here for?'

'We're just his toys – something he could laugh about happening in the future.' Callie lashed out angrily with her foot, sending a pile of papyrus books tumbling across the floor. 'I hate him. *I hate him!* We're trapped in this nightmare, and the only way out I can see is us getting killed.'

Nick looked as if he didn't know what to say. The torchlight reflected off the pile of books Callie had just upset. Three silver stars arranged in a rainbow, the Seer's own distinctive symbol, were marked along the top of one of the scrolls she'd just uncovered. 'What's that by your foot?'

Callie reached forward to pick up the scroll with trembling fingers, afraid the delicate papyrus would disintegrate. It made a stiff crackling sound as she unrolled it.

She gasped. 'It's from him... *Dear Callie and Nick,*' she read out with trepidation. '*I think of you as my friends, even though we shall never meet.*'

Nick stared at her in astonishment. 'Flipping heck, Callie. You're getting really good at translating his messages!'

Callie's heart missed a beat. She hadn't translated it at all. 'It's not in hieroglyphs,' she stammered. 'It's written in English. And he's using our proper names.'

'What?' Nick stared at the scroll.

Callie went on reading: '*You have found this chamber as I knew you would. I counterbalanced the lift for your exact weight, so only you could visit.*'

'Bit of a show off, isn't he?' said Nick.

'*From here you must take one last journey.*' Callie's heart sank once more – just as she feared; there was more for them to do. '*Take the eastern road through the hills. In the pyramid, the Eternal Mountain, in the region of Lake Anubis, you shall discover the source of eternal youth, my greatest secret.*'

'A pyramid? The Eternal Mountain,' spat Nick. 'Aren't pyramids kind of massive? You know, the sort of things that stand out a bit? And Ssin's never found it, even though she's been looking for three and a half thousand years?'

Callie slumped back in her chair, allowing the scroll to

re-roll itself. It did seem impossible. 'The pyramid must be hidden somehow.'

After a long silence, Nick said: 'He's not going to be waiting there for us, is he? If this pyramid contains the source of eternal youth, he could still be alive, and in a lot better condition than his pharaoh.'

Callie shook her head. 'But he just said, didn't he? "Even though we shall never meet."' She thought about Omar's book: *Egypt's Greatest Astrologer.* Everyone thought that the Seer had drowned or been eaten by hippos when he was just seventeen. He must have managed to record his secrets before that.

Nick let out a deep sigh. 'Come on, then. There's nothing more for us here, is there?'

They passed through the doorway with the arrowhead pattern – and took their places on the stickleback and squirrel symbols in the empty room.

Horrifyingly, nothing happened. The floor remained exactly where it was. Callie glanced at her brother. He was fiddling with the huge book that showed how to build a pyramid.

'It's that book, you idiot.'

'What's that book? What are you talking about?'

'It's making you heavier.'

'But it shows how to build stuff without cranes!'

'Go and put it back, otherwise we'll never get out of here. This thing needs our exact weight, remember.'

'Fine!' Nick went and plonked the book down on the nearest wooden lectern with a loud thud. He was muttering when he came back into the empty room: 'You can carry half the books ever printed round with you – but if I want something to read I can't have it.'

'I'll buy you a copy of *The Gruffalo* when we get home,' said Callie sarcastically. 'Now get on that symbol.'

Nick stepped onto the carved stickleback, and, with a reassuring grating sound, the entire room began to rise again. Centimetre by centimetre the view of the secret chamber disappeared behind them. Callie bent down, and then squatted to watch the priceless collection of Egyptian knowledge slipping away from their grasp. There was a rumble and their 'escalator' settled on the opposite corner of the library from where they'd descended. As they stepped out, the room instantly began to descend, the original upper room easing back into place above it.

The wind was howling through the inner section of the library ruins and Callie glanced up through the missing floors to the open square of sky above. It was darkened by swirling clouds of sand. While she was watching, the sky cleared for just a second, and a brown, hazy light seeped in through the open roof to illuminate the grey-green walls. She screamed. They were surrounded by Followers of Ssin.

'Seize them!' screeched the pharaoh.

Crocodile Head lurched for Callie, a dreadful silhouette as the light was blotted out again by the sand clouds. Callie felt his sharp nails gripping her arm and dragging her and Nick into the room where they had sunk into the secret depths of the library. A wooden wheelchair was already upended there, and Gobb, his bandaged stubs sticking out behind him, was scraping at the floor with dirty fingernails in an insane attempt to open the subterranean room. They must have found the symbols, and been trying to work out the mystery when Callie and Nick had reappeared. Gobb was mumbling to himself, as though sheer madness had overtaken him: 'Gobb must find the secret of eternal youth for her.' He licked his wide, fat lips, his mismatched eyes rolling oddly. 'Yes... The pharaoh will be pleased. Ssin will forgive Gobb if he succeeds... Ssin will allow Gobb back into her affections.'

Ssin, Crocodile Head and Horse Face crowded into the room behind Callie and Nick. Horse Face had been punished for being tricked off the cruise ship, because all four fingers from his left hand had been removed. The remaining stubs were coated in black tar. Callie shuddered.

A yell from Ssin dragged Callie's gaze away from Horse Face's hand: 'How? How did you reach the lower level?'

'The room descended when we stood on the squirrel and the stickleback symbols. That other room,' Callie pointed through the door, deciding honesty was the best policy, 'was the way up.'

'Show me! Stand upon the symbols again.'

'It, it won't work with anyone else in here,' stammered Callie desperately. 'It needs my weight and my brother's exactly.'

For a moment the only sound was that of the raging sandstorm that was now lashing the outer shell of the library, while Ssin raged inside, thwarted by the Seer once again.

'Weapons!' she screeched suddenly. 'Tear up the floor!'

Curved swords zinged out of their scabbards as Crocodile Head, Horse Face and others set to hacking at the stone floor. As the blades rang out in the gloom, Callie wondered why there were so few followers. Some forty men had left Medphis, now there were less than twenty, including those standing in the main chamber.

'What's happened to the rest of them?' she whispered to Nick, her voice masked by the clanging of swords. 'Her army?'

'They couldn't have all made it. They lost three chariots the first night, didn't they? And another couple crashed when she blew that trumpet thing to stop us escaping.'

'What are you whispering about?' shrieked Ssin, rounding lividly on Callie. 'You know where the Eternal Mountain is, don't you? You saw a map, co-ordinates written down?' She sounded insatiable, her greed making her fire off question after question. 'Tell me!'

'We didn't find a message,' lied Callie. 'It's only old scrolls.'

'Liar!' It was a dreadful wail. Ssin gesticulated dementedly. 'Seize her! Beat the truth from her.'

Gobb pitched forward on his hands and knees before Crocodile Head or any of the others could move. But he stopped suddenly, his face frozen. He turned his hand over. Something was squashed on his palm, the remains of its segmented sting pumping a final spurt of venom into his exposed wrist. He bellowed now, ripping away the scorpion with the fingers of his other hand.

'Pharaoh, help me!' he stared desperately at Ssin, who did nothing to aid him. Gobb fell to stabbing at his own hand with a blade that had been lying on the floor. He was gouging out strips of his own flesh to stop the venom spreading, intermittently sucking hard on his wrist. Fountains of bright blood were soon staining the stone floor in a halo around him. Crocodile Head and the others crowded round to watch, licking their lips ghoulishly at the giant priest's possessed struggles.

'The floor! The floor! Don't stop!' shrieked Ssin fiendishly.

Gobb froze with the blade in his hand to turn a stricken expression towards his pharaoh. She cared nothing for him, his death throes were a mere interruption.

'Move his useless carcase to one side!' Ssin commanded remorselessly.

Crocodile Head and Horse Face, jamming his fingerless hand under Gobb's arm, carted the priest cursing and snarling to the side of the chamber, and work on the floor recommenced.

'Hurry! Hurry. Waste no time!' screeched Ssin impatiently.

Gobb's protuberant, bloodshot eyes were still fixed upon her. A dribble of brown vomit ran from the corner of his mouth, and thick, frosty green snot hung from both nostrils. The deadly scorpion venom pulsed through his bloodstream.

'You would abandon me thus...? After all I have done in your name?' Gobb heaved himself forward on his knees reaching his arms towards Ssin.

Crocodile Head ran over to him and began to rain heavy, thudding fists onto Gobb's misshapen brown skull.

'Good, Moldo.' There was the trace of a smile on Ssin's puckered lips. 'You shall be my new Grand Priest. Now, finish the scorpion's work.'

Crocodile Head drove his sword deep into Gobb's abdomen, and the priest sank finally and motionless to the stone floor.

Momentarily forgotten in the darkness of hatred and greed, Callie pulled her brother slowly towards the low window – and out into the storm.

A maelstrom of sound assaulted their eardrums, intermittently roaring and howling – a deafening tumult. They were blasted by walls of flying sand, the roughness of it scouring the exposed skin on their arms and faces. Dust blinded and choked them as they struggled to breathe.

'That way,' Nick managed to gurgle. He waved round the corner of the ruins, away from the Nile and towards the hills –

neither visible through the thick curtain of sand. 'The message said take the eastern road . . . East is away from the Nile on this side of the bank. ' Callie forced a nod – the Seer, or Fate, had left them no choice. She held on firmly to her brother, and together they hugged the outside wall of the library, staggering along and trying not to be blown in the wrong direction by the storm.

A clattering sound started – so loud it momentarily drowned out the storm. Callie threw them both sideways, seconds before a flying chariot smashed itself to pieces against the wall in front of them.

'Thanks,' gasped Nick breathlessly. Two white stallions galloped past, whinnying in terror before the wind. They stumbled after them, fighting hard to keep their balance. Finally reaching the corner of the ruins the wind pushed them round, and afforded them a temporary respite.

'Nick?' Callie swallowed a mouthful of sand and grit.

'I'm all right.' He was leaning his back against the storm. Callie's eyes streamed, reacting to a lifetime's dust blasting into them in one go. Her ponytail had broken loose, so that her dark hair was whipping around her face.

She thought Nick was saying: 'Cover your face,' and definitely saw him yanking up the top half of his T-shirt, so that it covered both mouth and nose. She nodded that she under-stood, and with an effort to control her flapping hood, finally managed to drag it over her head.

There was a scrap of path leading away from the ruins and up a slope. 'We need to get going,' she screamed. 'Ssin won't be far behind us.'

'Did she cause this storm?'

Callie shook her head. 'No. She wouldn't risk her chariots, would she?'

Nick nodded and they plunged back into the full fury of the storm, feeling their way up a path they could hardly see. Just occasionally there was a break in the swirling, biting sand when they glimpsed a jagged slope climbing higher into the hills. By some miracle, the storm was blowing them the way they wanted to go.

'Just keep going,' Callie willed herself every ten paces or so. Each step was another step away from their enemies, another step towards the end – whatever that might be. They would live or they would die – only the Seer, the boy who'd seen them so far into the future, knew which it was going to be. 'Just keep going,' she repeated again. Each new blast of wind penetrated to her bones, seemingly freezing every blood vessel.

The terrain was dotted with palm trees which had a habit of looming out of the flying sand like attackers. Callie tried to calculate how far they'd gone with the storm hurtling them along like a couple of feathers: a kilometre, maybe two? She thought it had been about half an hour. Yet still there was no sign of a lake or pyramid, not that she could see much at all.

'How long before they come after us?' Nick called out to Callie.

'They won't be able to follow us through the sandstorm,' said Callie, shielding her eyes from the sand. 'Their chariots would be smashed to pieces. But, as soon as the storm abates, they'll be coming.'

'They'll break into the hidden library now they know it's there,' said Nick. 'And then they'll know which way we went.'

'We should have destroyed the Seer's message,' called out Callie, angry at herself for not thinking of it when they'd had the chance.

The wind moaned around them, as if someone's soul was departing the earth.

Arm in arm they battled on through the storm, hoping they were heading towards the eternal mountain.

22

Nemesis

Fortune climbed out of the river half a mile down from where the large male hippo was protecting its young. Whistling softly, he started making a small den for himself in the fresh green reeds, then lay on his back to dry out and rest in the heat of the midday sun. He noticed there was still clay upon his feet from where he had climbed out of the river. It was good quality clay, the type he had used as a potter's son, and it made him yearn for his old, lost life, and more especially for the love of his murdered parents. But all that had been taken from him by Pharaoh Ssin, the she-devil who he had once imagined himself to be in love with.

Before he had swum away, Fortune had watched from behind the cover of a floating log. Ssin had sacrificed two more of her sailors, forcing them into the murky depths on rope lines to search for some sign of him. But the hippos, outraged at further intrusion, had attacked twice more until the water around the war galley had been dyed scarlet with human blood. By then Ssin was faced with mutiny by the rest of her crew, if she sent but one more of them to a fruitless suicide.

So the galley had finally sailed away, its royal occupant

railing loudly against the gods, and her crew equally, for betraying her. She would now have a long wait in store for that which she desired. And she would not seek Fortune again; this he had ensured. In five weeks' time she would have completed the long journey back up the Nile, to her palace at Medphis, for the first time since his escape over a year ago. She would tear his quarters apart brick by brick hoping to find even a fragment which would reveal the location of the eternal mountain, and she would fail. What she would find instead was his prediction of Squirrel and Stickleback: where and when they would appear, and that they would be able to lead her to eternal youth. It was fate, all of it, that they should come and that he should write to them, and that Ssin should follow them. It was a pity that he could not make it easier for Squirrel and Stickleback, whom he liked, but he could only guide them. He could not change their fate, and they had an important role to play.

He lay back on his soft green mattress with his hands cupped behind his head and closed his eyes. The lapping of the water against the bank set free the sweet earthy aroma of the mud; the coot-like call of a purple gallinule squeaked from a nearby lily pad. Alternating waves of red, yellow and orange broke across his eyes as the sun passed through his eyelids.

He could see Squirrel and Stickleback in the future, battling against the violence of a sandstorm, their strange modern clothes flapping and whirling about them. It was the final leg of their terrifying journey. They had held on together, protective, loyal, but for what? He had not seen their ending yet, himself. Could he help? Maybe. Fate was fate.

A kind of thwacking noise in the reeds twenty paces from Fortune's nest made him open his eyes, and the purple gallinule went clacking across the water. Someone was searching the riverbank, but Fortune was unafraid, he had foreseen this.

'This way,' he called. 'I am over here.'

'Oh...' A minute later, a boy a few years younger than Fortune, came pushing through the reeds that remained standing around Fortune's den. He presented a shaven head, and was wearing a yellow and red striped kilt of the finest cotton, and expensive well-made leather sandals. He was also carrying a copper spear with a deadly looking point but made no attempt to threaten Fortune with it.

'You don't seem very surprised to see me,' said the boy, who was quite alone, and apparently as unafraid as Fortune.

'Why should I be, Nemesis?' Fortune asked. 'You are right on time.'

The boy gaped, sunlight sparkling in his unusually turquoise eyes. 'On time?'

'This moment was always set down to happen,' explained Fortune. 'Your future and mine are as intertwined as two strands of wild knot thorn.'

'I don't know about that,' said Nemesis, tossing down his spear and sitting on his heels face to face with Fortune.

Fortune smiled, he had taken an instant liking to this boy.

'I saw the way she threw you almost into the mouth of the great hippo.' Nemesis's hitherto friendly, open face suddenly became dark and violent. 'What did you do to deserve that?'

'I was her slave, and I ran away,' replied Fortune simply.

'Most masters would have just given you a thrashing,' remarked Nemesis. He stared off through the reeds and into the distance. 'Oh, how I prayed to Anubis that she would lose her balance on that deck and fall overboard, or that her sailors would turn on her and push her straight into Lady Taweret's gaping jaws,' said Nemesis viciously. 'I was watching from the bank for ages... I've been tracking her galley for several miles, hoping she would stray into range of my spear, but never once did she come close enough.'

The boy turned his ethereal, turquoise blue eyes back upon Fortune. 'She murdered my parents, you see: Intef and Anteepi. Four full cycles of the seasons ago. You've probably heard of them; they were joint rulers of Egypt – until she poisoned them to usurp their crown.' He spat into the nearby water. 'With them out of the way, she was next in line to the throne. She is my cousin.'

'Were you not next in line to the throne of Egypt?' asked Fortune.

'Yes. She sent soldiers to assassinate me, by stabbing me through the heart,' replied Nemesis. 'She believes that I am dead. But I am not, and I have sworn vengeance upon her.'

'Then why have you abandoned your attempt to slay her?' asked Fortune. 'Her galley sails further away as we speak.'

'While they were searching for you on the wrong side of the river I thought I saw you climbing out down here. Something told me that we could join forces against her.'

Fortune nodded. This was exactly as he had foreseen it.

'So, are you going to tell me who you are, and how it is that you were expecting me?'

'Besides being her slave, I was her fortune-teller, which is also my name: Fortune. I'm very good at it.'

'Did you realise that she was going to feed you to the hippos, then?' Nemesis asked in astonishment.

Fortune nodded. 'I planned my own death to stop her searching for me any more.'

Nemesis now grinned. 'So, do you know what will happen to her?'

'Yes.'

'Then you must know whether I succeed in killing her?' Nemesis's expression was one of desperate longing. He was willing Fortune to say yes.

'She cannot be killed.' Fortune disappointed him. 'Your spear, however well-aimed, would have no effect. She possesses eternal life. I'm sorry.'

Fortune saw the conflict raging within Nemesis. He made fists, his knuckles appearing white through the teak colour of the rest of his skin. After more than a minute he said: 'It is ironic then, is it not, that I possess the secret of eternal youth?'

'Yes.' Fortune nodded, unsurprised by the revelation. The twelve-year-old before him had not aged a single day since the death of his parents four years before. Nor had he succumbed to the assassins' blades. What was ironic was that Fortune had created eternal life for Ssin, only to learn later that eternal youth was already available, and so close at hand. Ssin had never really needed him.

Fortune gazed across the placid river to the yellow mountains beyond. He recognised them from his visions. Somewhere amid those peaks was eternal youth.

'Tell me, then,' he said to Nemesis, 'how it is that you possess eternal youth.'

'I was sent out alone into the wilderness as my coming-of-age trial. With only a bow, a sword and a spear I was to survive for one cycle of the year. I did better. I remained the same age by discovering a very special spring.

'It was on a late winter evening. I'd been hunting an antelope for most of the day, growing ever hungrier, but never getting close enough to be sure of a clean kill. I'd not eaten for days, apart from wild roots, and the hunt had wearied me to near exhaustion. Then this same antelope led me through a cleft in the mountains and to a hidden valley. Few, if any, must have known of its existence. Well, there I lost the antelope completely. I was pretty angry I can tell you, but too starved to even find the strength to cry. At first I thought about backtracking and climbing out of the valley where I'd entered, but it was growing dark, and I thought maybe if I carried on I might pick up the antelope's trail once more. I did not, but, around midnight and under a full moon, I saw a strange air rising from a small crater in the ground.

'It was a gift from Isis the goddess of magic: a vapour, a puff of wind to be breathed. And breathe it I did. It restored my strength instantly, and I was no longer hungry, nor even felt the necessity to eat.' Nemesis grinned. 'I spent my whole year of seclusion, in and around that valley, only eating for the pleasure of it, and breathing eternal youth again and again.

'But before I returned home, Ssin stole the throne, and my parents' lives with it, and sent her new soldiers after me.' Nemesis finished his story angrily. 'I have only just left the safety of the valley to wreak my revenge, and now you tell me that my destiny is to fail.'

'I only said that you could not *kill* Ssin,' Fortune reminded him. 'You will take your revenge in another way. In the way which fate intends for you.'

'Tell me!' begged Nemesis, his turquoise eyes appealing to Fortune to release him of his terrible burden.

'You must bury her alive in her palace at Medphis.'

Nemesis started. 'Are you serious?'

'Perfectly serious.'

'You will instruct me how to do it?'

'I will relate to you how it happens,' said Fortune. 'Nothing more.'

'I have but one gift great enough to repay you,' said Nemesis solemnly.

'Eternal youth,' guessed Fortune, devoid of any great desire to learn the secret himself. He had no wish to stay for ever young. His own murdered parents awaited him in the afterlife. But perhaps he could stay young for a little while.

Nemesis held out his hand. 'Eternal youth shall be yours, Fortune the fortune-teller. There in the wilderness, in the secret valley, I shall build you a secret pyramid.'

'I know you will.' Fortune nodded his agreement. 'And I shall make it disappear.'

23

The Eternal Mountain

))

Nick had looked for traces of moss on the rocks to establish which way was north, before they had continued their journey eastwards. At some point during the last hour the anger of the storm had gusted away into nothing, leaving shades of bronze and ochre in the torn clouds above. Finally, through a cleft in the hills, they saw a narrow lake, fringed by wild green marshland. A faint breeze was ruffling the water, bringing with it the scent of herbs from the surrounding fields.

Rocks and pebbles plopped into the water as Callie and Nick clambered down a last shallow bank.

'The pyramid's not here, is it?' said Callie crestfallen. 'This must be the wrong lake.'

Nick stared at the water with absolute conviction. 'It isn't the wrong lake. What if the pyramid is tiny, or at least fairly small? No one said pyramids have to be gigantic, and it'd explain why Ssin's never found it.' He looked back into the hills, seeming to contemplate the evil they knew was behind them. 'Shouldn't we at least have a proper look?'

Callie nodded slightly, using as little energy as possible.

All she wanted to do was lie down and sleep, yet having come all this way and through so much they still couldn't stop to rest.

They were almost a quarter of the way round when Nick's sharp eyes picked up something nestling among the shoreline rocks. 'What's that?'

'What's what?' said Callie. 'What are you looking at?'

Nick was staring at a strange formation of rocks a little way in front of them and at the side of the lake. 'It's a statue of a dog or something.'

'Huh?'

'Look!' said Nick exasperatedly. 'There's its head, and its back.' He started pointing out details.

'Oh my God, you're right.' The statue was carved into the rocks themselves, making it blend in perfectly with the surrounding landscape. Callie started running.

'It's not a pyramid, though, is it?' Nick warned, running along beside her.

'No, but it's *something*.'

They arrived, panting, at an enormous statue which was glaring towards the middle of the narrow lake. 'I don't think it's a dog, either,' panted Callie. 'I think it's a jackal, which makes sense, as this is Anubis's Lake. Anubis was a jackal god. The ancient Egyptians believed he presided over death, because real jackals used to hang around tombs and cemeteries – probably to eat the corpses.'

'Nice.'

Callie positioned herself between the two powerful outstretched front legs of the statue, to gaze up at its pointed hound-like head. 'I know I've seen this thing somewhere before.'

'It's a bit like that Sphinx thing in Cairo,' contributed Nick. 'Only that's a lion with a pharaoh's face.'

Callie shook her head, frustrated. 'No, I was thinking of something smaller.' She wracked her brains to place the statue, and it suddenly came to her. 'It's *exactly* like that stupid nodding dog thing Dad had in the car.' Their dad was always buying tacky stuff with a vaguely archaeological angle. 'Do you remember? Its head bounced up and down every time the car stopped, or started, or went over a bump.'

'Yep.' He looked uncomfortable. The thing had been on the back parcel shelf of their car for less than a week before Nick had broken its head off.

'Are you saying that thing nods?' he suddenly realised what Callie meant and stared up at the statue in disbelief.

'I'm saying it's another message.' Callie's gaze swept hopefully over the statue, hunting for squirrel or stickleback signs. But it appeared to be a fairly regular statue carved from a single lump of natural rock. She clambered up the jackal's haunches, so that she could stand on its back staring at the lake between its upward pointing ears.

'See if you can make its head nod,' said Nick seriously.

Callie wearily pulled herself up the statue's neck until she could balance on its head. Then she jumped twice, but nothing happened. 'That didn't work.' She slid back down again and stood looking up at the statue. 'How did you break the one in the car?'

'What?' Nick pulled his most innocent expression. '*I* didn't break it. Dad went round a corner too fast, and its head flew off.'

'Nick!' Callie said impatiently. 'I'm not going to tell him, am I? This has got to be relevant; the Seer knew everything about us, didn't he? He probably had a vision of you breaking Rover three thousand and odd years before you actually did.'

'I tried dismantling it,' mumbled Nick. 'To see how it worked.'

'OK. How did you *dismantle* it?'

'There was a screw...Somewhere there.' Nick lobbed a pebble at the statue's throat and it clicked against carved rock. He pelted three more stones – *click...click...click.*

Clack.

Callie's head jerked up. 'That sounded different...Hit it in the same place if you can.'

Clack...clack...clack.

'I think it's hollow at that point...Keep throwing!' Callie joined in with a volley of her own. She hit the statue's muzzle, one of its pointing ears and missed it completely twice. 'It's not funny,' she snapped at Nick, who couldn't help laughing at her pitiful attempts.

Crack. One of Callie's stones smashed straight through the statue's outer shell, and fine, dry sand began to dribble out.

'All that sand must have been holding up the jackal's neck,' said Nick enthusiastically.

The dribble became a rush, pouring onto the ground between the statue's outstretched legs. And, slowly, the massive jackal's head began to nod downwards with an excruciating crunching sound.

'Dad's nodding dog!' exclaimed Callie wryly.

It took exactly five minutes for the jackal's pointed muzzle to reach the ground and stop. But nothing, apart from the position of the jackal's head, seemed to have changed.

'I don't get it,' said Callie disappointedly. 'It must have done something more than just nod.' She sat down on one of the giant paws and stared at the overcast sky in frustration.

'Where's the water going?' Nick was looking in the other

direction, peering at the surface of the lake directly in front of the statue. Pieces of dead reed and a few dried-up balls of yellow Acacia blossom, which had been perfectly still a moment ago, were suddenly floating towards them.

'I don't know. Does it matter?'

'Of course it matters if we've somehow started draining the lake.' Nick got down onto his hands and knees to look for a pipe under the waterline. 'I can't see a hole or anything. But the water's definitely going somewhere now.'

'Why? What's the point of that?'

'Sometimes, Callie, I think you're really thick! The pyramid must be underwater! It's in the middle of the lake. I wouldn't put it past the Seer to build his pyramid and then flood the entire valley to hide it. He was full of tricks, wasn't he?' Nick looked as if he was about to explode. 'When the Seer said "In the region of Lake Anubis" he actually meant "*In* Lake Anubis".'

He took a couple of splashing steps into the dark water, till the matting of floating reeds was up to his knees.

Exactly where the jackal statue had been staring before bowing its head, something was breaking the surface of the water.

'It's the tip of the pyramid cap,' breathed Callie. Soft ripples of water rolled all the way across the lake to lap gently against the bank, and the pointed capstone looked ghostly under the streaks of shredded, brown clouds. 'How are we supposed to get to it?' she went on, even though she knew the answer already.

'We're going to have to swim,' said Nick gently.

Callie eyed the water with concern. 'You're Stickleback, remember. I'm only Squirrel.'

'We can't wait for the entire pyramid to surface,' said Nick logically. 'It'll take too long.'

213

'You mean Ssin and her army will get here first,' said Callie.

'I don't think they'll be far behind us.' Nick shrugged apologetically. 'Come on, it'll be OK.' He waded out until the water reached the waistband of his jeans. 'It's not even cold.'

'Wait.' Callie started emptying her pockets, placing all the things she wouldn't need – *Egypt's Greatest Astrologer*, *Hieroglyphics for Beginners* and her hairbrush – onto a rock, wondering if she would ever return for them.

She dipped a trainer-clad foot into the lake, and told herself that the water was pleasantly warm. 'I can do this.'

Nick had begun to swim, but he turned to wait for her, treading water with little splashing sounds. Callie felt her way in step by step, gasping as the water embraced her. She stretched forward, using a breaststroke and a strong kick, and keeping her head well above the surface.

'It's only like a couple of lengths of the school swimming pool,' Nick called back supportively.

'A...couple...of...lengths...of...the...school... swimming...pool...' She repeated the incantation as she swam.

'Come on, Callie; eternal youth.'

Her head still ached with the prospect of eternal youth. Staying thirteen for ever or succumbing to the wrath of Ssin? It was a choice between no future and an endless future – a lose-lose scenario. Was today the last day she would ever grow older? Or, worse, was this her last day full stop?

She could see the pinnacle of the pyramid more clearly with every stroke, and it gave her something to focus on. Though she could only see the nearest side, four identical triangles were obviously creating an exquisite point. The pinnacle seemed to float miraculously on top of the water.

'How are we going to get inside?' she called to Nick, who had already reached the pyramid, and was swimming round it.

'It's too slippery to climb onto, even for you,' he called back, his fingertips sliding across one of the exposed triangles.

Callie swam up beside him and tried scratching the pyramid's surface. Some of the ochre colouring was scraped away. What was underneath was even smoother, glinting even in the weak sunlight. 'The point's made of glass,' she said, splashing more water onto the section she'd just cleaned. There was a distinct transition between an upper section of glass and a lower section of pure white marble. 'We can smash through the glass.'

'Smash through it with what?' asked Nick.

'Here. Try using this.' The torch was the one thing she'd kept in her pocket, thinking it would come in useful; though she had been intending to use it to light their way once they were inside, not to use it as a hammer.

Nick took the torch from her and hit it against the side nearest to him, making a kind of clunking sound.

'Watch your eyes!' Callie warned him. 'That's a lot of glass.'

At the third attempt there was a tinkle, but it proved to be just the lens of the torch. 'Stupid pyramid!' complained Nick.

Callie swam round to put her hands on the torch as well.

'After three... One... two... three!' They stabbed together.

The entire diamond-shaped pinnacle exploded with a bang, spraying glass that was thousands of years old into the water. Callie winced as small shards slashed across her arms and the side of her face. She was checking Nick was all right, when a fine turquoise vapour seeped slowly over the pyramid's marble sill and enveloped them for a second before drifting across the lake eerily.

'What was that?' said Nick, his breathing slightly laboured.

'Condensation? From air that's been trapped inside for thousands of years?' said Callie, shaking her head doubtfully. She'd never seen coloured condensation before.

'We've just broken into a pyramid, though,' said Nick fearfully. 'Omar told me about stuff the pharaohs used to do to stop tomb robbers desecrating their tombs: like painting poisons onto the walls, or smearing them with deadly bacteria and funguses...'

'Isn't it too late to worry about it now?' said Callie. 'Unless you were holding your breath, because I wasn't.'

'No, me neither.'

'Then we carry on. Use the torch to get rid of some more of that glass before we climb in.'

Nick used the torch handle to chip away jagged splinters still embedded into the brim of the pyramid.

'That's enough.' Callie swam forward and dragged herself over the marble edge, easing down onto a wooden floor inside. More splinters from the broken pinnacle crunched under the soles of her trainers. She stood on tiptoes to help pull Nick after her, and he came slithering in.

Finally they were standing inside the Eternal Mountain. Callie rang out her sodden hair as she looked around.

The upper chamber, if it could even be called a chamber, was just a few metres square with a ramp along one side, sloping under the floor. Callie was about to follow it when an unexpected noise stopped her.

'Can you hear something?' She peered over the brim of the pyramid again to locate the sound. It seemed to be coming from a dip between the hills, a revving engine sound. A large red fuel tanker was clattering over the rocky terrain, stirring up considerable amounts of dust. 'There must be a road we missed,' she murmured, not really believing it.

'I don't think there is,' said Nick, squinting at the horizon. 'That thing's smashing straight through bushes.' In fact, the tanker was racing down the slope so haphazardly it was careering through everything in its path: rocks, bushes and a small, bare tree. It had to zigzag to avoid the steepest sections of the hill. 'Where did it come from?'

'There was a fuel tanker parked at the dock, when we got off *The Spirit on the Nile* this morning,' Callie remembered. But there seemed no reason for it to be coming out here.

They watched, rooted to the spot. They could hear the engine revving even harder as it bounced down the last kilometre of rocky hillside. The gigantic wheels were bumping up and down dangerously, the battered cylindrical gasoline section clanking. It skirted an area of green marsh and plunged towards the water before skidding to a halt in a swirl of sand.

The familiar form of Crocodile Head jumped down from the cab, before lifting Ssin after him. And now they could see at least six other Followers, clinging to the sides of the tanker.

'They've found a better way than chariots,' rasped Callie.

'Are they the only ones left out of Ssin's whole army?' asked Nick.

'It's more than enough,' replied Callie, afraid. 'Come on. We haven't got much time.'

24

The Lost Prophesies

T hey had to crawl on their hands and knees to follow the wooden ramp as it sloped underneath the floor and into the bowels of the pyramid. 'Watch out for broken glass,' warned Callie as a shard from the smashed pinnacle stabbed the palm of her hand, drawing a bead of bright red blood.

'Too late,' replied Nick. Blood was seeping through his jeans around both knees. But the broken glass only delayed them for the first few metres, until the ramp turned at a right angle and continued to descend between an inner and outer wall.

'We must be tracing the outside of the pyramid,' guessed Callie. The ceiling above them was angled inwards from left to right and brightly polished bronze mirrors were positioned at each corner to channel in light from up above.

After the ramp had turned at right angles another three times there was room to stand up. Callie's wet trainers squelched on the wooden ramp as she automatically broke into a run, Nick behind her.

Ssin had taken little time to discover Fortune's last message once they had smashed through the floor of the library. In his arrogance he'd even written it in the language of the foreigners, which was hardly a challenge for her. She'd learned many new languages in her 3,422 years. With most of her chariots shattered by the storm she had resorted to a more modern mode of transport. It stank horribly of the flammable oils the world now used, worse than the rank odour of Moldo when it was time to choose a fresh crocodile's head.

Now, perched on her portable throne, at the foot of the hill, she noticed that the water was draining slowly from the lake. Dry weeds were being sucked towards the very edge. 'Moldo, carry me over there.'

Moldo came running willingly, his crocodile-head mask flapping up and down, and he lifted her from the throne, as though she were a feather, and carried her closer to the lake. When they were almost upon it, Ssin observed the statue of Anubis, virtually invisible among the surrounding rocks. She studied its oddly drooping head, and then glanced at the water between its outstretched paws. The broken tip of a pyramid stood above the surface of the water. She bit her lip so hard that she drew a droplet of blood, which she licked pleasurably, relishing its metallic taste.

'The Eternal Mountain.' Ssin found herself drifting back in time. It was a long while to remember back to when Fortune had loved her, but during that time she had taken him to see the three great pyramids of her ancestors: Menkaure, Khafre and Khufu, and Fortune had called them mountains. She was gazing upon a *mountain, an eternal mountain. A mountain she guessed Fortune had constructed himself – and then hidden. She was almost at the end.*

'Put me down here, Moldo,' she ordered. 'Then return with the others to the mighty chariot.' She indicated the battered gasoline tanker. 'Ignite the liquid it carries.'

'Highness?'

Even through his crocodile mask, she could guess at his baffled expression.

'All must be consumed by fire. Yourself as well.' She would not share her prize with anyone. An eternally youthful Moldo? Not for a pyramid full of gold. 'Obey my command. It is the command of a god.' Her withered lips puckered into something resembling a smile. 'You will gain the rank of Grand Priest in the afterlife. All but pharaohs shall bow to you, Moldo.'

She heard Moldo swallowing a lump in his throat. 'Truly?'

'You have my word, and my love.'

Slowly Moldo began to return to where the enormous vehicle had been abandoned. He was igniting a bundle of dry reeds as Ssin waded into the water. She did not watch to see what happened, just heard the explosion and the screams as she started to swim.

Callie was still running when the wooden slope lurched beneath her, smashing her sideways against the wall. She cried out in pain, registering the sound of a muffled explosion. 'What the hell was that?'

220

Nick shook his head. 'I don't know. It felt like the whole pyramid shook.'

Callie saw her frightened expression reflected back at her from another light-channelling bronze mirror. 'Keep going,' she ordered hoarsely.

Her footsteps stuttered to a halt only fifty metres later. There was a triangular entrance cut into the inner wall, the first they'd seen. Callie tried to see inside but the light from the bronze mirrors penetrated no further than a few gloomy metres. 'I'll go first.'

Nick gave her a rather weak smile. 'Together?'

Callie nodded, and they stepped slowly through the opening.

An intense light lasered through to the back of Callie's eyeballs, making her yell out in pain. She had stared directly at something that seemed brighter than the sun.

'Nick, I can't see!' Callie fell to her knees, covering her watering eyes that felt as if they were bleeding. She could hear her brother groaning somewhere in front of her. 'Where are you?'

'I don't know. I can't see, either.'

Callie groped for him, aiming for the sound of his voice. Then she realised she could see a little; through her tightly screwed-up eyelids she could make out golden-edged shapes – everywhere. She tried opening her eyes a bit at a time, wincing at the intensity of the light as it still burned and drew stinging teardrops. A blurry Nick was at the centre of a ring of throbbing light, leading her further into the room.

There was a *clang* as Nick blundered blindly into something, and suddenly, thankfully, the brightness diminished. Nick was cursing, and Callie saw him more clearly. Blood was flowing

221

freely from a split lip. He was kneeling beside a mirror the size and shape of a satellite dish, which was reflecting and magnifying the weak sunlight through an opening in the ceiling. Nick waggled the mirror a few times on its mechanical arm as if he was flicking a spectacular light switch on and off, on and off.

'I found the light switch,' he said ruefully, wiping blood from his mouth with the back of his hand.

Callie came unsteadily to her feet, gasping at what she saw.

'Is this entire room made of gold?'

Even without the dazzling glare from the mirror, every wall, every surface shimmered in golden brilliance. Callie turned on the spot with her mouth wide open. 'It's a golden pyramid within a pyramid,' she breathed.

Under her feet was a vast square of golden tiles framed by triangular walls meeting in a point high above them. A glass-lensed eyelet fixed in the very centre was focusing sunlight onto the mirror directly underneath.

'The Seer!' whispered Callie. A human-shaped casket was standing upright on a set of golden steps. The front was painted brightly with the likeness of the occupant: a handsome teenager, with the muscles of one who had worked hard in the potters' fields, and the intelligent eyes of a true visionary. In place of the standard crook and fan of a pharaoh crossed over his chest he clutched a simple clay vase and a sheet of papyrus with four phases of the moon pictured on it – indicators of pottery and astrology – the two great influences of the Seer's life.

'That's him?' Nick had mounted the steps. 'He died that young?'

'He was seventeen or eighteen,' said Callie quietly. 'Not much older than us.'

222

'How do you know?'

'I finished reading Omar's book last night, and it said that Ssin recaptured the Seer, but that he fell off her war galley and drowned, or was eaten by hippos.'

'Why didn't you tell me that before?'

Callie felt guilty. 'Because it scared me that there wouldn't be anything for us to find, and I didn't want you to be scared as well.' She rubbed her forehead, her eyes still stinging.

Nick seemed to accept her explanation, because he nodded briefly and went up to the casket. 'I still don't buy it though.'

'You don't buy what?'

'That he'd let himself be captured, and then be eaten by hippos. Was he having an off day with predictions, or what? No, it's a lot more likely that he faked his own death.'

Callie's mouth fell open. 'That does sound like the sort of thing a boy would do.'

'It's just like us throwing those two pillows from the boat. He just wanted to get Ssin off his back so he could get on with his predictions and stuff.'

Nick was almost nose to nose with the ancient Egyptian face painted onto the casket. He started trying to prise off the casket lid with his fingernails.

'What are you doing?'

'Maybe the prophesies are in there with him.'

'It's sealed with some sort of wax,' said Callie. She started picking off the yellow-brown wax as Nick continued trying to lever off the lid.

After a lot of grunting the entire lid came off in Nick's hands. He struggled to slide it off the edge of the steps, and it went bumping down loudly to the golden tiled floor. Traces of

223

ancient chemicals leaked harmlessly into the atmosphere from the open casket. He and Callie leaped back as if half expecting the mummy to lurch out at them. When it didn't, they tiptoed slowly forward.

'Just his mummified remains,' said Nick frowning. 'No prophesies.'

Callie stared at the mummy in distaste. The once-white head-to-toe bandages were discoloured to a rusty brown, and the figure wrapped inside them smelled faintly of dust and herbs. There was a hint of a face beneath the cloth: sunken eyes, a shallow nose, and something of a wide mouth.

'The prophesies must be here somewhere.' Callie wandered gladly back down the steps. She noticed her reflection on the golden wall as she moved past it. Self consciously, she paused to look at herself, adjusting her hair. Unnervingly, her reflection remained utterly motionless: a snapshot of Callie staring back at Callie unblinkingly. 'What the...?'

She tiptoed forward, curiously, losing sight of the reflection for a moment before catching it again on a slightly altered angle. Then she realised – it wasn't a reflection at all, but a perfect picture of her, drawn in dozens of subtly differing shades of gold. The effect was both unsettling and brilliant at once. Every detail was perfect.

'Nick, look.' She tilted her head slightly, allowing the light in the chamber to ignite every thread of gold in the image. 'It's a picture of me!'

'A picture? You're kidding.' Nick peered over Callie's shoulder. 'It's *exactly* like you...'

Callie moved sideways, studying the rest of the wall properly. Another picture instantly emerged from the shimmering surface. 'It's of both of us!' she gulped.

Nick moved again to her side. 'That's really disturbing.'

The intricate image seemed to show them reaching up and turning a dial, a dial the size of a CD.

'It's like a page from an instruction manual,' said Callie. The Seer was showing them what to do. 'Look for that disc!' She dashed along the gold-faced wall, examining each side in turn and finding nothing. When she stopped in frustration, she realised Nick was still standing in the same spot, picking at the gold disc with his fingernails.

'It's the picture itself,' he said in awe. 'It's sticking out a bit. Come and help.'

Exactly as she was shown in the picture, Callie reached up to help Nick move the dial. 'It's turning.' Tiny shutters began to spiral back into the disc itself, revealing a crystal-clear lens behind. Nick leaped back with a startled yell, as a multicoloured beam of light burst through the lens, speared across the room and struck the mummified remains standing in the open casket. As the light continued to project, the Seer appeared to live again – the bandages a screen for a lifelike figure.

A boy, around eighteen years old, wearing a green kilt, smiled at them. His brown-eyed gaze worked eerily around the room as if he was familiarising himself with his surroundings after so many years. Callie edged back towards the base of the golden steps, and the mummy's gaze lowered slowly to meet her own.

'It's looking at you,' gasped Nick. 'How's it doing that?'

Her heart beating faster, Callie moved forward again. She could make out the Seer's face, even though it was textured and grainy from the bandages underneath it. The beam of coloured light was a film of the Seer, being projected directly onto his mummy. 'It's like an overhead projector.' She held up her hand to break the projection beam. A section of the green kilt appeared on her palm and right along her arm. 'It's incredible!'

'Since when did ancient Egyptians have home cinema?' Nick scrambled back to the top of the golden steps to get a better look.

'The Seer could see into the future, couldn't he?' exclaimed Callie. 'We know he predicted inventions – he just used the technology thousands of years before they were officially invented. We should have guessed!' Callie drew back as the mummy's projected lips parted and began to speak:

'*At last, Squirrel and Stickleback. Far-off visitors from a far-off time.*' The voice was remarkably clear – and speaking in flawless English. It emanated from all around the chamber, bouncing off the golden walls.

'We were thinking: ancient scrolls, and he was thinking Skype!' rasped Nick.

'*Yes, Skype.*' The Seer must have nodded his head during the recording, because the image on the mummy's face seemed to move distortedly from side to side. Callie and Nick both gulped.

'Did he just hear me?' asked Nick.

Callie shook her head. 'No. He predicted what you were going to say.'

'*I wish I hadn't possessed this gift,*' the Seer went on, as if in conversation. '*My life would have been very different.*'

'What does he mean by that?'

Callie thought she understood. 'Everything he achieved, everything he learned, all he prophesied – he would have traded for his old life, as the obscure son of a potter working on the banks of the Nile.' The images on his painted casket confirmed it: the clay vase crossed over the phases of the moon – the two elements of his life at clashing odds. 'He wished he could have stopped seeing things in the future,' she added simply.

'*Exactly*,' Fortune agreed. '*I was eighteen summers old when I finally escaped Ssin, by making her believe I was dead. I helped Nemesis, her cousin, another she thought was dead, to take her place. He was a good pharaoh, and a grateful one. As you can see, he rewarded me well.*' Fortune grinned boyishly, his gaze travelling around the golden chamber. '*Not this shiny stuff – the reward was eternal youth. His own prize, he gave to me.*' Fortune grinned again. '*I don't look bad for one hundred and thirteen, do I?*'

'A hundred and thirteen!' exploded Nick.

'*It was long enough to see as much of the future as I ever wanted to. I could not be asked to wait around to alter fate.*'

'How did you die, then?' Callie demanded the projection directly. 'We thought eternal *meant* eternal.'

'*There's a get-out clause.*' The Seer winked at her, and her mouth dropped open.

'A get-out clause?'

This time the Seer ignored her question. '*I have many prophesies and secrets to reveal – before she comes.*'

Callie twisted round to stare fearfully at the triangular-shaped entrance, half expecting Ssin to come in then.

'*I'm sorry. I cannot change that fact,*' said Fortune.

'What use are the prophesies to us if she's going to kill us anyway?' demanded Nick, moving round to where he could keep an eye on the entrance.

Once more the Seer disregarded the question.

'Just listen to him,' said Callie.

'*On 20th January 2019, an Icelandic volcano will erupt near the city of Sigurdsvik... A devastating tsunami will reach the*

Greek island of Opinos on 19th June 2026...US-EURO AIR flight 272 from New York to Rome will crash on 1st December 2021... 7th August 2046, the largest ever recorded earthquake will strike Pinzhou, Central China... The London to Glasgow express will derail at midnight on 13th October 2022...'

Callie suddenly realised something spectacular was going on. The Seer was giving them predictions about the future. What was the point, unless they were going to live?!

'We've got to remember the dates!' she shouted to Nick. 'Everything he tells us.'

'Why?'

'We *can* change fate. We can change it by warning people. That's why he's telling us! There's a reason to all this, Nick: to save lives! Just like he has saved ours by guiding us here.'

'A meteor will strike the Russian town of St Petersburg on 3rd June 2014... A nuclear-power explosion, Carlos Grande, Argentina, 11th July 2052...'

'I'll never remember them all,' choked Nick.

'You must!'

'Your parents. A fatal car accident on 14th February 2016.'

Callie's heart stopped and she cried out. 'Mum and Dad! We have to survive. That's why it's us! We have to warn Mum and Dad, Nick.' Tears were streaming down her face. 'We *can* change fate! If we *know* what's going to happen, we can avert it. I'm sure that's the secret – the Seer's greatest gift.' She swallowed a lump in her throat. *'February the fourteenth, 2016.'* She wouldn't let her parents go anywhere near a car for the whole of 2016.

The Seer's mummy had ground to a halt.

'Is it done?' stammered Callie.

'Today Squirrel and Stickleback will die at the hands of Ssin.'

Callie spun round. The voice was not the Seer's. She staggered back, too late to stop the flashing golden blade slicing deeply across her throat. She felt only numb as she fell to the golden tiles, and watched helpless as Ssin drove the same blade into Nick's chest right up to its jewel-encrusted hilt. Her brother collapsed beside her.

Ssin lurched up the golden steps. She lifted a hand to interrupt the projection, just as Callie had, and pronounced: 'A trick, a modern trick.' She addressed the mummy: 'Speak again. You said nothing of the source of eternal youth.'

The projection stared back impassively for a moment before obliging her:

'*The breath of eternal youth blows no longer through the eternal mountain. It is a spent force. The well that created it has long since run dry. Those who entered the pyramid first, breathed the last.*'

Ssin twisted round in horror. Incredibly, Callie was helping Nick to remove Ssin's copper blade from his chest. Both of them were completely unharmed. 'I, I don't understand,' he was stammering, his hands shaking. 'We should be dead. Are we ghosts?'

'We're *eternal*, Nick,' said Callie breathlessly, the ethereal turquoise light of eternity sparkling in her eyes, and mirrored in Nick's.

'But we haven't done anything.'

'We didn't have to. That vapour we breathed in when we smashed the tip of the pyramid. Not poison, not a deadly bacteria: eternal youth.'

'Them?' screeched Ssin. 'Slaves? Eternal? You have denied me for *them*? My entire army lost in the sands – for this!' She flung herself onto the Seer's mummified remains. 'Fiend!

Vile ghost!' She found another dagger from beneath her white robes and plunged it two-handed into the mummy's chest. With an angry shriek she wrenched the blade through bandages, dust and dry flesh with a great ripping sound. The image continued to project onto torn linen and bones. 'You have made me wait an eternity for Hell!'

She screamed louder than before, as she realised she could never take her revenge on he who had tricked her.

25

Jackal-Headed God

K

As the scream subsided, Ssin turned slowly to Callie, blazing hatred from her sunken eyes. A calculating look had replaced the revulsion. 'You were only minutes before me. The air in your lungs, spreading through your bodies, sustaining your life – it is the breath of eternal youth. It belongs to me! I shall devour it from your thieving innards.'

She sprang at Callie, rejuvenated by the lust to bring back her youth and beauty.

Callie crashed back onto the tiles, the depraved monster on top of her sucking out her breath in a vile kiss. Callie's screams for help were stolen.

'Get off her!' Nick swung the blade he still held at Ssin, but it bounced uselessly off her immortal head. She hissed, possessed, and flew at him in turn.

'*Ssin.*' The Seer's image began to speak afresh. '*You are more foolish than I ever believed. The breath of eternal youth preserves youth, nothing can recreate it. The ravages of time are your reward for your wicked, sinful life. You have paid the price for your cruelty.*'

Ssin's mouth slid slowly away from Nick's, and she glowered at the mummy as though it were a real, living thing. 'But you promised me!' she wailed.

'*I promised you nothing. You assumed! Had you discovered this place when young and beautiful you would have remained the same. You are too late, too late by three thousand, four hundred years. All that awaits you here is death.*'

'What?' screeched Ssin, her puckered lips in a snarl. 'You can't kill me, you potter's dung, you orphan, you foul, unworshipped, forgotten cockroach! Did you not grant me eternal life?'

'*And now I grant you eternal death... Yes.*' The image smiled vengefully, its reflection glittering off the four golden walls. '*Observe your hands, crone! See how they blacken.*'

Ssin gaped at the palms of her hands in horror. Sooty black, the withered skin was beginning to peel from her fingers in ugly strips. She cried out in a terror she'd never experienced before, holding the hands away from her as though they were not hers.

'*I was most specific about the poison painted onto the inside of my tomb,*' Fortune's projected image went on. '*And that the poison was so profuse that none could fail to touch it. The colour of the yellow appenia leaf, and the mountain-wasp honey blends beautifully with gold and masks the real poison: worm root, ground sea-snail shell, pink fluorspar, viper venom, the wine of the Amun-berry, vampire-bat saliva... The list goes on; Nemesis and I searched the whole world over for all those rare ingredients: the antidote to eternal life.*'

Callie stared at her own hands. They'd touched the walls as well. Hers and Nick's hands were smeared with the same poison! 'Us?' she demanded of the flickering projection. But the

Seer was shaking his head, making the image on the tattered bandages blur again.

'*No, my friends. Not you as well. You never drank the original elixir of eternal life.*'

There was a clatter as Ssin threw herself at the upright casket once more: different this time, a desperate supplicant. 'Save me, Fortune. Don't allow me to die thus.' The peeling blackness was now advancing up her arms. 'You loved me once.'

'*I was mistaken.*' He stared at her with hatred, and Callie wanted to vomit as skin continued flake off Ssin's cursed body like a plague of black dandruff: her face, her throat, her breast. The creature sagged, then rolled dead down the steps, finishing at Callie's feet. Callie stood transfixed.

The Seer's voice came one last time: '*Thank you, Callie and Nick. Reveal my lost prophesies... Now go, before it is too late.*' Then the projection flickered into nothing. The Seer was gone.

'Too late? Too late for what?' asked Callie, tearing her gaze away from Ssin.

'Too late to get out,' guessed Nick, dragging his sister through the triangular opening.

The walls of the sloping corridor seemed to be pitching and tossing like waves, as the pyramid groaned with a great rumbling sound. Their way was blocked by a stone panel.

'We've gone the wrong way,' gasped Callie.

'No, we haven't. The pyramid's sealing itself off!'

Nick turned decisively. 'We have to go down instead.'

'What if "down" is still underwater?'

'Then we'll swim for it!' He grabbed her arm again and pulled her back towards the other end of the sloping passage.

233

Another rumbling sound came from somewhere ahead of them.

Callie clattered on down the wooden ramp for several moments. Then Nick's voice reached back for her, and she realised he'd lost his grip on her and she'd fallen behind: 'Callie! Callie. Come ON!' The rumbling noise reasserted itself in her brain, and she saw another stone panel slowly descending in front of her; a gap of just a metre remained.

'Roll under it,' commanded Nick, demonstrating by flinging himself through the diminishing gap. Callie did as she was ordered, scraping the skin off her knees and elbows, but coming out on the other side of the panel.

'Don't stop!' yelled Nick, his voice echoing oddly in her brain. Callie staggered on. Another block was descending in front of them already – scraping loudly, shaking the pyramid. It was five metres away...Four...Three...Two...One.

'Hurry!' shouted Nick, to urge his clearly frightened sister on. They slithered under the block together on the last beat of the last second. Callie stood up half dazed and nauseous, as the panel slotted into place behind her with an almighty thud.

Panting hard, she looked about her. They were in a small chamber – empty and with plain stone walls. Daylight showed dimly through a large triangle of pale green glass. Callie could make out rocks and puddles beyond – the lake bed at the bottom of Anubis's Lake, drained of all its water.

Nick ran the palm of his hand over the glass. 'It's the same as the pinnacle,' he said, 'we can smash our way out.'

Callie nodded and tried kicking the pane, the *bang-bang-bang* sounds hurting her already aching head. The thickness of the glass resisted her blows. Nick took a few steps back, then aimed a flying kick at it to see if that would work. It worked spectacularly, the resulting explosion shocking the life out of both of them. Splinters of glass smashed around them.

Nick picked himself up, little cuts marking his cheeks, the left side of his nose, and blood trickling from incision under his chin. 'I think the word is "ouch." Come on.' Callie watched him step out into sunshine, brushing shards of glass out of his hair, and started to follow him.

'I do not think so.' Someone was standing in Callie's way. Blackened skeletal fingers tightened around Callie's throat. 'Stay with me for eternity,' hissed Ssin, her hate-filled milky eyes all that remained remotely human in her black, skinless skull.

'No-oh.' Callie felt her lips swelling, her eyes bulging.

Another block began to lower, sealing off the way out. Stone grated upon stone. The lake bed slowly disappeared from view. Golden sunlight was replaced by the eerie bronze glow from the mirrors. The block settled into place with a heavy thump.

Ssin began to laugh dementedly: 'I shall share my eternal death with your eternal youth. Together we shall be forever. That is my revenge.'

Callie gurgled in horror. But the grip around her throat loosened a little as Ssin seemed to be staring at something new. 'My... My Lord,' she stammered, uncharacteristically respectful. 'I have no quarrel with you... This girl has offended me grievously and must pay. You have no cause for anger.'

The bony fingers around Callie's throat lifted a fraction more, enabling her to turn and take in what her enemy saw. Looming above them both, five-metres high, was a colossal man – with the head of a jackal: Lord Anubis, god of the dead... His terrible image swam before Callie, tears falling and soaking her pale cheeks.

'Nick!' she sobbed. She wanted her little brother to come back and save her. They'd made it so far.

The god Anubis regarded her with interest through dark jackal eyes, set deeply above a dog-like snout – this was something new, this was something unfamiliar to him.

'My Lord... My Lord...' Ssin continued to burble, through her blackened lips. 'She is nothing to you. She is mine. Do you not understand why I must make her suffer? Three thousand, four hundred years I have waited – for what? My own destruction at the hands of a slave. Some small revenge must be my reward, Lord of the Underworld.'

Anubis ignored her, stooping from his great height to sniff at Callie – following the contours of her face without touching her. Callie pressed herself against the wall as the jackal god's warm breath ruffled the ends of her fringe. Large brown eyes fixed upon the amulet, which she had quite forgotten, was dangling around her neck. 'This little one is protected,' he growled in a doggish voice.

'But, my Lord, I am Pharaoh!'

'You are Cruelty and Hatred. And this child observes old magic, a shield against your evil.'

'A trinket!' The sarcasm rose in disrespectful tones. 'A coloured bead!'

A deafening howl reverberated around the chamber. Callie ducked, sobbing in fear, great, painful beats of her heart. And with a ferocity that was shocking, Anubis attacked. He dashed Ssin first against the wall with a mighty crack, then beat her remains against the floor – smashing her charcoal form into broken pieces. His howls continued as black dust rained down.

When it was over, he turned again to Callie.

'Tell my mum and my dad that I love them,' she whispered

a prayer to him as he took hold of her in one giant paw. She felt herself being lifted off the ground and, for some reason she could not explain, she was no longer afraid. 'Tell Nick I love him too,' she murmured. She smiled at the thought of her younger brother. Hopefully sometimes he would miss her. And he would warn their parents about 14th February 2016.

She glanced up in surprise as she felt herself moving across the chamber. Anubis's gentle hand was carrying her to the entrance of the pyramid. 'But the block,' she told him. 'It's sealed the pyramid.'

With a smile, Anubis lifted that too and slid her softly underneath.

Callie heard a final thud behind her...

Callie jumped. 'Ow! Did you just slap me?' She glared accusingly at Nick, her cheek stinging from the blow.

'I've been trying to bring you round.'

'Bring me round?' Callie was leaning against a damp ledge at the base of an impressive, white pyramid: the eternal mountain, now visible for all to see. The sky above her was almost clear, all traces of the recent sandstorm erased, and the temperature had soared.

'Why didn't you come straight out?' Nick asked in an impatient tone. 'You were nearly trapped in there.'

Callie looked back at the pyramid to make sure that it had definitely sealed itself. The sudden movement made her head spin. 'Ssin pounced on me at the last minute. I couldn't get out.'

Her explanation produced a puzzled look from Nick.

'Callie, she was poisoned. We saw her shrivel and die.'

Callie frowned. 'Yes, but somehow she came back to life, or it was her ghost. But then Anubis finished her off.'

'Anubis?' Nick screwed up his face. 'The jackal person...? Callie, *I* dragged you out. Me. And you're a lot heavier than you look.'

The cloudless sky appeared to pulse above them. Callie swallowed a massive lump in her throat. What had just happened? She looked down and noticed her hands, coated in the yellowish-gold slimeThe Seer had had painted on the walls of his tomb. 'Could something in that poison stuff painted on the walls have affected me? Made me hallucinate?' She scrambled unsteadily from the block she was leaning against and made it to a muddy puddle on the ground, where she started vigorously washing her hands.

'It's possible,' said Nick. 'But it didn't affect me.'

'Mum always says you've got the constitution of an ox. Nothing ever makes you sick.'

When Callie had finished scrubbing her hands, and drying them on her skirt, she tried focusing on the rather changed view. The lake was now a valley, set between tangerine-hued hills. Nick shielded his eyes from the sun to peer up at the pyramid.

'You realise we're stuck like this for ever don't you: aged twelve and thirteen?'

Callie shook her head. 'No, we're not.'

'What do you mean, "no, we're not"? We sucked it in, didn't we? Eternal youth. That blue vapour when we smashed our way into the pyramid. And we didn't die when she stabbed us, so that pretty much proves it works... That was pretty cool, actually!'

'The Seer told you himself,' said Callie. 'There's a get-out clause. And we got out, didn't we? When you leave the eternal mountain eternal youth stops working...Nemesis didn't remain the same age for the rest of his life, did he? Omar would have told us. Your eyes are already returning to normal.'

'What's that supposed to mean?' Nick said, looking baffled.

'They appeared almost turquoise while we were inside the pyramid. I think it was the light of eternity.'

Nick gulped, squinting at Callie's intensely blue eyes before the light faded altogether. 'Yeah. Yours too.'

'Anyway,' Callie went on, 'there was no more of the breath of eternal youth left, was there? The last of it leaked out when we opened the pyramid. The source had run dry over thousands of years.'

Nick seemed to take a minute or so to catch up. 'Oh well, that's good then, isn't it?' He sounded a bit unsure. 'Didn't like the idea of spending the rest of my life in Year Eight. Another two and a half terms of maths with Garbitt is bad enough!' He wrinkled his brow thoughtfully. 'What are we going to do about the prophesies?'

'Well, we make sure Mum and Dad never get in a car again,' said Callie heartily. 'But I don't think the rest are down to us.'

'You can't be serious!' gasped Nick, looking scandalised. 'We could save, like thousands of lives.'

'I didn't mean that.' Callie pointed up at the glistening white pyramid, rising up against the sun behind them. It was a heavenly form of the flawless mountain, a colossus of utter perfection. 'Experts are going to want to study that thing, aren't they? All we have to do is tell them how to switch on the Seer's recording. We revealed the Lost Prophesies when we revealed the pyramid. The Seer must have always known that it would happen this way. But he told us about Mum and Dad. That was his prediction for us. The thing that mattered most to us. '

'Like a reward for everything we'd done?'

'Something like that.'

'Wow.' Nick blew out his cheeks. 'It's a relief really cos I'd already forgotten most of the other prophesies. There was something going to happen in Argentina, but I can't remember when.'

Callie scrutinised her hands again, and all traces of bat saliva and ground-up sea-snail shell appeared to have gone. 'I'm sorry there were no lottery numbers for you, though, or something you could discover before the real inventor did.'

Nick shrugged. 'I've always got Danger Tennis to fall back on.'

'Yeah. Good luck with that.' Callie contemplated the distant hills to the west. Beni-Sami and the Nile lay somewhere in that direction. But how were they ever going to get all the way back to Cairo?

'There's one prediction I wish the Seer had made,' Nick said.

'Hmm. What's that?'

'That there'd be a McDonalds around here somewhere. I'm starving!'

'Oh no! Look!' said Callie quietly.

'What?'

Callie was still staring at the rocky horizon. A crest of dust was following the rapidly turning wheels of a small convoy of vehicles: three identical, hi-spec black jeeps spearing towards them. Callie recognised them almost at once – the jeeps that had forced them off the road when they'd been trying to drive to

240

their parents, and then delivered them into Gobb's clutches.

'How the hell have they found us?' demanded Nick. 'Have they been following Ssin all along?'

'I don't know,' said Callie anxiously.

'They're not going to be very happy when they find out what's happened to Ssin and the rest of her army, are they?'

'Maybe they will,' Callie said with a note of hope. 'Ramy said Gobb forced them to work for him, and that they were scared of Crocodile Head.' She automatically fingered the amulet Ramy had given her. 'They *might* thank us.'

'Oh yeah, people are always thanking *us,* aren't they?'

The three black jeeps continued across the lake bed, spraying out the remaining puddles from under their tyres; the roar of powerful engines reached Callie and Nick on the warm breeze.

'Come on, let's run for it,' said Nick, starting to turn.

'It wouldn't do any good,' said Callie, 'even if I had any strength left.'

It was already too late. The first of the jeeps neatly blocked off their retreat. The other two vehicles skidded to a halt, forming a triangle around them. Car doors were flung open, and Ramy was the first to reach them.

'Where is she? Where is Ssin?'

Callie gulped. 'In there,' she muttered, pointing over her shoulder at the eternal mountain. 'She's dead, along with the rest of her army.'

'How?' demanded Ramy.

'Poisoned in the tomb. The giant, Gobb, was killed by a scorpion. What happened to her army I don't know, but she said she'd lost them in the sands.'

Ramy looked relieved, along with the rest of his people.

Black Robe, the man who seemed to be their leader, nodded to Ramy before waving his men towards the pyramid.

Callie waited until they were out of earshot then asked Ramy bluntly: 'How did you find us?'

Ramy reached forward to catch hold of the amulet around Callie's neck, his sudden movement startling her. 'This bead contains a small transmitter. We have been tracking you.'

'You used us!' flared Callie, blushing angrily. 'All this time!'

'*Fate* used you,' corrected Ramy, letting the bead fall again, his eyes meeting Callie's. 'I'm sorry.'

Callie tore the amulet off and threw it at him. 'Then why didn't you come sooner? We could have done with your help on a dozen occasions.'

'It wasn't that easy,' replied Ramy. 'We kept losing your signal. Then last night we tracked your boat but could not get on board. And this morning it was too dangerous to go on in a sandstorm.'

'We've spent a lot of time underground,' said Nick, picking the amulet out of the sand and handing it to Ramy. 'I bet this thing wouldn't work in most of the places we've been.'

'No, it wouldn't.'

'Why did you follow us anyway?' Callie still hadn't finished feeling angry. 'Are you here to rob the pyramid?' Black Robe and the rest of Ramy's people were scouting the base of the pyramid.

'No, we are not here to rob the pyramid!' said Ramy, just as angry. 'We are here to see justice done.'

'Justice?' Callie didn't understand. 'You mean you want the prophesies!'

'No. Our justice is to see Ssin dead. For that we have

waited a long time,' said Ramy, and Callie thought he meant to be free of their yoke, but he went on: 'My people are the descendents of Neb.'

'Neb?' asked Nick for both of them. 'Who's Neb?'

'He was a potter's son, a friend of the Seer. And the Seer saved his life by killing a mighty crocodile. It was that act which brought the Seer to the attention of the pharaoh.'

Callie remembered reading about it several days ago in Omar's book. 'You're descended from *that* boy?' She was too curious to be angry any more.

'Yes, and we have always held the Seer as our saviour. The person to whom all descended from Neb owe their lives. From generation to generation we have vowed to repay Neb's debt to the Seer.'

'Then you were only pretending to serve Ssin,' guessed Nick, 'so that you could get close enough to kill her?'

'Yes,' confirmed Ramy, 'but she was always protected – until now.'

'Well the Seer took her life himself,' said Callie, 'by luring her to his pyramid and then using his skills as a chemist to poison her.'

'Then it was justice,' said Ramy with satisfaction.

'What about the other Followers of Ssin – at the Palace?' asked Nick. 'Will they still be dangerous?'

Ramy thought about it for a moment. 'How can they be? They have no one left to follow.'

Nick looked relieved. 'What are you going to do with us now?' asked Callie. All she really wanted to do was sleep.

'We will take you back to Cairo, to your parents,' said Ramy. 'They are there, scouring the city for you for the past five days.'

'They didn't get our email then,' said Callie.

Nick shrugged. 'Told you they never check them.' He was peering into the nearest jeep. 'I don't suppose you've got any more of those lamb, sultanas and onion things with the stuffed vine leaves, have you…? We can pay for them.' He held out a large, blood-red stone in the palm of his hand.

Callie almost fainted. Nick was offering Ramy a huge ruby. 'Where the hell did you get that?' she hissed, as Ramy climbed into the jeep to find them something to eat.

Nick turned his back to Ramy and lifted his T-shirt a little to reveal a golden dagger with a jewel-encrusted hilt, missing a large ruby, thrust into the waistband of his jeans. It was the dagger Ssin had tried to kill them both with. 'She gave it to us, didn't she?' reasoned Nick, but then added a warning 'Shhhhh' and pulled his T-shirt back down.

'You're going to end up like Uncle Omar,' Callie told him disapprovingly.

'What, with my own secret stash of treasure?'

'No. In prison probably!'

Ramy was waving Egyptian flat bread, grilled chicken and a bottle of green sugarcane juice. Callie smiled at him this time, and took one last look at the pyramid they'd found before climbing into the jeep. She wondered if the Seer had predicted this ending…

THE ISLAND OF THIEVES

JOSH LACEY

Buried treasure. Ruthless gangsters. An ancient clue . . .

Our Captayne took the pinnace ashore and I went with hym and six men also, who were sworne by God to be secret in al they saw. Here we buried five chests filled with gold.

Tom Trelawney was looking for excitement. Now he's found it. With his eccentric Uncle Harvey, he's travelling to South America on a quest for hidden gold. But Uncle Harvey has some dangerous enemies and they want the treasure too. Who will be the first to uncover the secrets of the mysterious island?

Praise for other books by this author:

'A delight'
The Times

'Smart and pacy'
Sunday Times

9781849392457 £5.99

OUTLAW

Stephen Davies

The rules are there to be broken

Fifteen-year-old Jake Knight is an explorer and adventurer at heart but this often gets him into trouble. When a stuffy English boarding school suspends him for rule-breaking, Jake flies out to Burkina Faso where his parents are living. He is expecting a long, adventure-filled vacation under a smiling African sun. But what awaits him there is kidnapping, terrorism and Yakuuba Sor – the most wanted outlaw in the Sahara desert.

'A strong desert setting and a corkscrew of a plot make this a terrific page-turner.'
Julia Eccleshare, LoveReading4Kids

'Stephen Davies writes brilliantly'
Writeaway

'Exceptional talent'
The School Librarian

9781849390880 £5.99

HAUNTED

**A FANTASTIC COLLECTION OF GHOST STORIES
FROM TODAY'S LEADING CHILDREN'S AUTHORS**

'A chilling slice of horror. An excellent balance of
traditional and modern and a perfect pocket-money
purchase for winter evenings.' *Daily Mail*

Derek Landy, Philip Reeve, Joseph Delaney, Susan
Cooper, Eleanor Updale, Jamila Gavin, Mal Peet, Matt
Haig, Berlie Doherty, Robin Jarvis and Sam Llewellyn
have come together to bring you eleven ghost stories:
from a ghost walk around York; to a drowned boy,
who's determined to find someone to play with; to a
lost child trapped in a mirror, ready
to pull you in; to devilish creatures,
waiting with bated breath for their
next young victim; to an ancient
woodland reawakened. Some will
make you scream, some will make
you shiver, but all will haunt you
gently long after you've put the
book down.

9781849393218 £6.99

WILL GALLOWS

& THE SNAKE-BELLIED TROLL

DEREK KEILTY

ILLUSTRATED BY JONNY DUDDLE

It's time for revenge!

Will Gallows, a young elfling sky cowboy, is riding
out on a dangerous quest. His mission? To bring
Noose Wormworx, the evil snake-bellied troll, to
justice. Noose is wanted for the murder of Will's
pa, and Will won't stop until he's got revenge!

'Wow, what a brilliant read.
Fresh and original – and very
funny too. This cowboy's
riding to an exciting new
frontier in fiction.'
Joseph Delaney, author of
The Spook's Apprentice

9781849392365 £5.99

NIGHT ON TERROR ISLAND

It's the scariest movie ever and they're stuck in it!

PHILIP CAVENEY

Have you ever wanted to be in the movies?

Kip has, and when he meets mysterious Mr
Lazarus he thinks his dream's come true. Because
Mr Lazarus can project people into movies! Films
like *Terror Island*, full of hungry sabre-toothed
tigers and killer Neanderthals.

When you're in a film, everything is real: real
bullets, real swords, real monsters. But beware . . .
if you don't get out by the time
the closing credits roll, you'll be
trapped in the film forever!

Can Kip rescue his sister
before the sabre-toothed tigers
get her? And if he can – how
is he going to get back?!

9781849392709 £5.99